The Holiday Killing Spree Complete Collection

Labor Day Weekend Massacre
Opening Season Massacre
Christmas Day Massacre

K.A. Meng

Blurbs

First Comes Love

Jolene Argall and her friends escape to the lake for Labor Day Weekend. Three days of drinking and parental free fun turns deadly when a friend is murdered. Jolene calls the police but by the time they arrive the body has disappeared. The friends try to convince the police that they're not lying. Jolene and her friends need to find the killer before they're next.

Then Comes Death

Jolene Argall and her boyfriend, Bob Ghul, have been on the run since a fun Labor Day weekend turned deadly. Now their hiding in a remote cabin but soon deer season will begin bring hunters to the area. Jolene fears they'll be recognized. She faces the grim task deciding to flee or kill.

Then Comes the Trial

Ho, ho, ho! Christmas is coming and so is the deadline for Jolene Argall and her boyfriend, Bob Ghul. While all the good girls and boys get presents, Jolene and Bob face multiple first-degree murder charges and a domestic terrorism charge. The story behind the massacre comes out, but is it the whole truth or a fabricated lie? Will Jolene and Bob get what they deserve or the freedom to open presents on Christmas Day?

To all the horror fans.

Character Profiles

The Holiday Killing Spree Book 1:
Labor Day Weekend Massacre

Jolene Argall – the main protagonist. She would do anything for a friend, and she loves animals. She is currently single.

Abigail "Abby" Miller – the annoying friend. She thinks everything is so great. She is in drama and is always upbeat. She is currently single, but she used to date Hank Pratt.

Monte Jackson – the rich kid. His family own the cabin where the story takes place. He helps those in need, and also, flaunts his wealth while helping others. He is in an off-and-on relationship with Corrie Summers that is currently off. He is forced to bring his little brother Conrad Jackson on the trip.

Hank Pratt – the all-star. He is good at every sport imaginable and loves to party. He is currently single, but he used to date Abby Miller.

Conrad Jackson – the annoying kid brother. He's Monte Jackson's little brother, who is forced to hang out and make sure his older brother isn't doing anything stupid by their parents. He loves dark metal music and dresses in dark clothes. He is currently single.

Corrie Summers – the queen B. She is the most popular girl in school. If anyone crosses her, they will feel her wrath. She cheated on Monte Jackson and they are currently not dating.

Bob August – the new kid. He meets Jolene Argall in the middle of the lake with his friends at the pontoon party. They hangout and bond over what happens. He is currently single.

Brad Holmes – the sports star. He along with Hank Pratt are the biggest stars in school. He is currently dating Lindsay Wood. He and Lindsay are like the old married couple, and everyone believes they'll be together forever.

Ned Ryan – the smart kid. He is the smartest kid in school. He's the captain of everything geek. He is currently single.

Tabby Abbott – the bestie. She is a best friend of Corrie Summers. She doesn't do anything without Corrie's approval. Tabby is currently dating some guy in college, at least she says so.

Lindsay Wood – the other bestie. She is another best friend of Corrie Summers. Lindsay spends too much time with her boyfriend Brad Holmes so her status of best friend has dropped to the other bestie. She and Brad are like the old married couple, and everyone believes they'll be together forever.

Kaylee Ghul – the good friend. She slept with Monte Jackson who was dating Corrie Summers at the time. She was ousted from the group because of this.

Detective Rebecca Gibson – the no nonsense detective. She is the primary that is called to the cabin. Nothing else is known about her. Her partner is Willmar Morgenstern.

Detective Willmar Morgenstern – the asshole detective. He is way too full of himself. He is being trained by his partner Detective Rebecca Gibson. Nothing else is known about Detective Morgenstern except for he is an ass.

The Holiday Killing Spree Book 2:
Opening Season Massacre

Jolene Argall – the main protagonist. She will do anything for a friend, and she loves animals. She is dating Bob Ghul.

Bob Ghul – the tough guy. He is in love with Jolene Argall. He will do anything to keep her safe and keep other men away from her. He is dating Jolene.

Glen Jager – the grandpa. He is the patriarch. He is married to Betsy Jager.

Marc Jager – the pervert. He is the son of Glen and Betsy Jager. He is a dick and is dating Bridgette Hornsby.

Bridgette Hornsby – the idiot. She looks like she is stuck in the 1980s with big hair and tanned skinned. She is dating Marc Jager.

Betsy Jager – the grandma. She is the matriarch and the kindest member of the family unless she has to deal with her son's girlfriend. She is married to Glen Jager.

Logan Jager – the grandson. He is the youngest member of the Jager Clan. Not much else is known about him.

James Jager – the father. He is the father of Logan Jager and the son of Glen and Betsy Jager. James is married to Lindsay Jager. Not much else is known about him.

Lindsay Jager – the mother. She is the mother of Logan Jager. Lindsay is married to James Jager. Not much else is known about her.

Roger Jager – the uncle. He is the uncle of Logan Jager and the brother of James Jager. Not much else is known about him.

Pat Jager – another uncle. He is the uncle of Logan Jager. Not much else is known about him.

Candace Jager – the aunt. She is the aunt of Logan Jager. Not much else is known about her.

SUV that arrives later - 5 occupants. 3 men and 2 woman. Nothing else is known about them.

The Holiday Killing Spree Book 3:
Christmas Day Massacre

Jolene Argall – the main protagonist. She will do anything for a friend, and she loves animals. She is dating Bob Ghul.

Bob Ghul – the tough guy. He is in love with Jolene Argall. He will do anything to keep her safe and keep other men away from her. He is dating Jolene.

Shelly Nicholson – the psychologist. Jolene Argall's psychologist, who keeps on saying she wants help Jolene, but is she really? She appears to have a crush on Roger Dangers.

Roger Dangers – the best lawyer. Jolene Argall's lawyer. He is working pro bono because he believes in Jolene. He's practical and is honest if he will lose a case or not.

Conrad Jackson – the friend. Conrad is the only person besides Jolene Argall to make it out of the Labor Day weekend massacre alive. He has given up his rebellious ways.

Katherine Hayes – the no nonsense judge. She won't take crap from anyone. Don't let her hear your phone in court, she'll take it away from you and toss you jail.

Eleanor York – the gorgeous lawyer. Bob Ghul's good-looking and court appointed lawyer. Don't let her good-looks fool you, she knows what she's doing. She does her very best for her clients.

Alex Turnbuckle – the jerk state attorney. He has been prosecuting defendants as long as Jolene Argall and Bob Ghul have been alive. He can't wait to earn another victory under his belt.

Sharon Sullivan – the second state attorney. She is nicer than Alex Turnbuckle, and she does know what she's doing. In order to be second chair, she had to climb her way to the top.

Detective Willmar Morgenstern – the asshole detective. He is way too full of himself. He is still a jerk and doesn't feel too much remorse for his partner, Rebecca Gibson's death. Not much is known about Detective Morgenstern except for he's an ass.

Kim Ji-yong – the coroner. One of the many witnesses called to the stand. He knows a lot about dead bodies by figuring out how they died, but he leaves finding the motive to the detectives.

Contents

Labor Day Weekend Massacre

The Holiday Killing Spree Book 1

K.A. Meng

Chapter 1

Monte Jackson steered his new black SUV onto a dirt road and then onto the path in the woods into a clearing. He parked on a patch of grass in front of a two-story lake house.

Wow, I thought. Each time I saw this place, it amazed me. *Must be nice being rich.*

I staggered from the vehicle. Half my butt tingled from it falling asleep. I held onto the door until feeling returned. The sixty-minute car ride almost bored me to death, but it was well worth it. I'd be spending the next three days away from my parents, my teachers, and everybody else except for my friends. I didn't count Monte's annoying little brother, who had come with us. This should be the best Labor Day weekend ever.

"Jolene, isn't this great?" Abby Miller's voice sounded way too upbeat for the afternoon, and she smiled. She gracefully slid from my side of the SUV to join me, using her hand to shield her eyes from the sun as she stared at the lake.

The muddy water shimmered through a gap in the trees. A patch of grass was missing from the higher ground. If I remembered correctly, that was the path to the boathouse and the shore.

"We'll have so much fun. This will be great," Abby said.

Monte glanced at me and rolled his eyes. He must not enjoy Abby's repetitive use of the five-letter word like me. Did he gesture stem from an alternative cause? Nah.

Abby took my hand and shook it, saying, "Come on guys, I'm saying we need this after—"

"We're not talking about *her* here." Monte cut Abby off, and his voice dripped with venom. He pocketed his keys before heading to the front door.

"He can be such a dick sometimes. I don't get why Corrie or Kaylee want him. We're not taking his bags inside." Abby's nostrils flared and released my hand.

"Hank or Brad can grab them." I unlocked the hatch to Monte's SUV and rummaged around for my duffle bag. I gave Abby hers first. Where was mine?

"Where's everyone else?" She glanced at the path behind us. A few birds sang in the trees, and a cicada buzzed in the tall grass near the woods. I'd hate to mow the area around the lake house. The job would take hours, even on a riding lawn mower.

"Brad's been here before. He won't get lost." Despite my words, my stomach twisted into a knot. What if they had a car accident?

Abby mirrored my worry, but she said the words out loud.

"Call Corrie to see where she is. God isn't that cruel. He won't kill our friends after one died. This isn't a horror movie," I said.

"Kaylee wasn't killed, and we're not supposed to mention her." Abby shifted away from me and brought her phone to her ear, telling me we were done with this conversation.

Stupid bitch. The thought popped into my head before I could stop it. At least I didn't say the words. I didn't want to hurt Abby's feelings, no matter how much she annoyed me.

"Yes, because we had nothing to do with Kaylee's death." I released a loud, frustrated sigh and dug for my bag. Our group forgave Monte's indiscretion while Kaylee's was not.

Hank Pratt appeared by my side and asked, "Argall, what are you doing?"

"Jesus! You scared me." I jumped as my heart raced. I touched my hand to my chest to help steady the thumping. He had ridden in the front seat. I should've known he'd come for his bags instead of being startled.

"Why are you tense? We're supposed to be having fun." He placed his hands on his hips, puffing out his chest.

"I'm waiting for the so-called fun to begin."

He laughed and patted my back, saying, "We'll have time. If we hurry, we can pick a room before everyone else gets here. I'll take Monte's things inside." Hank nudged me on the shoulder and lifted four bags easily with his massive arms. He had the ability to carry mine and Abby's, too, without breaking a sweat. He was all-state in every sport: hockey, baseball, football, and wrestling. If our high school had fishing, he would've mastered that too.

"Good idea." With the duffel bags out of the way, I found mine and swung the strap onto my shoulder.

Abby ended her call and walked over to us before saying, "The rest of our friends stopped for gas. They'll be here in ten to fifteen minutes, max. What are we planning? It had better be great."

"We're deciding where to sleep," I answered. She sought different entertainment.

"I won't share a room with Corrie. She won't be great until she forgives Monte for sleeping with...well, you know who."

"Me either," I said.

"We should room together," Abby said.

"Everyone can have their own bedrooms if they want. This place is enormous." Hank saved me from having to tell Abby no.

After I flashed him a thank-you smile, I headed inside behind him. I halted in my tracks.

Abby bumped into me.

My mouth popped open, and I couldn't speak.

The lake house was gorgeous. The open-concept kitchen would be a chef's dream, with dark marble countertops, stainless steel appliances, and tall cabinets. I'd forgotten how amazing and new everything looked. The Jacksons possessed wealth, yet this property seemed excessive for its infrequent use.

Monte sat on a stool at the island and stared at the screen on his cell. A bottle of beer was already open in front of him. He was still Mr. Grumpypants and would be until Corrie forgave him.

Serves him right.

Monte didn't even glance at us as he said, "Pick where you want. I'm in the master on the second floor. My bro probably took his normal room that way." He pointed at the archway next to the kitchen.

"How far is the nearest lake house?" I asked.

"Three to four miles. We can head to the closest town tomorrow if anyone needs anything."

"Cool." I could unpack and make a list. I might've forgotten something in my hurry to get away.

Abby headed to the floating staircase with the glass railing. The panes showed no smudges or fingerprints. The ceiling was two stories above us.

"Are you coming?" Abby asked me as she stood on the middle landing, ten steps up.

"I'm down here." I wanted to stay as far away from her as possible, even if that meant rooming near Conrad, Monte's younger brother.

Monte's threat prompted Abby to cease her incessant talking during their journey. I needed a break from her. She'd been much more excessive lately. I reminded myself that everyone dealt with grief in their own way, but damn.

"Hank?" Abby asked. Her perfectly plucked eyebrow rose into the air.

"My room is upon this level," he stated.

"Whatever." Abby didn't sound too thrilled with us and ascended the rest of the stairs.

"This way," Hank told me. We headed down the hall where Monte said his brother's room would be. Where did that brat disappear? I hadn't seen him since we arrived.

Hank winked prior to entering the initial chamber on its right side, bidding me farewell.

Did I desire proximity to him? He might forget his room and enter mine, or purposely visit me for a late-night hookup.

I selected the left, most distant room, opened its door, then stepped inside.

"Mine," Conrad said. His tone radiated with his displeasure. He hadn't spoken one word in the SUV since we left East Garfo. For a second, I was unaware of his ability to speak. One word didn't make a sentence. He lay on his bed, the sheets already in disarray. The Jacksons had similar appearances: brown hair and dark eyes. "Get out."

"Sorry." I backed out and closed the door.

Ass hat.

Music blared through his speakers a second later. Hopefully, he would lock himself in there for the entire weekend. He could be such an asshole.

I picked a room away from him and closer to Hank's. After setting my bag on the bed, I yanked open the curtains for some light. The glass doors led to my own private deck. Giant windows made up the rest of the wall.

How great was this? Dammit! Now I used Abby's word. I shook my head to clear my thoughts and enjoyed the view. Boats and people dotted the lake. I couldn't wait to join them.

I put on my green bikini that matched my eyes and a white T-shirt to cover myself. I slipped into a pair of short shorts, stuffing my phone into a pocket. I'd explore my space later tonight and unpack, post-swim. I needed to do front crawls until my limbs ached and I couldn't think anymore. I missed Kaylee a lot.

Tears burned my eyes. If only Kaylee had called, I could've talked to her. I could've stopped her.

No, no. Stop thinking.

I switched my tennis shoes out for flip-flops and tossed a beach towel over my shoulder. My sunglasses rested on my head. I was ready for the lake. After one final look over the space, I departed.

"Hello, neighbor. You look good," Hank remarked within the corridor. He had a gleam in his pretty, cornflower blue eyes.

Lucky bastard.

My heart went pitter-patter, and I opened my mouth to speak, but nothing came out. Never before had someone rendered me without words.

He gave me a shit-eating grin, like he knew how my body reacted to him. He wiggled an eyebrow at me, saying, "We should probably see if everyone is here, unless you want to do something else?"

"Yeah, sure. Let's go check on everyone else." Heat flashed across my cheeks and my neck. I didn't like Hank, or did I? He was hot, but he was a meathead. I liked to have a conversation with a guy. I wouldn't mind making out with him and running my hands across his rock-hard abs. He had an eight-pack. I trailed behind him, staring at his fine ass.

"We should go boating," Monte said when we entered the kitchen.

"I want to swim." Corrie Summers' hands were on her hips as she faced Monte, to continue their pissing match.

Everyone else sat on the couch or the chairs, except for Hank, Conrad, and me. No one dared to get between the current argument, and I kept my mouth shut too.

"You can swim where I stop the boat," Monte said.

"No! I don't even want to be near you," Corrie said.

"Why did you come here, then? This is my family's lake house."

"You know why we're here, and what you did." Corrie shoved her pointer finger into his chest.

"Don't blame me. You're the one who cut Kaylee out. You're the reason she—" Monte stopped himself from saying more once he glanced at Corrie's face.

Her lower lip quivered, and tears shimmered in her eyes.

"Baby, I'm sorry. You did nothing wrong." Monte wrapped her in his arms and rubbed circles along her back. "Once you're feeling better, we'll go swimming."

"I want to take the pontoon." She swiped at her tears.

"We can do whatever you want."

Conrad entered the room and stood next to me, saying, "Whoa. The cold, spoiled, heartless bitch has feelings."

I pressed my lips together to keep myself from coming to Corrie's defense. Conrad had an excellent point.

A hot guy maneuvered his boat alongside our anchored pontoon with his three other equally good-looking friends. "Ladies, may we join you?" he inquired.

Corrie invited them aboard, preventing Monte from refusing.

"Tie us to your boat." The guy threw a rope, and she caught it.

She glanced around for something to tie it to. Corrie grunted and counted to search. She remained clueless regarding anything except cheerleading or feminine pursuits.

Hank helped her.

My friends and I introduced ourselves to the guys except for Conrad and Abby. He refused to come, and she stayed behind suffering from a migraine. Their absence represented no loss.

Our little party grew bigger when four more groups joined. By that time, I didn't remember anyone's name. I sat between someone and Hank, drinking a beer. I contemplated jumping into the water or sunbathing.

Monte played D.J. and kept away from Corrie. He wore horribly colored swim trunks. The pink with blue and yellow pattern didn't fit together, but somehow, it worked on him. He had selected a light blue tank top and ridiculously expensive sunglasses. He had a keen sense of fashion.

A couple of girls danced next to him, trying to get his attention.

He avoided them. He likely avoided further angering Corrie. She would flip out if she saw him with them.

"Come join me," Corrie said to me.

The two girls near Monte scattered.

"Okay," I said after I raised my hand to block the sun.

"We should talk since we haven't in a while." Corrie didn't look pissed or happy. What did she want?

"What's up?" I plopped onto the bench in the corner. Where did our friends who always tagged along with her go?

"How are you doing after Kaylee?" Corrie sat next to me and stretched her long legs out.

"I'm fine," I lied. I kept my tone even and stopped myself from hitting Corrie in the face. Our group should've never have gone along with her plan to ignore Kaylee.

"We had nothing to do with Kaylee's death, right?"

"I don't know. Has anyone talked to her mom?" I asked. We departed the wake following one hour's stay. Less than two days later, we were here.

"Sweetie, you know Kaylee had issues." Corrie touched my arm and gave it a squeeze.

"What kind?" This was news to me.

"Her brother, for starters. He's been at boot camp for the last five years after he killed their neighbor's dog."

"Didn't Monte run the dog over?"

"How should I know? Kaylee's brother fought with their stepdad and got sent away." At least this part was true. But why? Kaylee never got around to telling me.

"Why did he?" I asked Corrie. Bobby was nice. He was a scrawny dork, but kind to everyone, even his little sister's friends. He was older than Kaylee by two minutes.

"Does what he did matter? He's troubled and Kaylee is...was too." Corrie swallowed hard.

"You're right. I'm going in the water. See you later." I realized what she needed to hear. I blamed her, our friends, and myself for Kaylee's death. Before Corrie stopped me, I yanked my shirt off and removed my shorts, tossing them into a pile. I ran to the edge and dove in. The shocking cold sank into my bones. My teeth chattered.

A guy swam up next to me and said, "If you move your arms, you won't feel the chill anymore."

"Thanks. I'm Jolene Argall." I kicked my legs and swished my arms to let the warmth flood my limbs.

"Bob August."

"Nice to meet you, Bob," I said.

"Nice to meet you too, Jolene. Did some lady beg you to keep distance from her man? If I were seeing someone, she would need to."

I laughed despite the cheesy line. "You just used the worst pickup line I've ever heard. How might you respond if I were Carrie?"

"Are you fly?" Bob's right, bushy brow with a scar rose.

"Not at all. Unless you have a game and ask anybody to play." My mom used to blast the Carrie song whenever she got drunk. Did he know it? I would sound like an idiot if he didn't.

Bob smiled at me, revealing chiseled cheeks. He was handsome with stubble along his strong jawline. His eyes were a striking gray, like steel. His shoulders were broad, and he must have had a six-pack or more.

"Are you staying for the entire weekend, too?" Bob asked hopefully.

I nodded and chewed on my bottom lip.

"What's the matter?" Bob asked.

"Sorry, I'm fine. I came with my friends to relax and get away," I answered.

Bob tilted his head, treading water. "Get away from what?"

I studied his face, considering whether disclosure was wise. Before I decided anything, I blurted, "My best friend killed herself a week ago."

"How? Why? I'm sorry. You don't have to share anything with me." Bob sounded shocked, like I felt.

"She slit her wrists. Her stepfather came home and found her. Regarding the reason, I have no knowledge. I'm still trying to figure everything out." I paused and took a deep breath. Why was I spilling my guts to a stranger? I required something, yet my parents and companions declined any attempt. I didn't keep a diary. "Our group shunned her for sleeping with another friend's man, but I spoke to her. I told her to give our leader time. I...I wished Kaylee would've called or said something to me." Tears brimmed in my eyes.

Bob said nothing and wrapped his arms around me.

"I'm sorry. Near you, I lose my shit. I'm not cool," I said after I composed myself.

"You seem to be pretty fly to me," Bob said.

"You are too, for a white guy." I laughed and splashed water on his face.

His arm snaked around my waist.

I squealed, and he pulled us under. My mouth filled with water. When we bobbed to the surface, he leaned closer like he would kiss me, but I spat the liquid at him.

He laughed and wiped it away.

"Hey, Jolene! We're heading back to the lake house to party," Hank called with extra emphasis on the last word. He tucked in his arms and swayed his hips. He sucked at dancing.

"Are you coming?" I asked Bob.

"I'll have to see what my friends are doing first."

We swam to the pontoon's side. I used the ladder to climb back into the boat. Water streaked down my body. Did I look hot? I hoped so. I did not stumble on the deck after reaching it.

Score one for me.

I picked up my shirt and shorts and put them back on after drying myself off with my towel. My cell was still in my pocket. Nobody had stolen it.

"Is everyone here?" Monte asked.

I counted my friends and gave him a thumbs up.

Other captains duplicated this action. We ensured everyone's attendance without parental supervision.

Abby's brother once replied 'here' instead of another when their mother asked, leaving the absent child behind. She was madder than hell when she found out. My mom went and got him. Abby's mom surprised me; it didn't happen more since she had eight kids.

I wouldn't have a lot of kids. Two or three max. Kaylee would have none. My heart ached, and I shook my head. If I didn't think about her, I was fine.

Monte pushed the throttle, and I stumbled into Bob.

"Hey, I'm going with you." He caught my shoulders and smiled at me.

Bob's presence improved the journey toward the lake house. We kept the conversation light until he helped Monte anchor in the boathouse.

Hank, plus others, unloaded beer coolers from the pontoon.

Everyone walked up the hill to the lake house. Once we were inside, Monte blared music through the speakers. Some people danced while others sat on the couches or chairs talking. Even Conrad joined the party.

"I'm going to wake my friend," I said to Bob after the fourth song ended. She was a massive pain in my ass this week, but she'd be less annoying once she dealt with her emotions. If someone didn't get her up soon, she'd be pissed. I could use the time to wash my hair before the fish stink from the lake clung to it. My skin had tiny green patches underneath my bathing suit from the seaweed. I should've been like Corrie and sunbathed instead of swimming.

"I'll come." Bob set his beer on the coffee table.

I hesitated and then agreed. What if Abby didn't dress appropriately? Sometimes she slept naked.

"Stay. I'll go. You can't be wandering this place with Jolene. You two might not return to the party." Corrie downed her beer before setting the empty bottle next to Bob's.

"Really, Corrie?" I asked. My eye twitched. I didn't plan on sleeping with Bob after meeting him today. We could have kissed, and we required no room for it.

Some party attendees kissed on the couch's far end.

Bob hadn't made a move on me. He might not like me.

"I'm helping you, silly." Corrie hooked her arm in mine and led me to the steps.

After we climbed the stairs, I glanced down both hallways. Several doors were on either side. I asked, "Do you know what room Abby chose?"

"Nope. We'll have to find her," Corrie declared, heading right along the longest route. She opened the first door right, calling Abby's name. "Not this one."

Next to Corrie's search location, I found the bathroom.

"Do you like the guy you're talking with? He's cute."

"I do. Why?" I halted by the next door and narrowed my eyes on her. If she had any interest in Bob, I'd be in trouble.

"Just asking. Cease your defensiveness. Aren't you into Hank?"

"No, he's cute and hot, but he has more muscles than brains. I prefer being able to have a complete conversation with a man."

"Jocks can be fun. Too bad you don't like him. I was thinking you'd make a cute couple."

I cleared my throat to stop myself from saying anything else. Corrie's matchmaking came true a lot because she forced it on us. Ned, another friend here this weekend, and I saved ourselves by saying we were third cousins. We weren't related. I hadn't seen him since we returned with the pontoon. He was probably reading a book or something. He often wandered away like I wanted to do right now.

"Think about it, okay?" Corrie asked.

"Sure." I opened the next door and gasped.

Abby lay on a bed. Her right hand skimmed the floor, and red soaked her blanket. The color matched her hair; a knife protruding from her chest.

A blood-curdling scream filled the air. The sound hadn't come from me, but from Corrie, who stood behind me.

A stampede pounded the stairs.

I entered the room to check if Abby was breathing.

Her chest didn't rise, and her lifeless, blue-green eyes stared at the ceiling. She was dead. Her killer had scrawled 'great' on the wall next to her body.

Chapter 2

"Abby!" Corrie yelled once she composed herself. She ran to the bed.

"We're too late for CPR. We have to call the police," I said, after stepping in front of Corrie to stop her from touching Abby. Blood pooled on the floor. My stomach churned, and an acidic taste filled my mouth. I choked it back. Who killed her?

"And tell them what? Our friend died, and we had no clue?" Corrie's voice rose more for her next words, and only dogs were capable of hearing what she said next. She touched her cheeks with her hands. Should I comfort her?

Friends gathered in the tiny room or hallway. One of them could help Corrie.

"Stop freaking out, Corrie. Jolene's right. Someone murdered Abby. I'm calling the cops," Monte said.

Conrad pushed his way inside and placed his hand on his brother's, stopping the call by saying, "We can't have the police come here yet. We never met everyone at the party."

"Who cares? You killed Abby." Corrie's hands fell by her sides.

"What? I didn't leave my room until the party started."

"You were the only one here with Abby while everyone else was on the lake, and you play violent video games," Corrie said.

"Yes, killing zombies is like killing someone in real life, dumbass," Conrad said. His voice filled with anger, almost more than sarcasm. If I weren't so upset, he would've impressed me.

"One of us killed Abby, or someone who attended our school did," I stated before Corrie had a chance to reply.

"How? I don't follow." Conrad stared at me with his cold, dark brown eyes.

Who else, besides us or some classmates, knew Abby often says 'great'? I couldn't imagine my friends being the killer, but we meant things, though to my knowledge, we have never committed murder.

"Jolene has a point." Monte glanced at the wall.

I shivered after reading the word again. The five red letters looked like someone had used their finger to write them.

Is the blood on the wall Abby's?

"You're still the number one suspect." Corrie pointed a finger at Conrad.

"And you're number two." Conrad held two fingers in the air. He definitely had some balls for a freshman.

"Why? I wouldn't kill my friend." Corrie's face fell, and she chewed on her bottom lip.

"Accusing someone of murder doesn't sit well, does it?" Conrad asked.

"Knock it off, both of you. I need time to think." Monte raked a hand through his brown hair and unlocked his phone. He pressed his lips into a thin line as he stared at it.

"Conrad's right. We require everyone's names. Let's inform the authorities. How far is the nearest town? Ten or twenty miles?" I asked.

Brad shrugged his shoulders and drew his girlfriend closer. He kissed her forehead. She whimpered and buried her face in his chest.

Poor Lindsay. She and Abby were always doing things together whenever she didn't hang with Corrie or Brad.

"Fifteen miles. Calling the cops and asking for everyone's name won't give us much time. Everyone will hear the sirens," Monte said.

"We can lock the doors." Even after I said those words, I didn't like the idea.

"You want to stay cooped up with a killer?" Monte asked.

"Let's put this to a vote. Who will fetch the names, then contact authorities?" Conrad asked.

"Why are you calling the cops?" Bob asked in the hallway.

My friends and I turned in surprise and stopped our conversation.

Ned and Hank shifted to block Bob from coming into the room.

"What's going on? Everyone downstairs is curious about the reason for a scream. They sent me up here to investigate," Bob said. The two big galoots continued to block his entrance.

"Let him in before more come. He can help," I said.

"How?" Conrad asked, unsure.

"I don't know. I'm calling the cops." I dialed 911 on my cell.

"911. What's your emergency?" the operator on the line asked.

"My...my friend is dead. She has a knife in her chest." Tears filled my eyes. This seemed unreal until I uttered those words. I covered my mouth to hold back a sob.

"Is she breathing?" the 911 operator asked.

"No, she has a knife in her chest." How dumb might this 911 operator be?

"What's your address?" the operator asked.

"I don't know. Lake something or other. We're sixty minutes away from East Garfo in Minnesota." Monte spoke the name, yet it eluded my recall.

"Give me the phone." Monte held his hand out, and I gave him my cell. After he gave our location, he explained what had happened. "We have a problem. We have a party going on downstairs." He listened to the guy on the other end. "Okay. We can try."

"We need to hide the beer. I can't get into trouble for underage drinking. My parents will kill me." Corrie rubbed the back of her neck.

Monte glared at her. He covered his ears and walked to the window for further instructions.

"The cops won't give a shit about the liquor. They'll want to know why a dead girl is at my lake house," Conrad said to Corrie. He shook his head and looked away from Abby.

"What if the cops do care?" Corrie placed her hands on her hips.

"Someone died?" Bob asked. His tone sounded shocked.

"Let him in," I told my friends.

The behemoths shuffled out of the way.

"Did someone call the cops?" Bob stared at Abby and then glanced at each of us.

"My brother is on the phone with them now," Conrad said.

Bob inquired, "What is their desired action from us?"

"Touch nothing. We need to stop the party and tell everyone to stay here. The cops will want statements." Monte covered the phone's speaker when he spoke. After we nodded at him with our instructions, he returned to the call.

"I can't go downstairs," Lindsay said. Her skin paled, and she trembled.

Corrie inquired, "Will you remain here with Abby?"

Lindsay shook her head.

"I will escort the girls elsewhere. The boys will speak to our guests, and Jolene will help Hank." Corrie led Lindsay by her shoulders away from the room.

Tabby trailed behind them.

Corrie's idea of bonding with a guy involved death.

"Let's get this over with." I walked into the hall, my knees gave out, and I sank to the floor.

"Breathe," Bob said as he raced to my side.

"I got her. Follow operator instructions, and go with the group." Hank kneeled next to me, rubbing my back. His hands resembled enormous foam index-finger gloves, and the action intensified my discomfort.

I bolted to the bathroom and vomited into the toilet.

"Get it out. You'll feel better after you do," Hank said. At least he didn't touch me while I puked.

"Thanks," I muttered after he handed me a towel to wipe my mouth. I had pulled my hair back, so that I got nothing in it.

"I can't believe Abby's dead. She was with us this afternoon."

"Kaylee was with us once, too." I stood and flushed the toilet, and my condition improved significantly.

"Her death isn't the same."

"Why not? Kaylee's dead and now Abby. Who's next?"

"No one, I hope." Hank sounded sad. I forgot he and Abby dated last year.

"Me, too." I washed my hands and gargled the mouthwash Hank gave me from the cabinet. My feet were steady for now. I could join those downstairs. "The police should be here soon."

Sirens sounded in the distance.

"Can you walk?" Hank asked.

"Yeah, I'll be fine. Thanks for helping me." I hesitated, then gave him a kiss on the cheek.

"If I carried you, would I get a full lip lock?"

"Whatever, asshole." I punched him playfully on the shoulder, and a giggle escaped my lips. The laughter was what I needed, despite the serious situation. He wasn't the class clown. Ned received that job.

"I hate seeing you upset."

"I don't like to be upset either." We stopped on landing in the middle of the stairs. "Why would someone kill Abby? She wouldn't hurt a fly."

"Her constant use of "great" led to our breakup within months."

"Would you kill her for saying that word?" I craned my neck to see Hank's face. He was the tallest guy at our school. I was five feet and two inches, and he was a full foot taller than me. He didn't look like a murderer. What did one look like, though?

"No, but she had gotten worse lately." Hank's eyes darkened for a moment, and he shook his head afterward.

"Abby was dealing with Kaylee's death. She would be less annoying soon."

"We're all dealing with what Kaylee did. Doesn't mean we have to be jerks."

"True, but someone didn't have to kill Abby for it."

"Do you think Kaylee's death is related to Abby's murder?" Hank asked.

"Makes sense, doesn't it? Kaylee's mother or stepfather could've come here and planned to kill us after what we did. Her brother might have done it too. Wasn't he supposed to be at the funeral?" I didn't remember seeing him there. My mother forced me to greet Kaylee's family, and he hadn't been standing with them. I had to bite my tongue to prevent myself from blurting anything out to them.

"Hold on, you're assuming they know what we did?" Hank placed his hand on my shoulder and yanked me into his arms. His massive biceps encased me, like he cocooned me in a blanket. His voice dipped low for his next words. "We'll let the police do their jobs. They'll figure out who killed Abby."

"Will we tell them everything we know?"

He took a moment to decide before quietly saying, "Yeah."

I sighed and returned the hug. He was warm.

"I like you, Jolene," Hank said after a minute.

"I like you, too. Why are you saying those words now?" I shuffled away from his embrace.

"After today, I have a sense that I won't be able to tell you."

Before I could inquire about the reason for his sentiment, two police officers entered the lake house with their weapons drawn. "Where's the victim?" One of them asked.

Monte pointed upstairs.

They ran past Hank and me.

"We should wait downstairs with everyone else," Hank said. We walked down the rest of the stairs.

"Where were you?" Monte asked after we joined him and our four friends. I included Conrad this time. Corrie, plus the two other girls, remained upstairs.

"I puked in the bathroom," I answered.

"Are you feeling better now?" Bob glided over to me.

I could only nod my head.

"Inform me if you need water or other provisions," Bob stated, then grasped my hand, bestowing a kiss upon its back. His lips were soft.

Hank placed a protective hand on my shoulder.

Bob squeezed my hand a little tighter.

"How did everything go down here?" I shook both boys off me. Currently, I lacked desire to interact with either individual.

"We dumped or put the beer away and told everyone what happened. We didn't tell them how Abby died." Conrad nodded at the entrance when an older woman and a younger man dressed in suits walked inside before whispering, "The real party is starting."

"I need everyone's attention," the man in a black suit yelled. Once the cliques quieted, he started talking again. "My name is Detective Willmar Morgenstern. My partner, Detective Rebecca Gibson, and I are here to investigate a suspicious death, not to stop the party."

Murmurs floated around the room.

"We'll try to make this easy on you. Cooperation from everyone proves necessary for this. We will endeavor to expedite your departure. Where's Monte Jackson?" Morgenstern asked.

Monte raised his hand, like we were back in our English II class with Mrs. Fitzgerald.

"I want to speak with you and your friends first. Come with me." Morgenstern weaved through the crowd, and I followed him.

At least thirty people were here. When had everyone come? Our pontoon boat held few occupants while cruising the lake. More teenagers must've joined once they learned we were throwing a party.

"Where's a quiet place?" Morgenstern asked once we were close.

Monte pointed to the hallway leading from the kitchen.

Morgenstern, alongside his partner, guided us through the area, directing us into a guest chamber located on the left. The bed didn't have anyone's belongings on it. This wasn't Conrad's or mine or Hank's room.

"Take a seat." Gibson delayed her actions until attendees formed groups, resting on the bed or floor.

The cops brought in two chairs from the dining room table.

"Is this everyone?" Gibson asked.

"Three more are upstairs," Monte answered.

Gibson waved to an officer in the hall and whispered to him.

Once they finished speaking, he took off.

Gibson returned to the room and sat in the open chair before saying, "We have a few questions for everyone, and then we'll speak to you separately. How do you know the deceased?"

"Abby Miller was our best friend," Monte said.

"How old was she?"

"Seventeen," Monte answered.

"Where did she live? What are the names of her parents and their number?" After Monte answered the personal questions, Detective Gibson asked one more question, "When did you see Abby last?"

"After she walked into the lake house, she went to pick a room. According to Corrie, Abby declined the pontoon trip, stating she had a migraine," Monte responded.

"This was according to Corrie?" Morgenstern twirled a pen in his hand.

"Yeah, I heard Corrie say those words. I retrieved the pontoon from its boathouse." Monte shifted in his spot and folded his arms.

"Did anyone go with Corrie? Or you?"

"I went with Monte," Hank said.

"And you are?" Gibson asked.

"Hank Pratt."

"Where's Corrie?" The investigator stared at me for an answer. Aside from her, I represented the sole other female attendee.

"She's upstairs with two other friends of ours," I answered. I also told her my full name, even though she didn't ask for it.

"Convenient." Morgenstern jotted in his notebook, and his partner asked the next question.

"Does Abby have any enemies?"

My friends and I shook our heads.

"Has she done anything to harm someone?" Detective Morgenstern asked.

"No," Monte said.

"Yeah, right? She and Corrie are the biggest bullies at our high school," Conrad said. His tone filled with bitterness.

"Shut up. Corrie and Abby aren't bullies." Monte clenched his fists at his side.

The detectives glanced at each other.

"What's your name?" Morgenstern asked Conrad.

"Conrad Jackson. I'm Monte's brother."

"What high school do you attend?"

"East Garfo High School, but Bob isn't from there. I'm a freshman and the rest are seniors," Conrad answered.

"Who's Bob?"

"I am. Bob August. I go to Greenwald in North Dakota. I just met everyone here at the lake today," Bod answered after raising two fingers in the air.

"And you tagged along because?"

"We're friends. I'm here for Jolene." Bob took my hand and gave it a squeeze.

I liked him trying to comfort me like this.

Hank performed a similar action, which I found less pleasing. He and Bob squished me between them.

"Conrad, why do you say Abby and Corrie are bullies?" Morgenstern asked.

"They hurt people. Not physically, but they made fun of other students' outfits or called them names," Conrad answered.

"Who have they hurt?" Morgenstern asked.

"Get the student directory for EGHS and pick a name. Corrie and Abby laugh... Abby used to laugh at everybody. They once stole a girl's clothes after gym class, and she was stuck wearing the smelly outfit for the rest of the day. They called her Stink-a-Beth and everyone else did from then on," Conrad said.

"Did they bully you, too?" Gibson asked.

"They stopped after Monte and my parents found out. I'm forever known as Con-Reject at our school. Abby claimed I asked her out, and she rejected me. I didn't ask her out, and I didn't kill her for being mean to me," Conrad answered.

"Why did you say those last words?" Gibson asked. her cheek twitched after she set her jaw. She sat near the bed. I could throw a wadded piece of paper at her and hit her despite my lack of basketball skills.

"Isn't checking if someone killed anyone the first thing police ask?" Conrad asked.

"Have the police ever questioned you before?" Gibson asked.

"I've seen TV shows," Conrad said.

"Real life isn't like television," Gibson said.

"No, shit. This isn't the apocalypse, and zombies aren't walking around. Abby's dead and I didn't kill her," Conrad said. His nostrils flared with his temper.

Bam.

He hit his head against the wall.

"You need to calm down. We're asking questions to sort this out. Did anyone want your friend dead?" Morgenstern asked.

"Kaylee Ghul's mother or stepfather might. Her brother would, too, if he were in town," I answered. The truth needed to be freed.

"What actions did Abby take toward Kaylee?" Morgenstern inquired.

"Nothing." Monte glared at me from his spot on the bed.

"What actions did Abby take toward Kaylee?" Morgenstern inquired again. His gaze settled on me for an answer, but when I said nothing, it bounced to everyone else.

"Abby's dead and two days ago, we buried Kaylee. My friends and I are involved in how she died." I breathed deep to continue with the rant that had been building in me for days. No one could stop me. I pointed my thumb at Monte. "This jackass couldn't keep his dick in his pants and fucked Kaylee. Sleeping with a best friend's boyfriend breaks the girl code, and Corrie ousted her. Kaylee couldn't handle the shunning, which we all did, and killed herself."

"Shit, you guys are like a fucked-up soap opera." Conrad shook his head. His calling us horrible meant we were.

"We're not sure why Kaylee killed herself," Monte stated.

"Why are you still in the group?" Morgenstern asked.

"Monte's family has money. Corrie would eventually forgive his stupid ass. She always does. He cheats on her a lot," I answered.

"Do you think I'm some rich, spoiled dumbass?" Monte sounded upset, and his face fell.

"No, I'm sorry. I'm pissed and confused. Our group wouldn't be the same without you," I told him. My heart pinged with guilt.

Monte proved much kinder than my earlier portrayal. He was the guy who would help another gather everything after a bully knocked their books and other items to the floor. Monte would brag after he paid for anything needing to be replaced two seconds later.

"Detectives, can I have a word?" A police officer interrupted the next question.

Morgenstern, following the officer's quiet talk with detectives, stated, "You children are past the age for playing pranks."

My friends and I glanced at each other. A few had their eyebrows knitted together. We had no clue what he was implying.

"Your friend isn't upstairs. Only three girls are, who are alive. Wasting an officer's time is against the law. I should charge you with obstruction," Morgenstern said.

"What? You're joking," Monte said, the first to recover.

The rest of us either had our mouths or our eyes opened wide in shock.

"Go see for yourselves." Morgenstern waved us out the door.

We ran upstairs and down the hall. Since I did track, I burst into the room first.

Abby's body was missing. Someone had tucked a new blue comforter in, and blood didn't cover it. The clean floor sparkled. A damp patch occupied the space where 'great' belonged, suggesting recent removal by water.

Chapter 3

Conrad ripped the sheets off the bed. Blood didn't soak the mattress, and it was bare.

What the hell? Where is Abby's body?

"She was here less than an hour ago." Conrad sounded confused, as I felt, and he scratched his head. "Who could've taken Abby? Did she fake her own death?"

"Abby wouldn't." Hank glanced at his flip-flops. Was he also unsure? She was there. We all saw her.

"If Abby did, she would've yelled 'surprise' by now. Her parents would ground her until she graduated from college if the police were called for no reason. Imagine what would happen if we got charged with obstruction of justice like Morgenstern threatened. Can detectives give tickets? Would the charge be a ticket? Or would we go to jail?" Monte asked. His tone grew more worried. His parents could buy his way out of almost anything. A party I didn't go to last year got busted, and he walked away with nothing, while others there had a minor in-possession charge on their record.

Hank shrugged his shoulders.

The officers listened to the investigators. If the detectives wanted to give us a ticket or arrest us, we'd get something, even if they couldn't give us one.

"Did anybody touch Abby's body? Or take a picture?" Conrad asked.

"Who would take a photo? Don't be morbid." Monte's face scrunched up.

"We need some proof of her being dead, or the cops won't believe us," Conrad said.

"Abby wasn't breathing when I got here. She was dead. If she didn't leave on her own, then the killer took her," I said. My friends stared at me like I had sworn for the first time again in kindergarten when Monte stole my crayons. "Who else would have moved her and made us look like idiots in front of the cops?"

"Someone who wouldn't want her death investigated," Conrad answered, the first to respond. He rubbed his chin, and his eyes darkened.

"And someone who wants to mess with us. Most of us belong to the popular crowd." Hank wasn't talking about Conrad and possibly Bob. I didn't know where the second guy fit, but he was hot. He should be somewhere within the top ranks at any school he attended.

"We'll investigate Abby's death on our own. Everyone but Corrie, Tabby, and Lindsay's whereabouts are accounted for," Conrad said.

"Not everyone." Hank squinted at Bob, who stood next to me.

"I was with Conrad, Brad, and Ned downstairs telling your guests what happened with Abby," Bob said.

"I didn't see you the whole time. Did anyone else see Bob?" Conrad glanced at the other two guys.

They shook their heads.

"Ha, you could've killed Abby." Hank snapped his fingers. He took a step back, and his eyes widened as if he realized the truth behind his words.

Idiot.

I nibbled on my lip. If Bob were the killer, he was standing right next to me. Maybe I should move away too? I dismissed that thought when a better one popped into my head. Why would he want to kill Abby? He didn't know us.

"Conrad or Brad or Ned or Monte could've murdered Abby. I didn't see them the whole time either. I was near the back of the lake house, keeping others from using that entrance to leave." Bob folded his arms across his chest. He made an excellent point.

The tension in the middle of my shoulders released. I didn't realize I was carrying the extra stress.

"Stairs there lead to the second floor." Hank also made an excellent point. Who should I believe?

"Where were you?" Bob squared his shoulders and stared back at Hank.

"Watching Jolene puke her guts out." Hank sounded smug.

"Like I believe Jolene got sick after seeing Abby. They barely got along, and Jolene handles dead animals. I was on the phone with the cops the whole time. I'm ruled out as a suspect." Monte searched his pockets and gave me my phone. I'd forgotten that I let him use it to call the police.

"I don't touch dead animals unless I put gloves on to get them off the street before another car flattens them. I called them in to animal control, so their owner will know. Unlike you, I care for poor, defenseless creatures like Abby. Besides, I was using your porcelain throne like Hank told you, you royal jackass." My temper and blood boiled as I held in my anger. I didn't want Bob to think I was a freak. I hated seeing a pet dead, and no one doing anything about it. If my cat died, I would want to know. Monte was getting one hundred percent of my wrath now. "You could have taken Abby and placed her somewhere else while you were talking on the phone."

With my last words, our group erupted into, once again, accusing each other of killing Abby. We'd forgotten anyone at the party could've murdered her.

I covered my ears and yelled, "This isn't working! We need to leave."

"You're not going anywhere until you answer more questions." Morgenstern must've been watching our reactions.

Scumbag.

"We'll do the interviews separately this time. Stay here. We're talking to your other friends first unless they're imaginary too." Gibson, his partner, waved to an officer walking the hallway. "Escort these kids to different rooms and have someone guard their doors. Find and separate the others."

"Whatever, bitch," I muttered once she left. They led everyone from Abby's room but me. How had I become the unlucky bastard to get stuck here?

After ten minutes of no one coming to ask me a question, my legs ached from standing. I sat on the floor and rested my back against the wall near the closet on the other side of the room. I couldn't sit on the bed where Abby had died. How did anyone clean everything in a few minutes? A thought triggered inside my brain. Unless they didn't.

I crawled to the bed and checked the floorboards carefully. No blood. I bent my head closer, sniffing. The wood smelled like bleach and floor cleaner. When was the last time Jackson's family came here? The scent wouldn't have lasted more than a week.

"What are you doing?" Gibson asked.

Wham.

"Ouch." I hit my on the bed frame after Gibson's words surprised me, and I rubbed the spot. "Checking for blood. My friend was dead when I came in here last."

"Come out. We have questions for you."

In my pursuit, I'd gotten halfway underneath the bed without realizing it. I crawled out and sat up, resting my back against the frame.

"Did you find anything?" Morgenstern asked. His tone sounded curious.

I narrowed my eyes at him. Was he mocking me, or did he want to know the truth? He didn't ask me another question, so I answered, "Nope, but someone cleaned the floor."

"Abby cleaned after she pranked you."

"Now you believe she's real?" I asked, surprised.

"An officer got a hold of her parents. Abby left with you. We're combing the woods for her, and we'll be searching the lake if we don't find her. They're staying home in case she shows up," Morgenstern said. The water would be a good place to hide her body. The killer could have weighed her down.

"Do you believe my friends and me?"

"Nobody's in the bed." Gibson waved her hand at the spot, and I glanced behind me.

"No shit, Detective Dumbass," I said under my breath.

"What did you say?" Gibson asked.

"Nothing." My cheeks heated.

"We have a few questions for you. How well did you know Abby?" Gibson asked.

"Well, our grandparents were friends, so were our moms, and now us. So, I'd say I knew her pretty well," I answered.

"You don't seem the type to be running around with everyone else here," Gibson said.

"Because I'm not rich, right? Money doesn't matter when you've known people since you've worn diapers together. Besides, my parents are middle class. We're not poor." I took a deep breath to calm my anger. The detectives were doing their jobs. They needed to ask a bunch of stupid questions to get to the truth.

"Sure, you're not." Gibson's voice dripped with sarcasm.

I glanced at my clothes. I hadn't changed after tossing my cookies. My T-shirt was dirty from whatever earlier, most likely vomit and dirt. And my hair was a mess.

"I don't care about my appearance when a friend is dead," I said. Despite my words, I raked a hand through my hair.

"Since Abby's dead, why don't you or anyone else have blood on your clothes?" Gibson asked.

"No one touched her body."

"Why not?" Gibson asked.

"I told them we shouldn't," I answered.

Morgenstern and Gibson glanced at each other. Why did detectives do that? They must think whatever I said was suspicious.

Gibson's next action confirmed my suspicion. Her right eyebrow rose to meet her hairline, and a smirk tugged at her lips. She could be pretty with her curly red hair, but the gray pantsuit she wore killed her figure.

"Abby had a knife sticking from her chest. I don't need to be a coroner to call her dead. She also wasn't breathing," I said. Why did the police constantly treat us like we were idiots?

"Who checked her pulse?" Gibson asked.

I hesitated, thinking back to everything and saying, "No one did. Abby's chest didn't rise."

"She could still be alive."

I covered my mouth to hold back a sob, and my next words shook with emotion as I asked, "Did I let my friend die?"

"No, you didn't. If Abby were dead, she'd be here." Morgenstern gave me a wadded tissue from his pocket.

"Unless her killer took her." I dabbed at the corner of my eyes with the tissue and blew my nose inside. Whoever murdered her could've used the window. The dresser was right in front of it. Hanging from the ledge and dropping a story wasn't difficult. I'd done it at my house more than once when my parents wouldn't let me go to a party or a friend's house.

"Really?" Morgenstern asked.

"Why not? Like you said, 'if Abby was dead, she'd be here.' Have you found her in the woods or the lake?" I asked.

"Didn't Abby play a part in a school play? Several of your friends told us she did." Of course, Morgenstern wouldn't answer my questions. However, I'd better answer his. The sooner I did, the sooner he and his partner could get off the silly notion that my friend had pretended she was dead.

"Abby was the lead once or twice." Was I the last one to be interviewed? I had shoved my phone inside my pocket, and I couldn't glance at it without them noticing. I didn't know how long I'd been searching under the bed for a clue. The detectives blocked my view of the clock next to the bed.

"Could she do stage makeup?" Morgenstern asked.

"I don't know," I answered.

"Do you see where we are going with this?" Morgenstern asked.

"You think Abby faked her own death and...and what?" I asked.

"Ran away when she heard the police sirens. Your friend probably got spooked."

"Have you found her in the woods?" I asked.

"We're searching. We'll go soon and return in the morning. Here is my card. Call me when Abby returns." Morgenstern said 'when,' not 'if.' He and his partner didn't believe me.

"Can I go join my friends?" I asked after pocketing the card.

"Go ahead." Morgenstern and his partner moved away from the door.

I raced from the room and descended the stairs.

"What's the rush?" Monte asked once I ran to him. A few of our friends weren't here.

"The cops are leaving. They think Abby will come out after they're gone," I said in between deep breaths.

"She isn't coming back. I've never seen a dead body until today. I'm sorry." Bob gathered me in his arms.

I returned his hug eagerly. He felt warm and safe. Once the detectives pushed past us, I let him go, asking, "Where did Ned and Conrad go?"

"Conrad went to his room, and Ned's outside talking to the police." Monte glanced at the locked liquor cabinet.

"We'll crack a beer or two once the popo leave. We'll discuss the prank later," Hank whispered.

"What?" I asked, confused.

"Later." Hank narrowed his eyes at me like he didn't want me to say anything more.

"Whatever." I took a water bottle from the fridge and plopped on the couch to drink it. Today had been such a mess. What had happened to the fun and carefree day we had planned?

"You okay?" Bob asked as he sat next to me.

I shook my head no and offered him my water. Hank couldn't stand Bob, so Monte wouldn't be playing host soon.

"Thanks." Bob smiled, and a dimple appeared in only his left cheek. The mark made him even more handsome. He was rugged, like a farmer. His dark brown hair needed a trim, and his steel eyes didn't sparkle with his smile. Was he worried about his safety? He took a swig from the water bottle.

"Where did everyone go?" I asked.

"Those here for the party left when the police let them go. They were gone by the time I got here. Monte was already here," Bob answered.

"Your friends left you here?" I asked.

"Yep. Great, aren't they?" Bob swayed his head disbelievingly.

"You can take a room here unless we're leaving tonight, or Monte can drop you off."

"I want to stay and make sure you're okay," Bob said.

Lights illuminated the walls from the outside. Night had fallen during this ordeal. The cars flipped around and left the lake house. The cops were leaving us.

"Abby, come on out!" Hank called once every light was gone.

Monte yelled the same thing a minute later.

"What are you doing? You saw Abby's body," I said in disbelief.

"You and Abby are pranking us. Your joke is good, but it needs to stop. We could get into serious trouble." Monte held an open beer in his hand.

"I'm not messing with you. Abby's dead," I said.

"You told no one to touch her body," Monte said.

"To not contaminate the crime scene. I've seen TV shows. You could've checked Abby anytime. I wasn't stopping you." I did to Corrie, but I didn't tell them.

"Detective Gibson said you and Abby pulled a prank, but it went too far," Monte said.

"You believe some cop over me? We've known each other for, like, forever? When have I ever done anything like this?" My nostrils flared, and heat and anger surged through me. I'd expected this from Conrad or Ned, but not from Monte.

"You've had your fun. Where's Abby hiding?" Hank asked me.

I glared at him in response rather than answering. Those knuckle-heads frustrated me so much that they brought tears to my eyes.

"Come on, guys, stop it. Jolene's not lying," Bob said.

I set my hand on Bob's and gave it a squeeze to thank him for everything.

"I'll be right back. I'm checking on Ned. He may have convinced the police to believe your friend's dead. Someone may have stayed behind." Bob kissed the side of my head.

"Thank you," I muttered. At least someone believed me. Did Brad also? He had been silent and not moving from his spot on the chair.

"Bob's an asshole. How can you like him?" Hank asked after Bob left.

"Bob's great. He understands I had nothing to do with Abby faking her own death." Why wouldn't my friends listen to me? I chewed on my bottom lip. I understood why they suspected me because of the stupid detectives putting the ridiculous notion in their heads, but this wasn't a prank. "We should leave. Abby's parents can come here and try to find her." I was done with this whole stupid trip.

Hank growled and pivoted away from me. He stalked to a door and pulled it open, revealing a closet.

Abby wasn't hiding in there.

Brad and Monte opened cabinets or anything big enough for her to hide inside. Did Bob just believe me?

"Are you really going to look everywhere?" I asked after ten minutes. This might be a good idea if the killer stashed her body somewhere. Before I could tell them to check upstairs, a scream filled the air from that direction.

My friends and I glanced at each other. Corrie, Lindsay, and Tabby were in danger.

Chapter 4

By the time my friends and I were on the second floor, Corrie was there. Her face was white as a sheet, and her whole body shook. She pointed to where she had come from, saying, "Killer." Her voice trembled.

"Where's Lindsay?" Brad had gone pale even more than Corrie.

"She's...she's with the murderer and Tabby," Corrie answered.

"You left them there?" Brad's tone rose, and he hurried down the hall with Hank and Monte running behind him.

I didn't know what to do. Three big men, who were tall like linebackers, could handle one assailant, not me. Although Monte was shorter than the other two guys by a few inches, he was taller than me still, and I would only get in the way if I tried anything. I should at least help Corrie. Did I want to be on the same floor as the killer though?

Conrad ran into the kitchen, looking up at us. "Did someone scream?"

Corrie sobbed and held onto the banister.

"Help Corrie to the couch. Your brother, Hank, and Brad are checking on the other girls," I answered.

"Why?" Conrad asked, after taking the stairs two at a time.

"Why can't you just do what I say? They'll explain everything when they return. I'll bring Corrie some water," I said.

Conrad muttered something I couldn't hear as he led Corrie down the stairs to a recliner.

I joined them on the same level, but I went to the kitchen instead. I opened the fridge, closed my eyes, and said a silent prayer for my friends to be okay.

"Are you coming or what?" Conrad sounded annoyed.

"Here." I handed Corrie the bottle. Why did Conrad have to be such a jackass? I should have tossed the unopened drink at his face.

"Why is Corrie freaked out? She's shaking. What happened to the cold, heartless bitch?" Conrad asked.

"Killer." Corrie leaned over and vomited on the floor. She dropped her water.

Conrad stared at me for an answer, but no words came out of my mouth.

I knew nothing other than what Corrie had said.

From the top of the stairs, Brad yelled, "You stupid, bitch. How could you leave Lindsay to die?" He sailed down the staircase and over to us. His hand clenched into a fist, and he raised it above his head.

"Hey, man. She was scared. Don't touch her. Are you really going to hit a girl?" Bob shifted to face the other guy. I didn't know when he had joined us, but I was glad he did. Brad had a temper and would punch Corrie without realizing he had done it until after the fact.

Brad glanced at his fist and lowered it. He collapsed to the floor. Giant tears rolled from his eyes, and a sob escaped his lips. I had never seen him cry. When he lost the shot in the big hockey tournament against our rivals for the championship last year, the whole team cried, but not him.

"Lindsay's dead?" I asked with a squeak.

"Where's Tabby?" Conrad asked.

"Go see for yourself," Monte, said solemnly. He had followed Brad.

"You can stay here if you like," Bob said to me.

I shook my head. I needed to see them for myself. My friends would have to believe me. I wasn't pranking them now. I didn't want another friend to die to prove it.

Without talking, Bob, Conrad, and I climbed the stairs.

Hank waited in the hallway. When we approached, he nodded at the door across from him. His cheeks had turned a pleasant shade of green. He was propped against the wall to support himself.

"Don't throw up for a minute? I'll go with you to the bathroom," I whispered to him. We should do everything in pairs.

Hank shrugged his shoulders and covered his mouth. A gagging noise came from his throat, but nothing spilled from his mouth.

I opened the door. Conrad and Bob had already gone inside while I had stopped to talk to Hank.

Streaks of blood splattered the wall like an artist had used it as a canvas. The smell hit me like I'd stepped in shit, and it almost knocked me to the floor. After covering my nose and mouth, I entered the room.

Tabby lay on the bed with her face against the mattress. Her back was bloody, and her green T-shirt ripped. Did she die first or second?

Someone, most likely the killer, had busted the window inward from the outside. I glanced outside. The roof to the porch that wrapped around half of the lake house was below me. The murderer must've climbed on top of it and come through here to do a sneak attack on my friends. They didn't stand a chance if they huddled on the bed. This room was like Abby's, except everything flipped; the bed was against the opposite wall, a dresser was near the window, and a smaller door for a closet was on the wall opposite that.

Lindsay was close to the door, and she stared at the ceiling. Her blood smeared on the floor like someone had held her.

I didn't remember seeing Brad with blood on him, but I hadn't been paying much attention to what he looked like. My gaze had been on his fist.

With trembling hands, I used my cell to snap a picture of Lindsay first. The image had blurred. I held my breath for the next shot. Her cheeks were still rosy, but her sapphire eyes spoke volumes for her state. No light. No sparkle. Nothing there.

Tabby was positioned on her stomach where I couldn't see her face. Her back should be evidence enough. I took a few images of her and her wounds.

"What are you doing?" Conrad studied me.

"Getting the proof that the detectives need. They should know Abby and I weren't playing a prank." I selected the best photo of each of them and inserted the files into a text message. I wrote a snide remark.

More dead friends, asshole.

I took out the card the detective had given me. After I typed in the area code for Morgenstern's cell, mine slipped and fell to the hardwood floor with a clatter.

"Give me your phone." Bob took it from me after I picked it up. It had missed landing in Tabby's blood by a mere millimeter.

"What prank?" Conrad asked.

"Morgenstern and Gibson convinced everybody Abby and I were messing with you all, since I didn't let anyone touch her body," I answered.

"I don't believe you'd fake her death." Bob handed me my phone. Next to the text, a little icon swirled around. The message was sending.

"Me either. Abby was dead. I get why you didn't want anyone to touch her since you found her." Conrad placed a hand on my shoulder and gave it a squeeze. "Did Morgenstern respond?"

"The piss ant had better call instead of texting." Bob's tone filled with anger.

"The message is still sending." My phone was only a year old, and it shouldn't have taken this long to send two pictures. The generation icon was gone and the words, 'No service', replaced it. I showed them and pressed the dial button. My cell didn't connect. "Can anyone make a call?"

Bob and Conrad shook their heads after checking their phones.

"We need to leave. I'll help Hank. You tell everyone else to pack their shit," I said. Without waiting for the two to respond, I hurried from the room and took Hank to the bathroom.

Hank immediately lifted the lid to the toilet and threw up inside. The room stunk like vomit and liquor.

I flipped the switch for the fan and tapped my foot, waiting for him to be done.

He tossed his cookies once more and flushed the toilet. Some of the smell flushed away with the water. The rest hung in the air.

"This is fucked up," Hank said, after washing his face. He gargled mouthwash from the bottle I gave him.

"Are you feeling better? We should pack our things and go," I said.

"Before we do, I want to talk to you." Hank would not ask me out now, would he? He cleared his throat and tried again. "Who do you think killed our friends?"

"Some psycho. I was with you when Abby's body went missing."

"And when Tabby and Lindsay died. Who wasn't in the room with us? Bob, Conrad, and Ned."

"You're forgetting Corrie."

"Do you think she's capable of murder?" Hank stared into my eyes. What did he think? I couldn't read anything in his blue eyes, besides calmness like the ocean as I peered back at him.

"I don't believe Corrie's as blonde as she likes to act." I folded my arms and leaned against the door. After covering my nose with my hand, I spoke again, "She saw Abby last, and Corrie was in the other room when Lindsay and Tabby died."

"We can't rule Corrie out as a suspect then."

"Agreed. Where's Ned? I haven't seen him since the cops were here."

"I don't know."

Hank and I stared at each other for a moment, and then we took off running to the staircase. We both had to be thinking the same thing. Ned could be dead.

"Has anyone seen Ned?" I asked as we joined our friends in the living room.

Monte shook his head and his gaze shifted to Bob, who sat on the couch, asking, "Wasn't Ned outside with you?"

"I was looking to see if a cop stayed behind, but as far as I could tell, no one did. I didn't see Ned. We should find him before we go." Bob glanced at the door.

"I'll tell my brother to monitor Brad. We'll search for Ned." Monte left the room.

Brad snored on the couch. Did he cry himself to sleep? He and Lindsay were like the married couple in our group. I thought they'd be together forever.

"Did you see the killer's face?" I asked Corrie.

Corrie shook her head. Tears spilled from her eyes and onto the hardwood floor.

"Would you recognize him again if you saw him? Or his clothes?" I asked.

"I won't ever forget him. He had on black tennis shoes, and his face was hidden like a ninja," Corrie said.

Hank and Bob were wearing flip-flops. I wasn't sure about the rest. I glanced at Brad and he had on sandals.

"Did you see the color of his eyes or how tall he is?" I asked. If we had some clue to who the killer could be, we'd do what? Run? Being safe wasn't entirely possible, at least not yet.

"I don't remember," Corrie said.

I pressed my lips together, finding what she said a little strange. How could she not recall? She could tell me the awful dress a celebrity wore the day or weeks after an award show.

"How do you know if the killer was a guy?" Monte asked when he returned with his brother. The Jackson brothers both wore sandals with two straps in the front and the one above their heels. They could have a pair of black tennis shoes here. I was with Monte when Corrie said she was attacked.

"I'm not sure. The killer could be a girl." Corrie's information wasn't helpful.

Monte dug through a junk drawer and set flashlights on the counter, saying, "We only have three."

"We can share or use our phones," I said. Would Corrie be coming with us?

She reclined in the big chair with her eyes closed. Her makeup wasn't smeared. She must not have cried unless she wore waterproof mascara. Although it would have left streaks on her cheeks because no brand could hold up to crying. Someone had cleaned up her vomit.

"Are you coming?" Monte asked Corrie, his voice gentle. He still cared for her.

"Where are you going?" Corrie was in the same room we were in and didn't hear the conversation? I would say she surprised me, but my words would've been a lie if I did.

"Ned's missing," Monte said.

"So? He'll come out soon. When are we leaving?" Corrie asked.

"After we find Ned, and *you* pack your bags." Monte would not do it for her, and neither would I. He hadn't bothered to do anything for himself, but this was his family's lake house. He could leave everything here.

"Can't someone else do it like Jolene?" Corrie asked.

"Stay here then." Monte took a flashlight and stomped his feet as he walked toward the door.

"Wait, a minute. Don't leave me here." Corrie bolted from the chair.

"Let's go. The sooner we find Ned, the sooner we can get the hell out of here." I took the remaining flashlights and handed them to Bob and Hank. I switched on an app for my phone. This way I could check it for service a few times during our search.

"Don't I get a flashlight?" Corrie asked.

"Use your cell like me." I grunted and left the lake house. Should we call out for Ned or not?

Monte called his name.

"Is yelling a good idea?" Hank shifted his weight between his feet and glanced around. "The killer's either near here or is one of us. He might even be watching us now."

"Or she." Corrie flipped on the flashlight Bob had given her and shined it at me. He was forced to use his phone like me.

"Whomever killed our friends is here, and he or she might have murdered Ned." I ignored Corrie. Her thought process was not lost on me. Holding my hand to my face, I blocked the light she shined on me.

"This isn't the time to be politically correct." Monte at least didn't get what Corrie hinted at. "Ned!"

"Do you believe one of us killed your friends?" Bob asked me as he walked next to me.

"I don't know. Where were the cops?" I searched the tree line with my light. No, Ned.

"I'm not sure. I think they all left. We should search in the other direction along the beach and the boathouse. Ned couldn't have gotten far," Bob said.

"Knowing Ned, he would've started walking," I said.

"Would he leave us here?" Bob asked.

"We'll find out soon enough," I said. We walked in silence until we were at the beach.

"We should split up," Bob said.

"Like that's a good idea," I muttered.

Bob furrowed his brow and stared at me. At least he knew not to shine the light on my face.

I sounded like a big bitch to the only nice guy here. I should explain to him why. "If we go our separate ways, the killer could attack," I said.

"We won't be far away from each other. Half of us will check the docks and the other half the boathouse. If anyone is in trouble, yell and the rest of us will come running." Bob glanced at everyone in turn.

"I'm with Jolene." Hank threw an arm around my shoulder, and his stinky sweat smell filled my nose. Before I could object or gag, he led me to the boathouse. When we were near the entrance, he whispered in my ear, "Who do you think killed our friends?"

"I don't know. Everyone has had an opportunity, right?" I asked. Corrie was in the room when the two girls died, but she didn't have any blood on her. She might've killed them and then changed her clothes afterward, in order to appear innocent. After she did, she screamed for help. Was she wearing the same outfit? I couldn't remember what she wore earlier besides the tiny two-piece bathing suit. When had she found the time to change?

"Besides you and me. We were together when Abby went missing and when Corrie said someone attacked her," Hank said.

I voiced what I thought about her to him.

"Anyone is a suspect besides you and me. Even Bob?" Hank asked.

"Yeah, even Bob," I agreed. Saying those words hurt me a little. He was a nice guy who got wrapped up in my drama. Although a better term would be nightmare.

"Let's check for Ned and then join everyone else. If we can't find him, we may have to leave him."

"Unless two people are murdering everyone."

"What did you say?" Hank stopped inside, and I bumped into him.

"I was wondering if we were dealing with more than one person. How else would someone murder three of our friends?" My eyes took a moment to adjust to the darkness. A small window allowed the light from the moon and stars to seep inside. The two thin beams from our flashlights illuminated our path. I didn't search for a light switch. Our location didn't need to be broadcasted to the serial killer.

"Four. Ned's not around. We can assume he's dead," Hank said.

"I'm not. I'm hiding." Ned peeked from behind a workbench.

"Shit, man. You scared the hell out of me. Get out of there. We're heading home." Hank placed a hand on his heart.

"How?" Ned asked.

"The SUVs, duh."

"Has anyone checked the vehicles? Someone removed the batteries," Ned said.

"What? Why were you inside our ride?" Hank's hand gripped the flashlight tighter. Would Ned leave us here? He would.

"To see if I could start one to leave. The detectives asked me to stick around and call them once Abby returned, but she was dead. She isn't coming back," Ned said.

"You were going to leave us here?" Hank's tone deepened, and he rolled his shoulders. Did he want to punch Ned? I did in this moment.

"You could've taken the pontoon to a neighbor."

The lake lapped against the five docks. The doors to the stalls were closed, and nothing was there.

"Where are the boats?" I asked. When we disembarked from the pontoon, the bays were full.

"Near the dock outside, maybe," Hank said, nonchalantly. He stared at Ned with such hatred on his face, that the other guy was cowering behind the bench.

"I saw nothing there." I crept closer to the edge and glanced into the water, shining the flashlight from my phone downward. Something was there. Something big.

Hank searched the bay next to mine and said, "Someone sunk the boats. Bob had time when he was searching for the cops."

"Ned's been hiding in here half the night. He had way more time to kill everybody," I pointed out.

"Is anyone else dead besides Abby?" Ned asked after coming closer to me. His lower lip trembled, and he pushed his glasses back onto the bridge of his nose after they slipped.

"Tabby and Lindsay died so Corrie could get away." I assumed the last part. Did she shut the door when she ran away? Or worse, lock it? I explained everything that had happened.

"Unless Corrie killed them," Ned said, when I finished. He had come to the same conclusion as me.

"We shouldn't be working with Ned. We should stick together, just the two of us," Hank said to me.

"Do you think I'm a murderer?" Ned rubbed the back of his neck.

"Everyone but Jolene and I are suspects, including you. You're on my list in the first spot because of what happened to the pontoon," Hank said.

"A killer would exclude himself," Ned said.

I sighed and shifted my body away from them to stare at the water. My friends' constant arguing was getting on my last nerve. We should let everyone else know we had found Ned. Having a moment to think was nice. My flashlight app shined on something in the water. Whatever was there wasn't a boat; it was not big enough.

"What the hell's there?" Ned spotted what I was staring at and pointed at it.

"I'll grab the hook. Monte uses it to bring the line toward him before he raises the boat from the water for the winter," Hank answered. Two cords dangled above the bay we were investigating. He took the massive pole thing off the wall above the workbench and crept along the tiny side of the dock. The space could only fit one person. He dipped the metal curved end into the water.

"You almost got it. Go to the left. Not my left, yours." Ned directed with his hands, despite Hank not looking at him.

"Whatever is there is pretty heavy. I got it." Hank's voice rose with triumph.

The object bobbed to the surface, and a screamed was ripped from my throat.

Abby floated in the water.

"Shit!" Hank lost his footing and fell backward into the other bay.

"Help Hank," I said to Ned when he wrapped his arms around me. I choked back tears and twisted away.

Ned hurried away from me and offered his hand, helping Hank from the water.

The poor guy was dripping wet. Water streamed from Hank's thick, blond hair. With his locks matted against his forehead, his hair looked longer than normal. He usually kept his hair buzz-cut short. He should grow it out like a lot of guys in our high school.

"Are you okay?" Monte burst inside the boathouse. He held a large stick in a hand.

"We're fine. We found Abby." I turned off my flashlight and snapped a picture. My last text had a failed to send notification. I sent her photo to Morgenstern with a mean caption.

Dead Abby, jerk.

The sign for sending kept on swirling. I still didn't have any service. The message would send unless it reached its maximum attempts like the last one.

"I'm glad to see you." Monte wrapped Ned into a giant hug.

"You too, man." Ned sounded confused and patted the other man on the back. Monte wasn't a hugger.

"Where are Bob and Corrie?" I asked once they finished. I wanted to hug Ned too, but I restrained myself.

"She took off when she heard you scream, and Bob volunteered to go after her," Monte said.

"Of course, he did," Hank said. His tone dripped with sarcasm.

"What's the matter with you? Bob's been a big help, and I don't want to deal with Corrie's shit right now. Can you believe she runs away in danger? What in the hell did I ever see in her?" Monte asked.

"She's smart enough to stay alive. She's sexy. We should run away too," Hank said.

"Shut up, man. Why are you wet?" Monte nudged Hank in the shoulder.

"I took a dip in the lake," Hank joked.

"You wanted to cool off, huh?" Monte asked.

"If you're done flirting, can we go?" Ned asked.

Everyone couldn't agree with leaving here more. We formed a line at the door.

Ned opened it and stepped out of the boathouse. An axe swept through the air, hitting him in the neck. His head rolled onto the floor.

Chapter 5

For a moment, nothing registered in my brain. Ned's head was on the floor. Blood poured from his body, and he fell to the ground. Once the images seeped into my subconscious, I opened my mouth, and a scream spilled out.

The killer gripped the axe's handle with both hands to yank it from the doorframe. Pieces of wood tore away. He was taller than I, and his shoulders were broad.

"Fuck," Hank said. The boathouse didn't have a back entrance. We were screwed.

"The water," I shouted. Time to take a lesson from Corrie. I ran to the edge, jumped in, and floated to the surface. Hopefully, I hadn't chosen the same bay as Abby's dead body.

Two splashes sounded behind me.

I prayed for the noises to be my friends and not the crazy axe-wielding psycho. I didn't dare look back to find out.

"Swim faster. We can dive under the doors. Be careful. You don't want to get your feet tangled in the seaweed below us. I doubt my brother cleared it like he was supposed to," Monte said to us. The doors must not close all the way because the water would freeze in the winter, and the metal would rust if submerged long enough.

I'd like to say I knew we could escape before I yelled at my friends to get into the water, but that would've been a lie. In my sheer panic, I jumped in to get away.

Hank bobbed next to me and within seconds he was in front of us, since he was all-state in swimming paid off. When he got to the doors, he went under the water.

What a jerk. What did I ever see in him? Corrie and he would make a cute couple.

"Stay with me," Monte said when we reached the door. He took my hand, and we went under together. We popped out on the other side.

"Thanks." My heart felt full for once on this trip. Monte had looked out for me, unlike someone else. Was the killer following us? I hadn't heard another splash, but with the commotion of us fleeing, another noise would be easy to miss.

"Don't thank me yet. Follow me." Monte steered us in the opposite direction of the beach. We kept going until we couldn't see the boathouse anymore. We swam for ten minutes in silence. Then fifteen.

"How much further?" My arms ached. I didn't want to complain yet, but I wasn't sure how much longer I could swim.

"Around the bend is a little path where my brother and I fish when we're too lazy to take the boat. We should be able to take the woods and enter the lake house unnoticed. Do you think Corrie is back?" Monte asked.

"With her survival skills, she's probably halfway to the next town," I answered.

Monte frowned and resumed swimming next to me.

"Corrie will be back at your place. She hates walking more than necessary." I did my best to cheer him up.

Monte was worried for Corrie when he should've been more concerned for us. We had a killer after us somewhere. We could see no one if they came from the thick grass along the shoreline. Anything beyond that was just a silhouette.

One bad thing about going to the lake was no light pollution from the city; everything was dark. If the murderer was already underwater with scuba gear or waiting for us in the woods, we were screwed.

Monte kept swimming at a fast pace.

My breathing came out ragged by the time we neared the bend. I didn't mention taking a break again. I wanted to leave the water and be on dry land soon.

Monte finally angled us toward the sandy beach. "Keep close," he said at the shore. His sandals squeaked, and he slipped them off, holding them in his hands.

During our fight for survival, Hank and I had lost our flip-flops. I hadn't remembered where or when I left mine. We kept following Monte through the thick forest. The trees ended, and we were at the back entrance to the lake house.

We ran to the door, and Monte tried the handle, but it wouldn't turn. He dug inside his swimming trunks, taking out a set of keys. He was lucky he hadn't lost them in the swim or the jaunt through the woods. We stumbled into a side entrance and ran to the living room, where our friends were waiting.

"What the hell happened to you?" Conrad's eyes widened.

"Why are you wet?" Corrie asked at the same time.

"Killer. Ned." I couldn't string two words together. My vision watered. In a few hours, I'd lost four friends.

This can't be real. Someone pinch me so I can wake up from this nightmare.

Bob hurried to me and wrapped me in a giant hug. This was what I needed. I cried on his shoulder for a minute or two.

Hank grunted.

"Is Ned dead or the killer?" Bob asked me. His tone sounded gentle.

I shifted out of his embrace and stammered on my words, "The killer cut...cut his head off."

"What?" Bob's eyebrows furrowed together.

Monte told everyone what had happened.

Hank and I filled in where we could.

"We were debating whether or not we were searching for you," Corrie said once our tale finished.

"Glad you cared." Anger seeped into Monte's voice. Corrie didn't care for him. Conrad nicknaming her a cold, heartless bitch was an understatement.

"Don't be like that. We're getting chased by a killer. Do you expect us to risk ourselves if you're already dead?" Corrie placed her hands on her hips. She puffed out her chest and pushed her shoulders back.

"How would you know if you didn't check?" Monte asked.

"Bob saw the blood at the boathouse," Corrie said.

"You went to search for us?" Monte asked Bob. His voice dropped the hard edge.

"After I caught Corrie and took her back here, I went to the boathouse. No one was there except for a body. I couldn't tell who it was without the head," Bob answered. Where was Ned's head?

"Thanks for caring, man," Monte said. The redness in his face disappeared, and his lips curved into a smile. He clapped Bob on the back.

"So, you were by yourself?" Hank asked Bob.

"I was," Bob said.

"You killed Ned." Hank jumped on Bob, who stood next to me in front of the couch. They fell on Brad, and I shifted out of the way before I got an elbow or knee to my face.

Stupid boys.

Monte's hand snaked around Hank's waist to yank him off, but he had over forty more pounds of muscle.

Hank held onto Bob's throat, choking him.

"Help me," Monte said.

Conrad took Hank's other side.

Corrie and I tried to loosen his fingers.

Bob's face turned purple. If he didn't breathe soon, he'd die.

Hank's fingers slipped, and the boys pulled him away. They fell to the floor.

"Why isn't Brad moving?" I asked, confused. Having two big teenage boys dropped on anyone should have awoken them. I'd once slept through a tornado across the lake until the tent fell on me. These guys were much heavier than the light nylon.

"Brad?" Monte let Hank go after he quit struggling.

I touched Brad's neck for a pulse. Nothing. I checked his nose for air. Nothing. His chest didn't rise. He was dead. When had he died? Why did his face appear peaceful? Every dead body I'd seen looked afraid unless embalmed. "He's gone." My legs gave out, and I crumpled to the floor. Tears burned my eyes. Five of our friends were dead. Who had murdered them?

Hank was with me for every death. He couldn't be the killer.

Wait. Abby might've died when the party started or when we left on the pontoon. Hank and I weren't hanging out the whole time. He was with me when the killer took her body and placed it in the boathouse. He might've stashed her somewhere else until he could get her there. I didn't think he had the time, though.

"Bob killed Brad, too." Hank interrupted my thoughts. He staggered to his friend and checked for a pulse, too. He shook his head when he was done.

"Bob wasn't near Brad. Bob dropped me here and took off to find Jolene...to find you guys. He couldn't be the killer. Why would he want to kill us, anyway? He didn't know us until a few hours ago," Corrie said.

"Unless we have more than one murderer," I said.

My friends stared at me. Their mouths flew open, and their eyes widened.

"Can anyone account for their whereabouts when everyone died? Corrie was with Tabby and Lindsay," I said.

"Hey, I didn't kill anyone!" Corrie yelled. Sweat dotted jer forehead along her hairline. The poor girl was going to ruin her makeup.

"Monte, Hank, and I were together when Ned's head got cut off." I narrowed my eyes at Corrie. Why was she stating that? What was she hiding?

"I didn't see a head in the boathouse." Bob shifted his weight between his two feet. Did he feel guilty for contradicting me?

He'd better.

"The killer could've taken it with him or kicked it into the water," I said. We weren't about to go searching for Ned's head just to prove me right.

"Jolene and I were together when Abby's body went missing. She was already dead, but we have to account for her body disappearing too," Hank said.

"Who wasn't in the lake house when Tabby and Lindsay died?" Corrie plopped into a chair and twisted the end of a throw in her hands.

"Ned and Bob, but Corrie's still a suspect." I set my chin on my knees and closed my eyes. Everyone could've killed someone at some point, even me. I wasn't murdering anyone, but I couldn't voice my innocence because murderers had the tendency to say they didn't kill anyone.

"I didn't murder anyone." Corrie pouted her bottom lip.

"You're a chicken. Besides, Ned isn't a killer," Hank said.

"Why not?" Conrad frowned, and he paced the room. On his second return, he spoke again. "If we have two killers, what's stopping three or four? Whoever murdered our friends may have killed Ned to keep him from opening his big, fat mouth."

Conrad had called everyone 'our friends'. I would have smiled at those words if the situation wasn't so dire. Death really brought people closer.

"Ned didn't do this. You should've seen him when Jolene and I found him. He was scared shitless." Hank sat next to me and placed a hand on my thigh.

Silence filled the room. Was everyone thinking who could be the killer like me? I hadn't marked off anyone.

Corrie broke the silence first by saying, "Why are we even staying here? We need to leave now."

"Corrie's right. Ned said the SUVs don't work and someone sunk the boats," Hank said.

"If the vehicles are working, we'll know for sure if Ned was involved or not. Any watercraft inside the boathouse is on the bottom of the lake," I said. On shaky legs, I stood with Hank's help.

"You should stay here with Corrie, since you're too chicken to check on everyone else," Monte said to his little brother.

"Bob and I voted to go search for you, ass. Corrie and Brad said no." Conrad ambled past his brother and left the lake house.

"Brad was alive then? How long ago?" I followed Conrad and placed my hand on his shoulder to stop him.

"Minutes before you burst into the room," Conrad said.

I now had three suspects: Conrad, Corrie, and Bob. I needed to keep a closer eye on them. Unless someone poisoned Brad earlier, and he finally died.

God, this sucks. I'm not a fan of real-life murder mysteries.

Hank led everyone else outside.

Corrie walked next to Monte while Bob brought up the rear.

I slowed to let Bob catch up to me. He must be wondering how in the hell he got mixed up in this insane life. I know I was. What did my friends and I do to deserve to be hunted? Someone was picking us off one after the other. A shiver ran down my spine.

"Cold?" Bob asked.

"I'm fine." I wasn't, but I would be once I was safe at home.

Monte climbed inside his black SUV and stuck the key into the ignition. He turned it, but the vehicle didn't do a damn thing. After the second try, he popped the hood.

Hank lifted the hood and set it with the metal thing to stand. Someone shined a light for him to see what he was doing.

"Someone stole the battery," Hank said.

"Let's check Brad's SUV." Monte climbed from his vehicle.

"Doesn't Brad have the key?" Hank asked.

"We can at least pop the hood to see if his battery is missing, too," Monte said. They did and got the same results.

Everyone shifted to stand in front of the vehicle instead of looking inside it.

"This may be a dumb question, but do you have an extra battery?" Bob asked.

"We can use a jet ski. What happened to the boats?" Monte scratched his head and glanced between Hank and me for an answer.

"Someone sank all your watercraft. Sorry, man," Hank said.

"Weren't the doors closed? The murderer had to know how to lower them. He could be from this lake," Monte said.

"Or he is smart enough to know how to throw a switch. Lowering the doors for the bays is easy," Conrad said. Thousands of dollars in damage didn't faze the Jacksons. They were that rich.

"How do we leave? Swimming at night isn't a good idea. Someone could get a cramp and drown," Monte said.

"Our best bet is walking." Bob didn't sound like he liked the idea one bit.

"Not until we get some evidence, so the cops believe us. Jolene had some, but our little swim in the lake destroyed our phones," Hank said.

Something sounded in the distance. I couldn't tell what the noise was with their planning, so I said to them, "Shut up for a second. Do you hear something?"

Everyone went silent. The wind blew the grass, and a few crickets chirped. The low purr of an engine sounded like it was coming closer.

"A car?" Corrie jumped up and down. "We're saved."

"Unless it's the killer's friend coming to get us." Conrad wiped his mouth to hide his smirk. I was thinking the same thing, but I wasn't joking.

"Shut up, asshole." Corrie shoved Conrad in the shoulder, and he staggered without falling to the ground.

We waited, staring at the path.

Lights shone in our eyes. The driver kept coming, and we scrambled away from the lot for them to park. The sedan screeched to a halt, and Detective Gibson climbed out. Her partner wasn't with her.

Rats. Wait, I hated Morgenstern more, or did I hate Gibson more? They were both jerks.

"Kids, I've been trying to call you. Why aren't you answering your phones?" Gibson asked. Her tone radiated with anger.

"We have no service, but we're glad to see you. We need to leave now," Monte said.

Gibson checked her phone and shook her head, saying, "A cell tower must've fallen down somewhere. Did Abby return?"

"Her body turned up, and someone has killed four more friends," Monte answered.

"Sure, kid. This joke is getting old really quickly. I'm going to write you up if you don't stop with it." Despite her words, Gibson removed her flashlight and drew her gun.

"This is a massive prank we're pulling on you. We love to pretend someone has murdered our friends," I said. My voice dripped with sarcasm. I wiped away the tears from my eyes. Gibson frustrated me enough to puke. Having Morgenstern here instead would've been much better. He was a total asshole, but he might've listened to us.

"You lead me to a *body*." Gibson pointed her flashlight at Bob. "The rest will wait inside my car."

"You'll not lock me up with a killer on the loose." I held my hands up and stepped back into Bob.

"The backseat is the safest place to sort everything out." Gibson stuck the flashlight end in her mouth and opened the back door.

"Can we leave if the murderer shows up?" I asked.

"Inside a cop car, we probably can't. It's designed to keep the criminals inside," Conrad said.

"Then I'm not going in there," I said.

My friends shook their heads too.

"Be that way. You lot are worse than kindergarten students. Let's go, studly. The rest wait here," Gibson said to Bob. She'd taken the flashlight from her mouth before she spoke and shined the light at him.

"Where's your partner?" Bob directed her toward the beach.

"Morgenstern's working an actual case. We got a dead body elsewhere. I got the short straw and had to come check on you lot when no one answered our calls."

"Don't you think teens not answering their phones is weird?" Bob asked.

"We figured you didn't want to get in trouble for your prank," Gibson answered.

I couldn't hear Bob's next question as they shuffled further away. After a few minutes, I sat on the ground.

Hank took the spot next to me.

I leaned my head against his shoulder. I hadn't forgiven him for ditching me, but at this moment I didn't care because I was so tired. My t-shirt was still wet near the hem.

"We should take the cop car and go." Corrie broke the silence first.

"And add grand theft auto charges to our record? Gibson will be back after seeing Ned, and she'll know what to do. We'll be leaving soon," Conrad said.

"You put way too much faith in the detective. What if she dies too?" Corrie asked.

"Gibson will be fine since I'm staring at the killer." Conrad's gaze shifted to Corrie.

Before Corrie could say a rebuttal, a gunshot sounded from the boathouse.

"Bob!" I ran toward the noise. Fresh tears sprang into my eyes.

Chapter 6

I burst into the boathouse to find Bob next to Gibson. She was bleeding from a bullet wound in her chest. Blood ran down her chin from her mouth.

"What happened?" I asked at her side.

My friends ran inside a few steps behind me.

"The killer came up behind us and Gibson shot him. The killer shot her back," Bob said. His voice shook. His hands trembled, and he put pressure on her wound. Blood splattered across his shirt. Was he injured too?

"Where did he go?" I asked.

"In the water. The killer took the gun with him," Bob answered.

"How do you know it's a man?" Corrie asked.

"He was big. Who cares right now? Will you help me stop the bleeding?" Bob asked.

Corrie shined a small light on the outline of a watercraft on the bottom of the lake. Whoever was there could hide, waiting to strike.

Gibson gargled on her blood and tried to lift her hand to me.

I leaned next to her to hear what she said, but I couldn't make out her words.

"Say it again, detective." I took her hand.

"Run," Gibson said. One last gasp escaped her lips before she died.

"She's dead. We need to take the cop car and go." I searched Gibson's pocket for her keys, taking them from her. Whoever was killing had claimed victim number six.

"Let me drive. You can barely stand." Bob held out his palm, and I dropped the keys into it.

I couldn't drive on a good day, let alone to escape here.

"We're letting Bob drive?" Hank asked in disbelief.

"I'm from around here. I know my way to the next town. Besides, someone's going to help Jolene to the car." Bob said.

"I can walk by myself." I'd been doing fine on my own until today. Why did guys always think a girl needed to be rescued?

"Why are you on the ground then?" Bob hovered above me.

"Oh." Hadn't I climbed to my feet already? I glanced at my lap. I was on the floor.

Hank offered me his hand and helped me to stand. We hurried the best we could with my shaky legs to the car.

I climbed into the backseat and scooted over.

"Get in." Monte opened the front passenger door for Corrie.

"I'm not sitting, bitch. Should we really be stealing a cop car? Why was Jolene okay suggesting it and not me?" Corrie asked.

"Shut up and get in the damn car, everyone. The killer is out there," I said before Monte could rebuttal. They could fight for hours.

Corrie grumbled, but listened to me.

The rest of our friends piled inside.

Bob turned the key in the ignition. The vehicle spurted as if it would start, but nothing happened. He tried once more. After it failed again, he glanced at me in the rearview mirror.

"Pop the hood." Monte climbed out of the vehicle. His little brother followed him. They went to the front and opened the hood. "We have a battery. Try starting the car again." Nothing. "I don't know what's wrong."

"You try starting the car while I'm under the hood. I know a thing or two about vehicles." Bob slid out and switched places with Monte.

Conrad shuffled to the other side.

I glanced at Conrad, and he shrugged his shoulders.

"Let me know when I can start it," Monte said about the car when he was in position.

Bob fiddled with something inside the hood and said, "Try now." Not even a sputter this time.

"Bob knows how to work on cars," Hank whispered to me. His words hinted at something more.

"So? Taking out a battery is easy. Even Corrie could do it. I'm not staying in here. Move." I shoved Hank on his shoulder. Corrie couldn't really do it, but he was getting on my last nerve accusing Bob of everything.

Hank climbed out of the car, and I followed him.

Although my new friend was alone with the detective. Bob could've killed her. Wouldn't she warn us to stay away from him instead of telling me to 'run'? Unless she couldn't with him there. I shook the thought away. I couldn't let my mind wander. Someone else was hunting us, I hoped.

"What does 'even I could do it' mean? Don't leave me in here alone," Corrie said. Her tone had grown high enough to hurt my ears. She slid out of the driver's side and followed me.

I shivered and waited while the boys tried to get the sedan going. At least Corrie didn't call me out on making fun of her. What would I tell her? I meant it as a compliment.

The gentle breeze off the lake cooled the air. What time was it? The unexpected swim ruined my phone, and I didn't read the clock on the dash. If the battery weren't working, I wouldn't be able to see the time, anyway. I stepped closer to Corrie and noticed from her phone we were approaching midnight.

"Here's our problem. Someone cut the timing belt." Bob held up a black piece of rubber with a pointed end in the light from his app on his phone.

"Did the belt snap?" Monte opened the car door and slid out.

"Someone cut it, but I'm no expert. If the end snapped off, fraying would occur, not a clean cut like this. This car won't start without a belt." Bob showed us the end. His words made the most sense to me.

"Can we grab a belt from an SUV for the sedan?" Monte asked.

"We can try. The belt needs to be the right size, or it won't turn. I'm not sure what will happen if the belt isn't the right one. We may get to town, or only a few miles from here, or nothing will happen. Do you have any tools?" Bob asked.

"Inside my lake house," Monte answered.

"Getting the battery out might be a better idea," Bob said.

"How did the killer get to the car? We were inside the boathouse for a little over five minutes." Conrad shined a light at the front door of the sedan. He shook his hand and yanked the handle. "Before we take the battery out, we should try the radio. A cell tower might be down, but the CB should still work." He climbed inside and rooted around in the front seat. After a few seconds, he cursed a lot.

"What gives, man? Six people are dead, and you didn't swear that much." Monte shifted over to the passenger side door.

"Someone cut the cord. Can we fix this?" Conrad held the end in the air and used his flashlight.

"Ned could have. Does anyone else know how?" Monte asked.

Everyone shook their heads. We should attempt to, though. Matching the colored ends shouldn't be difficult. We weren't leaving this hellhole without walking or help.

"Hold on, the killer didn't have the keys. How could he get inside?" Monte rubbed his hands against his thighs. He did that action whenever he was nervous.

"Now you understand why I'm swearing. Someone here is working with whoever is after us," Conrad said.

"Only three people were in the front seat," Hank said.

I glanced at Bob, Corrie, and Monte. I trusted only two. Well, one. Monte was bad or worse than Corrie.

"Three people stayed inside the car while we tried to fix it." Monte folded his arms.

"Corrie was alone in the front seat. Hank and I touched nothing there. We can vouch for each other," I said.

My friends stared at Hank to prove my story, even Bob. Their accusations hurt my heart, but we were doing the same thing to everyone. I shouldn't take what they said too personally.

"Jolene and I didn't go near the dash," Hank said.

"Are you sure?" Monte's eyebrow rose in the air.

"Jolene was never alone in the car long enough to touch anything on the dash," Hank answered.

"You think Corrie's a murderer? Does anyone?" Monte shifted to me.

"After what she did to Kaylee, Lindsay, and Tabby, yeah." I didn't even take a moment to respond. If someone could leave their friends to die or hurt them so they'd kill themselves, being a murderer wasn't that far off.

Monte glanced at his brother next.

"I've been saying Corrie is the killer all along," Conrad said.

Bob and Hank nodded.

"Come on, guys. I ran away because I was scared. You know me. I can't hurt anyone." Corrie glanced at everyone.

"Tell those words to Kaylee." My voice dripped with venom.

"I'm called Con-Reject because of you." Conrad shifted closer to his brother. "We should lock her up until we know for sure. Duct tape or locking her in a closet inside the lake house should work."

"I have nothing on me to cut the cord." Corrie patted her thighs. She wasn't leaving anything to the imagination. Her skimpy shirt didn't hide her hot pink bra. She didn't have any blood on her. She wasn't as dirty as me or anyone else here, either.

Selfish bitch.

"Unless you left it inside the car." Conrad searched the front seat but found nothing.

I stole the flashlight from Conrad and checked under the car. Nothing was there. I swept the light one more time to be sure, and something glinted near the front door to the driver's seat where Corrie had gotten out.

After dusting my hands and knees off, I ran to the side and picked up the knife, showing it to everyone. Corrie could've used this to cut the cord on the microphone. She wouldn't go underneath the hood, so she had nothing to do with the belt being cut.

"We'll tie Corrie in a chair until an SUV is ready to go. When it's done, we'll place her in the back. The cops can figure out if she's innocent or not," Hank said.

Conrad and Hank walked toward Corrie.

Corrie shrieked and ran toward the lake house.

"I'll talk to her. Corrie, you'll be inside a room where no one can get you," Monte called after her.

"We shouldn't split up. When the characters say those words in the movie, someone always dies." I wasn't into horror flicks, but the few I've watched while on dates had done what I said.

Pain flashed across Conrad's face, and he ran after his brother. Those remaining, including me, followed him.

"Corrie being the murderer seems unlikely," Bob said to me. Why did he change his mind?

"She might play stupid," I said. Corrie was anything but a moron. If she wanted to be a killer, she could be one. She could do anything she set her mind to. The first thing that popped into my head was when our classmates voted her prom queen when she was a freshman and the next two years. I had little doubt she would hold the title this year too. Even the upperclassmen looked up to her.

"Do you think Corrie's capable of murder?" Bob asked me.

"She's the reason Kaylee killed herself," I answered.

"Bob knows what happened to Kaylee?" Hank planted his feet and shifted on his heels to face me.

"Yeah, I told him. You assholes didn't want to talk. I needed to speak to someone before I went insane." I could tell anyone I wanted, and they had no right to stop me.

"We did nothing. Kaylee ended her own life." Hank's tone rose with each word.

"You don't feel a smidge guilty?" I asked.

"No. Why should I?" Hank asked.

"Do you know why Kaylee ended her life? Does anybody here know why? Our friend is dead, and now five more are gone. Over half our clique is gone." My voice matched Hank's until I spoke the last sentence, and what I said seeped into my brain. Kaylee's death and theirs had to be connected, right? Her stepfather was working with someone here to kill us. We had done nothing else horrible.

"Assume nothing until you speak to her parents." Hank's face softened to match his words, and he wrapped an arm around me, bringing me into a tight embrace.

I didn't shift away from him even though he stunk like wet dog and sweat.

"Who else would be after us?" I asked.

"Anyone who is jealous they aren't cool like us," Hank answered.

"Do you think they killed our friends for not being allowed to hang with us? Your idea sounds ridiculous. Have we hurt anyone else?" I asked.

"Not me. Corrie and Monte might have," Hank answered.

"Is there something going on between you two?" Bob asked.

"Yes," Hank said.

"No," I said at the same time.

Hank let me go and studied my face for a moment. He frowned, shook his head, and went inside.

"Are you into him?" Bob asked me when we were alone.

"I was planning on kissing Hank, but nothing else. He isn't my type," I answered.

"Who is?"

"If we live through tonight, I'll tell you." I entered the lake house.

Bob chuckled as he followed me inside. He took my hand and gave it a squeeze. The corners of his eyes crinkled.

"How can you laugh at a time like this?" I asked. We had tied Corrie to a chair in the living room. Giggle fits took me, and I placed a hand on my tummy. Tears sprang to the corner of my eyes from humor instead of sadness for once. She looked absolutely ridiculous tied to a chair.

"This isn't funny," Monte said.

"Look at Corrie." Conrad laughed too.

"I don't see the humor in this, do you?" Monte asked Hank.

"You weren't the one Corrie picked on a lot." Hank covered his mouth to keep himself from chuckling.

"I want to be locked inside a room. Jerks." Corrie struggled against the ropes holding her in place, but the cords wouldn't budge.

"Let's carry her." Hank and Monte lifted the chair.

"You've gained some weight, Corrie," Monte said.

"Shut up, asshole." Corrie's face went red like a tomato.

"What room does the royal highness want?" Monte asked.

"Anyone without windows. Jolene can hold the key," Corrie said.

I breathed deeply to gain control of myself. Why did Corrie want me to hold her key? Didn't she think I was the killer? She had accused me earlier.

"Jolene locks the door and keeps the key," Corrie said once I arrived. We placed her inside a storage room filled with boxes along the same hall as my bedroom. If it had any windows, we couldn't see them.

"Why do you want Jolene?" Monte sounded hurt.

"I've been thinking. I'm not the killer, and from everyone's talking earlier, only Jolene has been with someone when our friends died. She freaks after she sees them dead, and we know she can't act for shit," Corrie said.

"Whatever." Monte dropped the key into my hand.

"Why are you being so cooperative?" I narrowed my eyes on Corrie. She ran away a few minutes ago. Normally she would've put up a fight.

"You're with the killer, and I'm safe in here." A triumphant grin spread across Corrie's perfect pink lips.

"What if the murderer comes for you?" I asked.

"You won't let anyone get the key."

"They could break down the door," I pointed out.

"You'll hear it and come save me," Corrie said.

"You're putting a lot of faith in me." A little warmth filled my limbs. Corrie treated me the worst or second worst in our group. Depending on her mood, she forced either Kaylee or me to do things for her.

"When Bob was in trouble, you sprinted to the boathouse without thinking. Imagine how you'll be when someone you've known forever is in danger? Now leave me be. Go find the killer so we can go home." Corrie tried to lift her arm to shoo me away, but she couldn't move. She motioned with her head instead.

"Are you seeing the downside to your little plan?" I asked, curious. Anyone could harm her.

"Other men restrained me before. This is no big deal," Corrie said.

"Gross. I didn't need to know what you and Monte do," I said.

"Who said Monte had tied me up?" Corrie grinned at me. She and Monte were the perfect couple, both cheaters.

I blew raspberries at her and slammed the door. After locking it, I tested it and stuck the key into my bikini top. I should've changed my clothes earlier.

"What did Corrie say?" Monte asked.

"She thinks I can solve everything," I answered. As soon as those words, I didn't believe them either.

"You're the smartest one in our school." Monte took off down the hall, and I walked beside him.

"Hardly. That is...was Ned. I'm good with the science stuff. We can figure this out together." Did I think Monte was the killer? No, he was at the party when Abby died. He could've played a long song and left his DJing to murder her. Or he could have killed her before we left to go out on the lake. He wouldn't have had the time if he were taking the pontoon from the boathouse. Okay, I wasn't sure.

"Your plan will be our backup. We're getting an SUV started and leaving," Monte said.

"I love your idea better," I told him.

We joined the rest of our friends in the living room.

"What idea?" Hank asked.

"Nothing. The tools are in here." Monte dug inside a closet and removed a red kit.

"Leaving Brad on the couch doesn't feel right," Hank said.

"Do you want to put him on a boat and light it up to send him off?" I asked half-jokingly. What did I see in Hank besides his big muscles?

"Don't be funny. He's my best friend besides Monte," Hank said.

"Mine is swimming in the lake and the other two are dead upstairs. We need to leave them where they are to not contaminate the crime scene," I said.

"Who's going to investigate? We already have one detective dead in the boathouse." Hank pointed in the direction to get there.

"Morgenstern or some other pair. I doubt the nearest police station only has two detectives. Why are we arguing when we need to go?" This situation was beyond frustrating. How could someone cut us off completely? They could've used a device to take out our phones. A storm hadn't come while we were here. Abby had called our friends earlier today, technically yesterday. We had reception at one point. If any tower near the lake fell, the cell company would repair it right away. Didn't Detective Gibson say she had been trying to call us? The lines were obviously working then.

"I got the tools. Let's go switch the sedan's battery to the SUV." Monte held up the red case.

"Do you know how?" Bob asked.

Monte shook his head.

"I'll show you." They traipsed outside, and the rest of us followed them.

"Should we all be going to the SUV? What about Corrie?" I asked on the deck. Guilt swirled inside my stomach, making me feel queasy.

Damn it. She's right. Why do I have to care?

"Corrie will be fine. You have the key. If you don't lose it, no one can kill her," Conrad said. His next words convinced me even more. "Do you want to be alone inside the lake house if the killer comes?"

I hopped off the stairs and strolled with them to the sedan.

Bob removed a socket and tested it against the battery connector. It didn't fit. He tried another until he found the right one. He removed the two bolts.

"Shit," Bob said. Something clanged inside the hood to the ground.

"What happened?" Monte shined his phone's flashlight around the hood and searched for whatever issue Bob had.

"My hand slipped, and the socket fell to the ground."

"Grab another one. Who cares where it went?"

"You don't have another one inside this toolbox. Shine the light and help me find it." Bob motioned with his hand and bent.

"Good thing Bob is here, otherwise you guys would be lost," I said.

"Pretty convenient," Hank whispered. Only I was close enough to hear him. He needed to get over his petty jealousy. Bob was saving our asses again.

"Can it. You're worse than Corrie," Monte said. Someone else heard.

Good.

"I'm stating the obvious truth. I don't work on cars either. If Bob hadn't helped us, we'd be walking to the next town," I said.

"We still might if this battery's dead. There's something underneath here leaking." Bob touched the liquid and pulled his hand back with a yelp.

"Are you okay?" I rushed to him.

Monte shined the light on Bob, but he held his hand to his chest, saying, "I need to wash this off. I got battery acid on my hand." He ran toward the lake house.

"Should I go help him?" I asked.

"No, he'll be fine. Help me find the socket." Monte bent and used the light to scan the grass.

"Why are you searching for the socket? If the killer stabbed the battery, putting duct tape on the hole won't help," Conrad said.

"How do you know the killer did it?" Monte asked.

"We, like the idiots we are, left the hood up on the car. The battery is leaking now. We were inside. Who else could've done it?" Conrad asked.

"Speak for yourself. I'm not an idiot," Monte said.

"Yeah, we are," Conrad said. He puffed his cheeks.

"Is anyone going to help?" Monte asked. His tone sounded frustrated.

"Ah, guys." I tugged on Monte's shirt, and I couldn't tear my gaze away from the woods.

"What?" Monte looked at me.

"The killer." I pointed at him.

He dressed in black and brandished a knife.

Chapter 7

My friends and I scattered in different directions. A man's scream echoed in the trees a few minutes later. Had the killer killed my friend, or did my friend kill the killer?

I didn't dare stop running on the dirt road to find out. After a while, my side ached. I slowed and held onto it. The bottom of my feet hurt like a motherfucker. I lifted one and dusted the tiny rocks off. Minor cuts were all over my soles. I should've grabbed my tennis shoes inside the lake house earlier.

The lake house? Shit!

We locked Corrie inside a room. Although I was the only one with the key, the murderer could've broken the lock to get to her.

A massive wave of guilt washed over me. I had to go back. If not for Corrie, for Bob, a nice guy who had gotten tangled in my messed-up life. Someone wouldn't be killing my friends to get to him. They'd go after him first and leave.

Once I saw the clearing, I entered the woods. I planned to sneak along the back to enter the lake house. The killer had come this way. He wouldn't return, right? Unless he had his base somewhere around here.

Stupid, stupid, stupid.

I went three more trees deep and turned. I could barely make anything out in the clearing. Whoever was there might not see me either.

Damnit.

Anyone could see my white T-shirt, so I took it off, wadding it into a ball. The smaller the size, the harder to see.

I kept glancing around and listening to make sure no one was following me. Pretty far away from me, I noticed something. I stared and shifted closer to it, heading in the opposite direction of the lake house.

Someone sat with their back against a log, facing the other direction. I didn't dare call to them.

Whoever was there could be the murderer waiting for me. The dark hair didn't belong to Hank. The shade wasn't light brown like Conrad's.

"Hey?" I called after I edged closer. After no response, I touched his shoulder, and his head slumped to the side. I moved to stand in front of him.

Monte stayed still, but he might've lost consciousness.

"Please don't be dead." I touched his neck for a pulse. Nothing. I waved my hand near his nose, but he didn't breathe.

His chest didn't rise either. He was dead, alright.

I glanced at his body and covered my mouth to stop the scream. A sob escaped instead.

Monte's intestines had spilled out. The killer slashed open his swimming trunks, and his dick was missing. Someone had cut it off. Who would do such a horrible thing?

His shirt was bloody. Had he died from many stab wounds to his chest and legs?

I counted his wounds, but stopped after I got to twenty. His killer must've murdered him for revenge. Why else would they use such excessive force? Was this for Kaylee's death or something else?

Monte was a playboy, but he wouldn't be stupid enough to sleep with a married woman. At least I didn't think so. He wasn't eighteen yet. A father of one of his conquests might want him dead. Six other people wouldn't have died for him though.

I needed to get to the lake house to see who else was alive. I stepped back and something squished underneath my foot.

Oh, boy. Vomit rose in my mouth. Did I just step on Monte's penis? I took my foot off his dick, checking underneath my sole. Only mud was there. I hadn't stepped on his junk. My shoulders sagged with relief.

After wiping my tears away, I headed to the back entrance. A few minutes later, I tried the handle, but it wouldn't turn. I crept along the side to the next door, locked again. I fumbled my way, checking every window or door until I finally stumbled inside when Conrad opened it at the same time as me.

He caught me before I fell to the floor.

"You're alive." Conrad gathered me in his arms, giving me a hug. His voice filled with concern for his next question. "Have you seen my brother?"

"Has anyone else returned?" I avoided the question and his gaze on purpose. I shifted out of his embrace after hugging him back.

"Bob and Hank are here."

"Where's Corrie?" My mouth ran dry. What if she's dead, too? Her death would be all my fault. Why hadn't I come back here sooner?

"Locked in her room. We pounded on the door, but she refused to answer."

"She could be dead," I said.

"In a locked room with only you having a key? I doubt it," Conrad said. He had a point.

"Don't you have a spare key somewhere?" I asked.

"My parents keep a set in their room. Only Monte and I know where those are. He and I aren't the killers." Conrad shifted away from me and yelled inside, "Jolene's back."

"I'm so glad you're alive." Bob rushed to me and wrapped me in an embrace. He bandaged his right hand where he had touched the battery acid. When he stopped hugging me, Hank did the same thing.

"You had me worried to death," Hank whispered in my ear.

"Should we let Corrie go or search for my brother first? Someone screamed earlier and I'm worried for—" Conrad said.

"I'm sorry," I cut him off. My vision blurred, and my heart broke for the sixth time in a month. If I counted the detectives, the total would be seven. She had tried to help us. Gibson earned the right for me to be sad for her, even though she had acted like a total bitch.

Conrad crumpled to his knees, and he buried his freckled face into his hands. He and his brother didn't get along, but they were family. They cared for each other. I'd witnessed it on more than one occasion when they thought no one was watching.

I wrapped my arms around him, hugging him.

Conrad didn't shake me off.

I said nothing. Telling him I was sorry didn't feel enough.

"Where's Monte?" Conrad asked after a few minutes. He hiccupped and rubbed his dark brown eyes like his brother. He was a younger version, but with freckles and a lighter shade of hair.

"In the woods," I answered.

"I need to see him," Conrad said.

"I'll show you." If I had a brother or a sister, I would want to see them with my own eyes.

Conrad used my shoulder to help himself stand.

I climbed to my feet after him.

"Is showing him his dead brother a good idea?" Bob whispered to me.

"If I had a sister, I'd want to see her. I wouldn't believe she was dead until I did," I answered. Would seeing Monte do Conrad any good? No, but at least he'd know the truth. That knowledge wouldn't change anything.

A scream ripped through the lake house.

I stumbled as I ran toward the storage room where the sound came from and we had locked Corrie up. Someone had busted the door open. I entered and froze in my tracks, almost falling.

Bob bumped into me.

Corrie sat in the chair still. Her intestines were on the ground. Someone had gutted her like Monte. The two SUV batteries connected to jumper cables, and the red ends clamped to her and the black ends fastened to a metal bar.

The killer must've just murdered her, since she screamed. Where was he or she? Bob had said his attacker was a guy, but we must be against more than one person.

The Jacksons had stacked the boxes two deep and five or six high. Someone could hide in here, so sticking around would be dumb. The murderer could knock something over and give up their position. I glanced around. Nothing appeared to be touched besides Corrie.

Her killer must've run away when they heard my friends and I coming. They weren't in the hall when I approached. They could have ducked into another room.

My head swirled, and I used the door for support. My friends and I were talking the whole time while Corrie was being tortured. Why hadn't she made a sound besides the scream?

The smell of burned flesh, blood, and urine filled my nostrils. I gagged. Seeing Corrie, the prettiest girl at our school, like this was difficult. My chest tightened with pain.

Her blonde hair clung to her head. Her face was down, and I stumbled into the room. She had to be dead with a gallon or more of blood on the carpet, and her guts falling out, but I had to be one hundred percent sure. What if she had a faint heartbeat?

I bent down next to her.

Her blue eyes were wide open in shock, with no light in them. Her face, her once blemish-free face, now dripped with blood.

I felt a strange satisfaction at seeing the smudged makeup. I jerked my head, and the thought flew away. Corrie had her good points, some days. Checking her for a pulse would be pointless. She was dead. Gutted. Her death was worse than Monte's. Whoever was after us wanted them to suffer the most. This must be about Kaylee's suicide and the part we played in it. Her stepdad or mom wouldn't stop until my friends and I were all dead. No other mean thing Corrie or Monte did could compare.

"Can...can you bring me to Monte now?" Conrad asked. His voice shook when he spoke.

"We'll see Monte first before we leave," I answered. We left the room and headed to the living room. I hesitated by the archway into the kitchen. Those alive waited for me. I needed shoes, pants, and protection. I took a kitchen knife from the block. "Stay here. I'll be right back."

"Where are you going?" Hank asked.

"To get my shoes." I exited the room.

"You shouldn't go alone," Hank called after me. He didn't come with me.

What did I ever see in him?

"I'll go with her." Bob followed me.

I ran into my room and dumped my suitcase onto the bed. I laid the knife next to me on the mattress as I shoved my legs into my pants and my feet into my shoes. My T-shirt was dirty, and I discarded it.

"We should've cleaned your feet first." Bob kneeled next to me.

"No time, and I don't want to die." I held back the cry and wiped my mouth with the back of my hand. I put on a clean shirt.

"You won't. I'll protect you, always."

"Why do you care? We barely know each other."

"We've been through eight deaths in a single day. I'd say we've gotten to know each other rather well." Bob lifted my chin to see my face. His gray eyes stared at me, calm and collected.

"You're right."

He offered me his hand, and I took it.

My heart beat wildly in my chest. After we were safe and away from this horrible nightmare, we could talk about us. Until then, I wasn't ready. At the door, I released his hand and returned for the knife, sticking it in my waistband of my pants at my back. I used my black T-shirt to hide it. Once I was done, I took his hand again.

Hank's eyebrows furrowed together, and he asked me, "You ready?"

I nodded and went outside the back door, holding Bob's hand. I led them through the forest. We were a good way in without coming to Monte's body. I opened my mouth to say we might have gone the wrong way, but then the back of his head came into view. I sucked at directions.

"Monte?" Conrad ran to his brother. He collapsed to his knees and pulled Monte into a tight hug.

Tears sprang into my eyes watching them. No matter what we did, we didn't deserve this. Kaylee took her own life. We didn't force her to.

"This is fucked up," Hank said. His voice radiated with bitterness.

"What do you mean?" Bob asked.

"My friends and I didn't talk to Kaylee for a few days. Big freaking deal. She killed herself, not us," Hank answered.

"I know little, but your friend dying has to be more to the story," Bob said.

"Like what?" Hank asked.

"Maybe she had a rough home life? Maybe she was depressed and not being with you made her even more upset?" Bob shrugged his shoulders.

"Or maybe Kaylee got what she deserved." Hank's hands shook by his side. He walked to Conrad and helped him to his feet. "Grieve later, man. We need to get the hell out of here. Our lives depend on it."

"Kaylee didn't deserve to die, and what she did is inexcusable. We need to tell the cops what we did so they can find the killer. This killing spree might have nothing to do with Kaylee." Even as I spoke those last words, I didn't believe it.

"Let's go." Hank walked between Bob and me, breaking our hand-holding.

"Asshole," I muttered. Did Hank have to move between us? He wasn't into me until today. He acted as if he owned me, but he didn't. We were friends, nothing more.

"Sorry, I'll go talk to him," Conrad said.

"Let him be. We'll walk on the road and head to the next place. You know where it is, right?" I placed a hand on Conrad's shoulder, stopping him.

"Over three miles away," Conrad said. His eyes were downcast, and his face was pale.

Bob took my hand, giving it a squeeze.

"Are you coming or what?" Hank paused in his tracks, glancing back at us.

"Let's go," Conrad said.

Hank continued walking, and a knife flew at his back.

I screamed, but the sound came too late.

The blade stuck between Hank's shoulder blades.

I traced the path the knife took.

Bob, next to me, still raised his arm. His other hand held mine.

"I told you Bob's the killer." Blood ran down Hank's chin. He wiped at it before he staggered and fell onto his stomach with the knife attached to his back.

I was too scared to do anything.

Bob released his hold on me and walked the few feet to the knife, yanking it out. He used the blade to cut Hank's throat.

"Why Bob? Why?" I asked once I found my voice. I had done nothing to save another friend. My heart ached.

"Your group killed my sister," Bob said.

"Who?" I had to be sure.

"Kaylee," Bob answered.

"You're Bobby Ghul?" My mouth popped open. Bobby was a scrawny kid who appeared nothing like the beefy Bob. What happened to him these last five years?

"In the flesh," Bobby said.

"Are you working with Kaylee's stepdad?" Conrad edged closer to me, and his fingertips grazed mine.

"I'd never work with that bastard." Bobby spat on the ground after he said the last word. "Do you know what the bastard did to my twin? Do you know why he sent me away?"

"Kaylee never told us." I had asked her at least a dozen times or more why Bobby left, but she refused to tell me anything. After a while, I stopped bugging her, believing she would spill everything when she was ready, but she never did. My right arm shook, and I held onto it.

"Our stepdad raped her every day. When I got old enough to put a stop to him, he had me thrown into a boot camp. He even gave me this with a beer bottle that he threw at my head." Bobby ran a finger against the scar on his eyebrow.

"I'm sorry." My chest squeezed tight. Why didn't Kaylee tell me the truth? I could've helped her. I could've saved her.

"I'm sorry, too. We didn't know. Why didn't your mom stop him?" Conrad asked.

"My dad dying messed up my mom. She doesn't care, and she went along with our stepdad for years. I killed her first," Bobby said. His tone lacked any warmth.

"You killed your stepfather next?" Conrad asked, even though he and I knew the answer.

"Do I really need to answer? I tortured the bastard worse than Corrie," Bob said.

"Are you murdering everyone alone?" Conrad asked.

"Yeah, Abby was easy. After the party started, I snuck upstairs and killed her in her sleep. Corrie took more ingenuity. I broke the door since she was easy pickings, tied to a chair. She believed I was there to flirt with her until she saw the knife. I got her scream recorded and set it to go off when I called my phone," Bobby answered.

"Wait, Hank, you, and I checked the door. I could have sworn it was locked." Conrad took my hand.

"Was the door locked? You believed me when I held the handle and pounded on the door," Bob said.

"What did you do to Monte?" I asked.

"I hunted and mutilated him before Corrie." Bobby sounded proud.

I could easily attribute everything to him. Why didn't I make the connections until now? He could've cut the cord to the radio in Gibson's car while he was in the front seat. He killed her in the boathouse. She told me to 'run', but I didn't realize until now that she meant for us to run from him.

Conrad clenched my hand enough to hurt it, and his shoulder blades tightened.

"Keep cool," I whispered to him. Bobby was a psycho. Anything we said could set him off.

"How will I kill you?" Bobby asked. After no one said anything, he raised the knife by his right ear.

"Don't kill Conrad. He had nothing to do with Kaylee's death. He never hung with my friends until today." The lie rolled off my tongue easily. He did at parties, but I would not tell Bobby the truth. I shifted to block Conrad.

"Get out of the way," Bobby said.

"Don't, Jolene," Conrad said when Bobby spoke.

I slowly walked to Bobby and put my hand on his in the air. I forced it down. My proximity to him made throwing the knife difficult unless he wanted to hurt me. What the hell was I doing? I backpedaled until my back hit a tree.

Bobby raised the knife to my head.

I closed my eyes. I couldn't escape him, and I couldn't get away. If he killed me, at least Conrad might live.

A thump sounded as if the knife hit something. I didn't feel any pain. I dared to open my eyes and check. Bobby had stabbed the knife into the trunk inches above my head.

I stared at him.

The hard edge in Bobby's eyes softened. He touched my cheek and ran his thumb across my lower lip. "I've always loved you." He pressed his lips against mine.

I was too shocked to move. He had tried to kill me minutes ago, and now he was kissing me.

What the hell?

A branch snapped in front of me. Bobby's lips left mine.

Conrad halted his advance and stared at us. His chin trembled.

Seeing my remaining friend scared melted my fear away.

Bobby yanked the knife out.

I touched his hand to stop him from throwing it. When Bobby turned back to me, I moved closer and pressed my lips against his, pushing him against another tree.

Bobby's tongue slipped into my mouth. We made out for a bit.

When my lungs burned, I pulled away from him to breathe. I wrapped my arms around his neck and gave him a hug.

Conrad was still there, not moving.

I mouthed to him, "Run," over Bobby's shoulder.

Conrad ran past us. His shoes crunched over the foliage.

Bobby grunted.

"Let him go, Bobby. No more killing. I can't be with if you do. I love you," I said after he took the knife from the tree.

"You love me?" he asked, unsure.

"Since the moment I met you." The lie was easy. I liked him as Bob August, but as Bobby Ghul, I couldn't. How could I? He had killed my friends.

The knife clattered when it hit the ground. Bobby swept me into his arms and kissed me along my jawline until he found my lips.

I could make out with Bobby and let Conrad run to safety. At least someone would leave this Labor Day weekend massacre alive.

***

The cops had searched the woods for hours.

I curled myself in Bobby's arms, keeping warm inside an abandoned hut. Trees and plants hid the entrance. No one could see it unless they knew where to look. We had stumbled onto the small cabin by pure accident when I tripped on a root. We squeezed through the crack in the door to hide from the police.

I could call for help and risk Bobby murdering me, or I could stay here in his arms. He promised me he wouldn't kill anymore unless I wanted him to.

When someone drew closer, I collected my breath.

The officer and whoever he was with were not far away. I could hear them speaking.

"The kid said they were in the woods, right? They couldn't have gotten far on foot," someone said. He paused near the entrance. Through the crack in the door, I could make out a few things. He scratched his head, and he wore a dark blue shirt like a cop.

"Are we dealing with a hostage situation?" his partner asked.

"The Jackson boy said the girl went with the culprit to let him escape. The guy killed eleven people. He could've murdered more. Didn't someone find a body out here? Would any girl go with a serial killer willingly?"

"I hope we find her alive. Where could they be? We've been here since early this morning," the partner said.

"We're moving onto the next grid. The captain wants us to double back later this afternoon," the cop said.

"We'll be here all day, won't we?"

"The dogs should be here soon. Hopefully, they'll…" What he said next drifted into the wind as they walked away.

If the dogs came, they'd smell Bobby and me. We would be in trouble. I waited for a few more minutes in the silence before I whispered, "We need to go."

"How? We can't keep running like this." Bobby frowned and wrapped me in a tighter embrace. "I won't let the police take you away from me."

"The fastest way to leave here is by boat or by car."

"The cops will have the road blocked."

"We'll have to steal a boat and cross the lake."

"How? The cops are searching the area," Bobby said.

"We'll steal a police boat," I answered.

"What do we do if an officer is using it?" Bobby wasn't making this easy on me.

"I'll kill them." I smiled at Bobby. Everyone had something bad inside, and I decided it was time to let mine out.

Opening Season Massacre

The Holiday Killing Spree Book 2

K.A. Meng

Chapter 1

The smell of smoke filled the air. The ax slipped from my hand, and the sharp blade stuck into the ground, missing my foot by a mere millimeter. I would've cursed myself, but my mind spun, my heart pounded, and my mouth ran dry.

I held my breath as I glanced around for any signs to run. No animals fled. No birds flew in the sky. A trail of smoke lifted into the air, although it was not quite enough for a blaze. Someone must be at a cabin nearby. Bobby wouldn't like that. And, frankly, I'd rather deal with a fire.

I picked up the ax again.

Whack.

The log split in two, not perfectly in half. Should I continue or stop? I set another piece of wood into place. This time when I cut it, the halves weren't close to being equal.

My stomach tied into a giant knot. I needed to get the wood done before a blizzard came. The weather service had been threatening one for weeks now, but I didn't dare continue. I'd probably hurt myself. I could distract Bobby for a bit, but he'd soon find out we had visitors nearby. If I managed him right, he wouldn't try to meet anyone tonight.

After I set the ax down, I wiped the sweat from my brow. The woodpile would have to wait. I hustled into our cabin and took off my boots.

Bobby wasn't in the main room. He could be in our bedroom or out back.

I hung my jacket up and called out, unsure, "Bobby?"

He rushed into the room from our bedroom and gave me a quick kiss before asking, "Jolene, you called? Is the chopping done? Do you need any help?" He removed his coat and pulled off his hat. Sweat dripped from the curls in his blond hair. He needed a haircut and another dye job. The roots of his dark brown hair were already showing. He didn't wear contacts, and I was thankful. I loved his gray eyes. They looked like a storm brewed underneath his lashes.

"Not yet. Before I tell you something, promise me you won't hurt anyone." I squared my shoulders and faced him.

"I have killed no one in a while. Why? What's going on?" His eyebrows furrowed together.

"You didn't murder anybody because I did." I feared if he did again, he wouldn't stop. He almost didn't after a guy tried to hurt me. I shuddered at the memory of five people or more dead and forced myself to think of something else. The image of me killing the cop to steal a boat flittered into my mind. A few more people who recognized us had died too, also by my hands. Bobby would've dropped more bodies if he had ended anyone's life.

"Just tell me," Bobby said. His tone filled with worry. He placed his hands on my upper arms, and his gaze searched for something in mine. His wristwatch ticked off a few seconds, and a log on the fire crackled.

I forced the panic attack that was rising inside of me to back down. I licked my lips before I whispered, "We have neighbors."

"I'll grab our guns." Bobby released me and made a beeline for the wooden box on the table in the kitchen.

"Can't we wait to see what they do first?" I placed my hand on the lid, stopping him from removing a weapon.

"What if they recognize us? Do you want them to disturb our peace? We've been here for three weeks, our longest time in one spot. We can't stay if they know who we are. I want to give you the life you deserve."

"What if they don't know us? We haven't been on the news for a while now. If you kill them, then the cops will get involved. Someone will miss them. I don't want—" I stopped myself from saying more, since I hadn't told him something yet.

"You don't want what?"

"Never mind. Not important." I glanced at my boots. Snow melted from them and left drops on the floor. I should've taken my footwear off when I came back in from chopping the wood. Oh well, too late now.

"Why are other people in our woods?" Bobby ran a hand through his hair.

"According to the shop owner when I went to town last, this weekend is opening season. I should've asked how busy everything got around here, but I didn't want to raise any suspicion," I answered. We rented our cabin from someone online. I drove the stolen car near town and then walked the rest of the way for supplies or work. We did what we could for free stuff like chopping wood, hunting, and whatever else.

"What's the big deal with hunting?" Bobby asked. He sounded unhappy.

My heart twinged. I wanted nothing more than to make him smile. I had grown up with hunters. My dad tried to take me several times, but I had no interest in hurting animals that couldn't defend themselves back then. He'd given up after a while. We both knew he wished to have a son and not me. However, I was an only child.

"Opening season is a holiday for hunters," I answered.

"How long will they stay?" Bobby asked.

"Through the weekend. They'll keep on coming back though if they don't fill their tags."

"What do we do?" Bobby wrapped his arms around my waist and set his chin on my shoulder.

I shuffled through several plausible scenarios and settled on one, saying, "We wait until tomorrow and go talk to them. If they recognize us or we suspect they do, we kill them. We'll have to leave right after they die."

Bobby swept my hair behind my ear and gave me a kiss at the base of my neck. "I wish you didn't have to cut your hair so short."

"Someone will recognize me if I don't." I might need to dye my roots too. We had changed our hair color at the same time. I looked quite different with my natural strawberry blonde hair dyed to a brunette.

"What should we do now? I need a distraction or I'm killing our neighbors."

"I have an idea." I kissed Bob. Since we wouldn't let anything or anyone disturb our peace, we deserved happiness like any normal couple.

"I like where you are going with this." His voice came out husky. He yanked my shirt off, and I unbuttoned him, letting his shirt drop to the floor. I ran my hand across his hard chest. He toned his body from spending years at boot camp. He kept his muscles since we had only a little food and not much else to do but have sex and work out.

I only worked for a few hours here and there. I couldn't leave Bobby alone for too long.

Pressing my mouth against his skin, I trailed kisses to his navel. A small patch of hair led from there and dipped below into his pants. I licked him until I got to the edge of his jeans.

"Don't stop there, unbutton me. I want my dick in your mouth and then in your body," Bob said.

I undid his button and zipper, releasing his penis from its prison. He never wore underwear. I wrapped my hand around the base.

"I can't wait anymore." Bob yanked me up and pressed his lips against mine with force. We tossed most of our clothes away. He slid inside me in a matter of seconds.

Sex with Bob was a perfect and massive workout. It left me satisfied, content, happy, and every other positive word that existed. He drew circles around my belly and my nipples. A shiver of pleasure ran from his touch to the tip of my toes. I hadn't realized we stumbled to our bed during our lovemaking. When had I kicked off my boots? I didn't remember.

"I love you, Bob," I told him.

"I love you, too." He pressed his lips against mine and dipped his tongue into my mouth. After our little make-out session, he slid his arm around my body.

This was the life I didn't want to give up. I sighed and raised my right arm above my head, sticking it underneath my pillow. Movement in the corner caught my attention. I yanked off my sock and tossed it, making whatever was there disappear.

Bob jiggled my boob some, and I laughed. He smiled for a moment. The next second, a serious expression crossed his handsome face as he said, "Do you realize you only call me Bobby whenever you're worried about me? I'm Bob when we're like this."

"I do? I'm sorry. I didn't realize. Can you forgive me?" I needed to be more careful. I didn't want to hurt his feelings, but he was like two different people. Bobby was the kid I met a few times before his mother and stepfather sent him away, and he returned to kill my friends at a lake cabin less than two months ago. Bob was the man I flirted with there and in whom I confided before they died. I never believed he was a murderer until he killed a friend right in front of me.

"Nothing needs to be forgiven. I enjoy knowing when you're upset, but I don't want you to fear me. You know I won't ever hurt you, right?"

"Yeah, I do." I didn't need to take a moment to answer because I trusted him completely.

"Good. Your eyes darkened, and I was worried you feared me." He sighed and his shoulders sagged.

"Sorry. I was thinking."

He raised an eyebrow.

"I was thinking about those we killed. Well, you killed," I answered his unasked question.

"They deserved it," he told me. Spittle built up in the corners of his sweet mouth, and he wiped it away.

We needed a much safer topic, and I was curious about something, so I asked, "Have you ever wanted to kill me?"

"Right after I read my sister's suicide note, I did. I even planned on how I would hurt you and your so-called friends, but I changed my mind when I saw you at the funeral. You were upset. No one else was. I heard your words at the lake. You're the one person in this world who I can never harm. If I'm not with you, I'll burn everything to the fucking ground." Bob's eyes were wide enough to show their whites.

"Let's be together forever, then." I wrapped my arms around him and lay my head on his chest. His heartbeat thudded fast until finally settling down. I could always calm him.

"We will. You can count on it." He lifted my chin and kissed me.

I kissed him back and then asked, "Kaylee left a suicide note? What did it say?" I didn't dare ask Bob if Kaylee had left a note until now. He mentioned nothing before. I'd been dying to know if my best friend did, but who could I ask? Her mom and stepdad were dead, killed by Bobby, my Bob. They deserved it.

"I don't want to talk about my sister's note." The playfulness fled his tone, and his gray eyes darkened to jet black. He sat up, moving away from me.

A shiver ran down my spine at the bitterness in his voice. My heart raced so fast that a sharp pain pierced my chest. "I'm sorry, Bobby—Bob. You don't have to tell me anything."

Bob looked at me. His nostrils flared, and he opened his mouth to say something, but no words came out.

"You…you don't have to say anything. I understand her death is still difficult for you to talk about." Kaylee died less than two months ago. Losing a sibling must hurt.

"You understand? No one understands. She was my twin, my other half. Every day," he stopped himself.

"Every day, what?"

"Nothing." Bob stood and stormed out of the room, naked.

With him gone, the cold seeped into my bones. Shivering, I pulled the blanket up to cover myself and lay there contemplating what I should do. Bob's wardrobe was in here with me. He'd been cutting trees into smaller pieces for me to chop and then stacked the wood I'd done into a pile out back. He said that if he had time, he'd put our dry clothes away. I sat up and noted the empty basket by the dresser we shared. Had it been full? I couldn't remember.

Our boots and coats were near the front door. Bob could put his on and leave if he found a pair of pants. I was pretty sure a couple pairs of his pants hung near the fire to dry, and the pair he wore before we had sex was out there, too.

The wind howled, and a window shook. Did the door creak? Did Bob leave? He would be back if he had left. One possibility filtered into my mind, and it bothered me. He needed to be left alone, but the last time I ignored my friend's feelings, she had killed herself.

The hair lifted on my arms and the nape of my neck. *Screw this.* I could sit here worrying, or I could do something. I shoved the blanket off me and went to find Bob.

He paced the big room.

After he made his second pass, I asked, "Can we talk?"

"I don't want to discuss my sister." Bob stopped for a second and rubbed his hands on his toned thighs.

"We won't until you're ready. I don't want...I don't want you to leave me." My stomach rolled, and I felt so nervous I could puke. Tears flashed in my eyes. I couldn't lose him over something so selfish. I'd been at a low point in my life multiple times and considered killing myself, but I never went through with it because of my friends. They were gone now, except for one, Conrad Jackson. The decision I made to stay with my lover meant I'd never see him or my parents again. Bob was my world now, and I just couldn't lose him.

"Oh, baby." The anger across Bob's face vanished, softening. He walked the three steps to me and wrapped me in his arms. "I'm not going anywhere. I'll do everything to keep us together."

"Me, too."

Chapter 2

The next morning, we melted the freshly fallen snow and boiled water for our baths. We dyed our hair again to hide our roots. We wanted to appear fresh when we greeted our new neighbors. Snow was in the forecast for tonight. As long as we made it home, we'd be fine.

"What's the plan?" Bob's cologne of marine air and sandalwood filled my nostrils. I had chosen that delicious smell for him from a dollar store. The generic kind based on some fancy brand fits better with our cheap lifestyle.

"We pretend to be hunters also and let them know we're out here, so they don't accidentally shoot us." I took a camouflage coat from the rack by the door. I purchased his jacket from the thrift store. After giving it a sniff, my nose scrunched from the smell of wet feathers. We should've washed it again. After squirting a fabric refresher over it, I handed it to him.

My coat was next to his and pink. Why women liked the color was beyond my comprehension. It clashed with the browns and greens from the leaves and branches, which were the more proper conceal-ment shades.

"We'll need to bring guns, then." Bob zipped himself up and then helped me with my zipper. He always did sweet things like this.

"How else are we supposed to be huntin' varmint?" My tone dripped with sarcasm and a poor attempt at a southern accent.

"I hope you don't talk like that in front of them." When I frowned at him and was about to get defensive, he added, "Your way of speaking is good enough."

"You sayin' I got an accent?" I asked. After hearing mine for the first time, I cringed.

Son of a bitch!

I did sound way too much like I'd come from the upper Midwest USA. "Don't you know?"

"God, I love you." Bob laughed and gave me a quick kiss. He took the rifle down from above the door.

"If you did, you'd let me have the big gun." I raised an eyebrow and stared at the beautiful weapon in his hand.

"And risk you hurting yourself again? No way! My job as your man is to protect you." The rifle had a wicked kickback. The first time I shot with it, I had a massive bruise on my shoulder for a week from the butt slamming into it.

"Or kill anyone you please," I muttered.

"If they harmed you, I would." Bob checked to see if the rifle was loaded before setting it down, then inspected a much smaller one and gave it to me. He cleaned the guns every night. I didn't have to worry about any jamming.

Or if they touched me, I thought. I kept those words to myself. If he found out how grabby the men at the late-night shift were at my job in town, Bob would've gone on another murderous rampage. We should keep our mass murdering of people down to once or twice a year.

"Here you go." Bob shoved a bunch of bullets and magazines into the left pocket of my jacket, since I was right-handed. That way, I could pull them out and load much faster with them on the opposite side.

"Should we bring anything else?" I glanced at the main weapon box on the table. We had a lot more guns, knives, and other killing instruments stashed around the cabin.

"Get us each two knives. I'll pocket a revolver. We don't want to look conspicuous. Besides, if we need to kill anyone, we won't do it until dark."

"Like you've done before?" I always wondered why he waited until then.

"Harder for people to see me."

"Unless they have night-vision goggles." I put my arm through the strap on the rifle and slung it on my back before taking out four knives. The blades of the knives ranged from four to six inches long. I rolled up my stonewashed jean legs and hooked a sheath above each ankle. After inserting the knives, I fixed my pants to hide them. No one could tell they were there.

Bob grabbed the 9 mm. He could do enough damage to a person without a gun. He carried on when he was against more than one person. A family or a group of friends could be at the cabin with the fire. If Bob and I were lucky, we might meet a loner. I could only hope.

"We need the orange vests." I took them from the drying rack near the fire. Once we learned neighbors were close by, we bleached and cut clothes to make vests. I dyed them before bed last night. The coloring wasn't as bright as I wanted, but it would have to do for now. Amazing how easily we lived with the guidance from a couple of how to survive in the wild books. I missed my city life with Wi-Fi, s'mores, iced coffee, and a hot shower that we didn't have to melt snow for, but I had Bob. He was plenty for me.

"Let's roll, babe," he said after he took his knives from me and sheathed them. He gave me another heart-melting kiss. We left the cabin together, walking hand in hand.

We didn't speak for the first two miles. Once we were at the base of a large hill, Bob said, "When we get to the top, we'll know where our neighbors are staying." We had scouted a good ten miles around our place, only finding six other cabins. We didn't dare go any further because of the town on one side and the shorter days.

"Looks like the big cabin," I said at the top. We didn't break in to see how many people could stay there. Now I wish we had. We wouldn't wonder. If I had to guess, I'd say ten or more.

Please be a lonely rich guy who likes to flaunt his wealth instead.

I crossed the fingers of my free hand for extra luck.

"I was afraid of that." Bob chewed on his bottom lip.

"Could the cabin be further away?" My tone sounded hopeful. The smoke from their fire didn't appear too far now, another three miles away at most.

Bob shook his head. He tugged my hand, and we continued on our path. This side of the hill was much steeper than the one we had just walked.

"Watch yourself." Bob slid his hands down to my waist and hauled me over a rather deep pile of snow.

Eighty minutes later, we could see the faint outline of the cabin. I glanced at the sky, and smoke filled it from a chimney. Yeah, people were there. *Rats.* Part of me wished the smaller one, about two miles further out, was being used instead, but no one took care of it, so I doubted anyone lived there or used it. Perhaps Bob and I could use it as a hiding place if we needed to.

"Have you ever greeted hunters before?" Bob stopped moving, and I did, too.

"Just my dad's friends. But I know we must declare ourselves. Once we get closer, we can call to them and let them know we're here. With our orange vests, they shouldn't shoot at us." They couldn't be as bad as us. What were the chances of two sets of serial killers in the same woods?

"I don't like this," Bob said.

"Me either. Let's get this done." I tugged on Bob's hand, and we crept toward the cabin. When we were close enough, we let each other go. We hid behind trees next to each other, watching our neighbors work.

An older gentleman, a grandpa's age, lifted a box from the back of an SUV parked next to a truck in the makeshift driveway. Another truck was behind the SUV. One truck had the attachment to move snow. Another two or three vehicles could fit in the spot they had cleared. Would more people show up?

The door to the dark gray truck opened, and a man as round as a barrel stepped out after shoving something into his shirt pocket. Smokes? His vehicle had a thin layer of snow on it. He walked to the SUV where a lady rummaged inside, older than me but younger than my mom. He gave her a kiss. They had to be a couple. This must be a family.

She set a duffel bag on top of a cooler. Even from this distance, I could see her tanned skin, although I couldn't tell if it was the fake kind or natural.

When the grandpa got closer to the cabin, a kid of about ten years old ran outside and took the box from him. They exchanged some words, but I was too far away to hear them.

My heart hammered inside its cage. The boy was too young to be hunting. He shouldn't be here. What if we had to kill his family? Could we kill him too? Bob could without hesitating. I didn't know if I would let him, though. An adult wasn't defenseless like a child.

"I see four people. What do you see?" Bob asked.

"Same as you. The damn curtains were drawn," I whispered. Could the occupants be in the cabin or out hunting? With three vehicles, there should be well over four people.

"We should introduce ourselves. They might notice us creeping soon and become suspicious. We can gather more information on our prey if we're with them."

I thought about what Bob had said for a second, and then something dawned on me. Has he done this before? So, I asked him, "Was that why you introduced yourself to me back at the lake?"

"One reason. I also wanted to get to know you. I've been in love with you since we first met."

My heart swooned at his words. I couldn't tell him I felt the same. When I first saw him, he was the scrawny, annoying brother of my best friend. He spent years changing himself. After I met him again, I liked him. Would that be love at second sight?

Bob grinned at me before kissing me on the forehead. He offered me his hand, and we stepped into the clearing. "Hello?" he called.

One by one, the people turned to us. Their eyes widened in shock at seeing us. Why?

"We saw the smoke from your fire and let you know we're here," Bob said to them. He let go of my hand to hold both of his in the air as he drew nearer.

I copied him.

"Where's your cabin?" the older gentleman asked once we were closer.

"Just a few miles from here." Bob pointed in the direction we had come from, but our little love nest wasn't there. We took a slight detour to get here.

"I didn't know anyone had a place near here." The guy sounded leery, and he touched his chin.

"Like I said, our cabin is a few miles away. We traveled more than a couple of miles to get here. We saw the smoke from your fire, and just wanted to let you know we're here for our safety and yours." Bob stopped walking once we were in the clearing. He opened his mouth to say something, but I spoke, preventing him from saying anything else.

"How many tags did you get? We got one." I stopped behind Bob and donned a smile, trying my best to put the family at ease. My arms grew numb from holding them up. I placed them down. My guy had dropped his.

"A few," the grandfather said. His tone sounded unpleasant. I wasn't getting much from him. Hopefully, this was his personality.

"What's going on, Glen?" an older lady asked as she stood in the doorway. Her hair had turned white. She wore a sweater, but not a jacket. They must plan on staying here for a while. Over the weekend, maybe longer. Why else would they make their cabin so comfortable?

"We got some neighbors."

"Really? Where are they staying?"

"Possibly the Milligans." Glen looked at us for an answer. I assumed that was the older gentleman's name. The chubby man didn't look like a Glen.

"Not sure. We signed up for one of those rental properties people can do on their own. Never got the owner's name for anonymity." I didn't lie or tell them more details than necessary. Bob and I would stay as long as we could. Using a fake name to rent the cabin was the simple part.

"Sounds like something the Milligans would do," Glen said.

"Or the Fonds," the older lady added.

"Is the hunting any good here? We plan on checking out several woods for the best one until we buy a place." I switched tactics to win the old man over.

"We've gotten a few twelve-point bucks, usually get an eight," Glen answered.

"Roger has gotten a twenty before. We forgot to tell you our names. I'm Lori Pratt and this is my husband." I held out my hand. My real name was Jolene Argall, and Bob wasn't Roger. He was Bob Ghoul. We weren't married, and I hoped one day he would ask me.

Glen stared at my hand.

"What are you doing? Greet our neighbors, and let's get in here and chat for a bit," the old lady called after a moment.

"Nice to meet you. I'm Glen Jager and this is my family." He finally smiled as he shook my hand. He named those who were with him and his wife, Betsy.

She held the door open for us as we knocked the snow off our boots before heading inside. "Does anyone want anything to drink?" she asked.

"I could use a beer," the guy named Marc said. He had to own the massive truck outside that he'd been sitting inside. The size of it screamed that he was overcompensating for something.

"You've had enough of those today." Betsy swatted his hand with a dish towel. She had to be his mother.

"But ma—" Marc said, but he was cut off.

"Don't but mom me. We have plenty left to do today before you hunt," Betsy said. I was right about their relationship.

"One more beer won't hurt me." Marc's tone whined.

"You should listen to your mother and stop your smoking, too. That'll kill you someday." Bridgette stood next to him. Glen had introduced her as Marc's lady friend. I couldn't quite tell if she was on good terms with his family or not.

"Stay out of this." Marc pressed his lips into a white slash, and he shifted his weight between his feet.

"This has nothing to do with you. I'll get you a beer, sweetie. Does anyone else want one?" Betsy didn't like her boy's girlfriend, and I wondered if her husband felt the same way.

"I'll take one." Bob glanced at me, and I shook my head.

I never developed a taste for the nasty beverage. Why anyone thought it tasted good was simply beyond my comprehension.

Betsy fished the drinks from the fridge and handed the beers to everyone except me.

"Have you been married long?" Glen stared at Bob for an answer. He settled into a recliner while Bob and I sat next to each other on the couch.

Bridgette took the spot next to me. Her tanned skin was the fake kind. Her short brown hair stood up on end, held there by a ton of hairspray. She looked like she was stuck in the eighties.

"Three years happily married now. We're high school sweethearts." Bob glanced at me and winked. The move looked more lovey-dovey than anything else to me.

I smiled at him.

"You're rather young," Betsy said.

"We get that a lot, but when you know someone is the one, you know." Bob took my hand and gave it a kiss.

Heat surged across my face from his intimate contact. I didn't need to fake my embarrassment.

"I bet your husband knows what I'm talking about," Bob said.

"I do. I do." Glen took a swig from his beer. Once he finished drinking it, he glanced at his wife. Their gazes met, and they shared something between them. I wished to one day be able to tell Bob everything with one look like that.

Bob and I spoke to the family for at least twenty minutes. I tried to think of a way to ask them if anyone else was coming here, but I couldn't find an opening.

Bob shook his empty beer and asked, "Do you have a garbage can?"

"I'll take it." Betsy took it from him, and she scooped up every empty bottle, sticking them in a trash can in the kitchen. Was I worried the family would run his DNA? Not really. With the trash can full, finding Bob's beer bottle would be hard. Marc had been drinking a lot. Maybe he'll be drunk later. He'd make an easier target if we had to kill him.

"So, is anyone else coming here to hunt with you? I don't want to accidentally shoot anyone," Bob said.

"We're here today, and more will join us tomorrow. We should all be in our orange vests and never alone," Glen said.

"We'll be wearing them too. It was nice meeting you all." Bob stood and took my hand. We said our goodbyes and left the group.

Once we were half a mile away, Bob shifted to stand in front of my path, stopping me from going any further. We walked side by side whenever we could. He always guided me and made sure I didn't stumble or fall.

"The neighbors didn't recognize us as far as I could tell. Do you think they did?" he asked.

"Yeah, or they will," I said, not needing time to think.

"What do we do?"

Corrie appeared beside Bob. He couldn't see her since she was dead and a ghost. Her whole body was translucent, and her guts spilled out, reminding me of what my guy had done to her. The first time I saw her, I almost peed my pants.

"You know what to do," Corrie said to me.

"We kill them," I told Bob.

Chapter 3

"**A**re you sure?" Bob asked. He shifted his weight between his feet.

"Yes, we...we can come back with our weapons. We'll have to kill them tonight." My mind spun. Once they were dead, we'd have more time to escape. What if they called the police? Shouldn't we run now? If they had known who we were, they wouldn't have let us into their cabin.

"What about tomorrow when more people show up? We don't know how many will come or when." Bob paled some.

"We'll deal with them when they get here. I want to be happy with you. We can't let people invade our lives. We'll be running forever if we do." Tears prickled my eyes. I would not cry. The cold air would turn my waterworks to ice, and I could get sick quickly.

"Shh, I got you. I'll protect you." Bob wrapped his arms around me. He always knew what I needed and when I needed it.

"Can we kill them?"

"Let's get back to our cabin and gear up. I've been dying to try out our night vision goggles on something." Bob had stolen them from a town we had driven through.

We held hands and returned the way we'd come. Corrie disappeared for now, but I knew she'd be back soon. She was like a severe case of foot fungus, always hanging around and watching. I shivered. When she was in the corner after Bob and I had sex, I tossed a sock at her to get her to leave. She had for a little while.

"Are you cold?" Bob asked.

"I'm fine," I lied. I doubted any antifungal could get rid of Corrie.

"What are you thinking about?"

"Nothing important." I was exhausted by the time we arrived home. My legs burned, and my feet hurt. Curling up next to Bob on our bed would be a much better idea than heading back to our neighbors. Night hadn't fallen yet.

"We should eat and take a nap." Bob went to the fire and tossed a log onto it. Nothing but embers remained. If we had been gone any longer, the blaze would've gone out, and our cabin would have become frigid; frost would pile up in the cracks and windowpanes.

"You don't want to do anything else?" I smiled at him. No matter how tired I was, I always found the strength to make love to Bob. He had the strange ability to return some energy back to me, like he was the opposite of a vampire. I might steal stamina from him.

"You bet I do." A bubble of laughter ripped out of his mouth, and his body shook with his amusement. He kissed me hard.

I slipped my tongue into his mouth, and he did the same with mine. I kept kissing him until I couldn't breathe. After pulling away from his embrace, I took a deep breath. I pulled the hat off his head. I couldn't wait to feel him inside me again. If we had any neighbors closer to us, they would certainly call the police because of the loud screams that would come from our cabin soon.

"We should stop to eat," Bob said after he helped me out of my coat and sweatshirt. He pressed his lips against mine.

"Not yet. I don't want this to end." My thoughts swarmed. What if this was the last time I would ever have Bob? We could die, or one of us could.

"Okay, I'll make love to you and then I'll feed you."

"Sounds like a brilliant plan. Now, no more talking." We no longer said anything except for some grunting and screaming. Once we finished, I closed my eyes, basking in the glow of happiness.

"Don't sleep."

"Sure. Sure." I couldn't say it a third time before sleep overtook me. Something startled me awake. Bob had shaken my arm to get me up.

"You need to eat," Bob said. His voice sounded gentle. He placed a plate next to me.

The smell of it made my mouth water. "How long did I sleep?" I sat up and stretched. The cold air hit my skin, and I shivered. After I pulled the blanket to cover my body except for my arms and head, I shifted my food into my lap. Bob had cooked a splendid feast of beans, meat, and onions with cornbread.

"Long enough for me to cook." He sat next to me, naked.

I enjoyed the view of him. All his muscles appeared toned and lean. I wished I could be as fit as he was. Someday maybe.

When I took a bite, I moaned. The cornbread melted in my mouth. Bob had added some butter to my plate to soften the dryness. We had few meal choices. Sometimes the canned food would freeze if we didn't keep it close to the fire. If we kept it too close, the food would cook.

Would I leave Bob for a more normal life? No way! I was madly in love with him. I couldn't imagine existing without him. He was a big part of me, more than my parents when I had lived with them. We never did the family meal or holidays. They were always too busy for me, so I became too busy for them. What would my man and I do for Thanksgiving or Christmas this year? We had celebrated our birthdays back in October. My man turned eighteen a day before me, like Kaylee, his twin.

My heart clenched thinking about her. I wished I could've done more. I blamed myself and I should have. Bob didn't. Maybe he did. I didn't know, and I was scared to ask him.

After her death, I searched for signs to make sure no one I cared about ever committed suicide again. I tried to find answers to why she did it. Kaylee went through every warning on the website.

She had told me more than once that she wanted to die. Of course, my friends had shrugged her words off. Kaylee had gotten blackout drunk at every party we attended. She had even slept with way more boys than before. Was she trying to fill in the pain and then when she couldn't anymore...she...she ended everything?

I bit back a sob and covered my mouth. If I told Bob my current focus, he'd get upset. Then I realized something awful. Without Kaylee dying, he and I wouldn't be here. We wouldn't be together. I didn't want her to die for us. Was I a bad person for even thinking this?

"You need to eat," Bob broke through my misery.

"Okay." I ate another sinfully delicious mouthful. He insisted I eat because he worried about me, not because he wanted to control me. We needed to keep our strength up. How much energy did someone burn killing people?

"What were you thinking?"

"How do you know when I have something on my mind?"

"Your brow ceases right here." He touched the spot in the middle of my forehead. After he removed his hand from me, he frowned. He asked his previous question again.

"I was trying to decide how to handle our neighbors." The lie rolled off my tongue. I couldn't tell him the truth. I didn't want to hurt his feelings, and I was worried he wouldn't understand. My mind went through so many thoughts in a minute or more. How could I start with one? He had offered to return me to my parent's house many times, but within a minute of saying those words or something similar, he'd admit that he couldn't handle being anywhere without me. He'd keep on killing until someone stopped him dead. I doubted even jail would prevent him. I didn't even want to talk about Kaylee.

"You and I will separate the Jagers and kill them one by one. If we can't, we take control over them and then pick them off. It'll be hard, though. They also have guns," Bob asked.

"Will we be okay?" My stomach tied into a knot. Bob had never hunted something that could hunt him back. I knew what my father showed me, but a deer couldn't use a rifle.

"Of course, nothing bad will ever happen to you. I'll make damn sure of it." Bob kissed me on my forehead before he dug into his food. He ate double my portion.

If I wanted more, I could get some. We always had a little extra in a meal, just in case. My plate should be good enough for now.

"Are we killing everyone?" I didn't wait for Bob to answer before asking, "Even the kid?"

"Even the kid."

This time, I frowned. Killing his parents or the old asshole grandpa wouldn't be a problem, but killing someone innocent didn't sit well with me. It felt wrong.

Bob and I finished our lunch, cuddled, and fell asleep in each other's arms. He set the alarm, giving us enough time to walk close to the other cabin before nightfall.

"Five more minutes," I muttered when Bob's alarm went off. I swear I'd just placed my head on my pillow a second ago.

"You had five more. Time to get up." Bob laughed and tickled my ribs when I didn't wake up.

A giggle escaped my mouth. I tried to wiggle away from him, but Bob stopped and pinned me to the bed.

"Are you awake now?" he asked, aware that I was. I knew he was, with him poking my leg that was underneath the blanket.

"What will you do if I'm not?" My pulse raced, and every cell in my body vibrated. I wanted him inside me. I needed him inside me. This might be our last time together. I wanted to remember it forever. We would kill our neighbors, but until they were dead, and we were a safe distance away, we wouldn't be free. Maybe we could even plan a more stable future elsewhere. Alaska might be far enough away.

"I'll have to wake you up then." He gave me a kiss that could melt the snow around our cabin. His tongue slipped into my mouth. He ripped the cover off me and slipped into me. Before he continued, he said, "We don't have time."

"We always have time." I wrapped my legs around his waist, pulling him in further.

"Then we'll have to be quick. We'll take our time later tonight or tomorrow." He pressed his lips against mine, and we were off to O-land faster than we'd ever gone before.

Once we finished, I breathed heavily like I'd run a mile in thirty seconds or fewer. Between breaths, I said, "What's the plan?"

"You do everything I tell you when I tell you." Bob gasped out a few words. He was worse off than me, but he'd done most of the work. He liked to be on top. Most of the time, I didn't mind. I was a virgin before I met him.

"Okay." I traced the scar on his right, bushy eyebrow. He was so young when he got it. His stepdad had done it after Bob tried to prevent the man from hurting his sister. My man had been through enough. I planned on making his life easier from now on.

Bob closed his eyes as I ran my finger along the mark again, and he smiled. He opened his eyes for the third movement. "I like it when you touch me there. Makes me feel like the scar isn't as bad as it appears," he said.

"You're the sexiest man alive. Don't you forget it," I assumed what he would say next. I told him many times not to belittle himself. He hated the fact that he couldn't work, but it was too much of a risk for us.

"You're the hottest girl alive."

"You mean, woman. I turned eighteen, silly."

"How could I forget? I am older than you. Do you like older men, Ms. Argall?"

"Just you." I giggled. "You're only a day older than me."

"That is a lot of seconds."

"Bah. Tell me that when you are twenty-one. Not like we can buy cigarettes anymore." Having a convenience store job rather than working in a diner would cut back on sexual harassment from customers and coworkers. I shivered remembering the cook at the place before the one in town.

Bob smiled and gave me one last kiss before getting out of bed. "Let's gear up." He patted me on the leg.

"What do we bring?" I asked.

"All of it," he answered.

"For five people?" I stumbled out of bed. The sheet twisted around my legs. I fell, and my knee hit the floor hard.

Ouch.

I'd have a bruise there in a few hours.

"Are you okay?" Bob rushed to my side and helped me to free myself. He held out his hand, pulling me to my feet.

"I'm fine." My cheeks heated.

"Can you move your leg? You sounded like you fell hard." He kissed my forehead and bent in front of me.

I tested my knee by bending it. It felt a little sore, but nothing a walk couldn't cure.

"We'll ice it while we get ready to leave," Bob said.

"We got plenty of snow for that," I quipped.

"God, you're funny." He wrapped me in his arms and kissed me on the top of my head.

"Do we need to bring everything for five people?" I tried to switch topics. I felt like an idiot for falling over sheets that I pulled from the bed. Only I could do something so stupid.

"They had three cars. They wouldn't have brought that many vehicles for so few people. I suspect some of their party was hunting when we got there." He made perfect sense.

"Like the boy's parents?" My heart skipped a beat.

"Most likely. I didn't think the middle-aged guy was his dad."

"And Bridgette most certainly is not the boy's mom. I got the impression that the Jagers weren't fond of her." Remembering Marc's suspicious behavior boiled my blood. What right did he have to be skeptical of his friendly new neighbors?

"He warmed up to you soon enough." Bob sounded jealous.

"You have nothing to worry about. I'm only interested in you." I snaked my arms around his neck. No other man could compare to my Bob.

"If you did, I'd kill the guy. You're mine, babe."

"I wouldn't have it any other way."

Bob's face relaxed. He ran a hand through his hair. "I'll be right back."

Before I could ask him where he was going, he disappeared out the back door. The cabin was small, but it had two entrances. I assumed both were in case of fire. Not having a window in our bedroom would make it impossible to get out. The fire marshal must've looked at the building plans and didn't approve of them without the extra exit. I'd be thankful for the double exits if Bob and I had a blaze. My dad once told me the fire marshal wrote up his workplace for not having a grounded power strip. Wasn't the second red light button on it for that? The other was for switching between on and off. *Stupid people.* Living with Bob meant I didn't have to deal with idiots.

Bob returned, carrying a pile of snow. The chilly breeze creased my skin before he shut the door. "Here, put this on your knee. I'll kiss it to make it better first, though." He did exactly that.

My face heated. I was glad he bent in front of me, so he couldn't see what he did to me. I should get dressed. After he tied his makeshift ice pack to my knee, I shifted to the bed.

Bob handed me my clothes and helped me dress. My jeans were difficult to put on, so we left that until after I removed the cold pack.

We scampered around the cabin, grabbing every weapon we owned and setting them on the table. I didn't gather as much as Bob.

"This sucks. Why did I have to get hurt? We're losing daylight." I dropped the handgun from the umbrella stand onto the table.

"Don't worry, babe. We're fine. We're just giving our neighbors time to return to their cabin for the night," Bob said. His tone filled with reassurance. Didn't he want to pick them off one by one? "I forgot to do something first."

"Thanks for making me feel better. What do you need to do?"

"Check the weather." Bob pulled out the little radio from over twenty years ago that still worked. Funny how everything from back then still worked. It sucked having to replace the burner cell phones every month since, with an update, we couldn't play the games we wanted.

"This is KNOT, the hottest radio station on land. Well, not right now." The host chuckled at his own attempt at a poor joke. *"We're at a cold twenty-one degrees and will continue to drop into the negative teens tonight. Expect flurries after sunup tomorrow, and then three to five inches of snow is expected throughout the rest of the day. Be ready for the first blizzard of the season. Now for your local sports update—"*

"I hate that guy," Bob said as he shut the radio off.

"No snow for now, that's good." I didn't care for the radio host either. I did like the jokes he told at the start of his show, though; not the best, but not the worst either.

"What were we talking about? Oh, yeah. I'd rather have you near me. I need to know that you're safe. Don't be afraid to pull the trigger."

"I haven't been so far."

"You make me proud when you do. I worry someone might make you hesitate." Bob slipped his hand to my waist. Did he suspect my thoughts were on the boy?

"No one ever could make me hesitate. I got this." Nausea swept through me, but I didn't let it overtake me. I would kill the kid. The act should prove to Bob that I could handle myself. He didn't need to always worry about me so much.

"We got this. We'll kill everyone and then leave. Before the police show up, we will have a respectful distance between us," Bob said.

"What if the cops know about us?" I asked.

"They'd be breaking into our cabin by now if they did."

"True."

"Ready?"

I nodded, took off the ice pack, and put on my pants. My leg felt better going easy on it. I could deal with the pain for tonight and any other until I could properly rest it, when we were in the clear.

Chapter 4

We were a mile from our neighbors before Bob stopped walking and turned to me. The red and orange hues from the setting sun shone through the bare trees. Most of the branches were empty except for the pine and a few young American elms. I remembered most of the plant names from the field biology class my parents forced me to take during my junior year. Like I'd ever be out in the woods, I had thought back then. But now I was thankful for the course. If I couldn't identify something, well, I had a handy little survival eBook for that.

Bob ran a hand through his hair. He did this whenever he wanted to tell me something and he wasn't sure how to say it.

I gave him the time he needed to plan his words. The worst-case scenario of him leaving me ran through my head. I wanted to be closer to the other cabin by now. I remembered little from the hunting trip my dad had taken me on other than his cautionary tale of nightfall in the woods. A forest at night was much harder to figure out directions, making it much easier to get lost in.

On a camping trip when I was little, I tried to take a shortcut through a grove of trees. I'd gotten hopelessly lost. I kept pushing through, hoping the white glint between the trunks was something I recognized. Instead, it was a road. The painted line had made the white glint. No entrance had been in my sight, so I turned around, heading back from where I came. Tears had been streaming down my face by the time I finally made it out. My limbs had gotten all scratched up from the branches, too. I promised myself never to do something stupid like that again.

"How's your knee?" Bob asked finally. Worried lines creased his brow.

"It's fine." I lifted to test it and stopped myself from wincing. The miles walking on it weren't as good for it as I had hoped it would be, but I didn't want to be a burden.

"Are you sure?" Concern filtered across his face, and he chewed on his bottom lip.

I nodded and gave him a quick peck. The cold and wind had chapped my lips. The next time we went to a store, I'd have to get some actual lipstick or lip balm.

"Use this." He handed me an unopened pink tube.

After taking it from him, I asked, "When did you get this?" I rubbed the balm against my lip, feeling the instant relief, but my joy didn't last long. The cold triggered me like the guidance system on a missile, and my mouth was the target. I shivered. I'd rather deal with winter than the ache. Being born in North Dakota, I could handle the chill.

"I have my ways," he answered. His tone teased. He rubbed my arms and kissed me. "This should help warm you up."

I moaned from another kiss. His actions gave me some heat, but not in the way he thought. After he pulled away from me, I whimpered.

"We'll have more time later," he promised.

"How do we approach our neighbor? Do the wounded routine?" I asked. We had once faked that someone had hurt me in the middle of the road. The motorist had stopped to help me. I had slit his throat when he bent to check if I was alive. His blood had gushed out all over my face.

Bob and I had dumped him in the ravine after covering him with leaves. We'd stolen his car for a few days, and lit it on fire once the police found his body.

One good thing about technology was that the news posted stories online, and people were nosy. They wanted or demanded more information about the victim. Unfortunately, I'd lost a good knife that day. My man got rid of it by throwing it into a lake. He was always cautious with evidence.

"If the Jagers are outside, yes. If not, we'll have to get them to leave the cabin."

"How?" I asked.

"Not sure yet." Bob smiled at me and offered his hand for me to take.

I took his hand, giving it a squeeze, and he returned the gesture. We got this. We could do this. I needed to be reassured more than he did.

I wrecked my nerves whenever we planned to kill. After we finished, I wouldn't feel normal again. I couldn't even force myself to calm down by telling myself with my normal saying of just two people or one needed to die. This time, we had an entire group. I could take on a few at most without Bob. He would do most of the killing. Would he stop once everyone was dead? The town wasn't too far away.

Bob would never hurt me. He'd said many times, but what if he tossed a knife or shot a gun and I impeded the blade or the bullet? Accidents happened all the time.

"Let's go," Bob said as he tugged on my hand.

The sun had set by the time we reached the clearing. The cabin lights shimmered between the trees. Smoke from the fire rose into the air.

"We'll need to creep closer since we can't hear anything from here," Bob said as he released my hand.

I immediately missed his touch and crouched low.

He shifted closer, using the trees for cover.

I stationed myself as he did and followed him along his path. Our boots crunched in the snow, but not loud enough to hear from far away. I had yet to don my night-vision goggles like him. One of us should see what could come at us, but maybe I'd be less anxious if I did. I took a moment to adjust the eyewear down over my eyes.

The world changed. I could see more than just the pitch-blackness and trees in front of me. Everything turned a greenish-blue, almost teal color; nothing like what I'd seen on TV and in the movies. They had the habit of using gray, which was more for cameras.

Light turned into a white blot that was coming from the windows of the cabin and the interior of a truck. Someone sat in the vehicle. I lifted the goggles off my face to check. I could barely see the glint from the cigarette. My gaze shifted to find Bob, trying to see him. I'd lost him.

I situated my night vision over my eyes again. This time, when I glanced around, I found Bob right away.

He focused in on the house a few feet away from me and then back at the truck. He must have been trying to decide what to do first. Bob ran a hand through his hair. Yep, he was. If we didn't kill the man, he could interrupt us inside, but if we did, he might scream and alert our prey.

Bob nodded, and I did back. He held three fingers in the air. He had decided what we should do.

I gave him a thumbs-up, telling him I understood and agreed. I took a deep breath before I moved. The third plan was simple. I distracted the guy. If I could kill him, I would; otherwise, Bob would sneak up behind him and take him out.

After creeping along the side of the clearing and putting my goggles away, I approached the truck from behind on the front passenger's door. My mouth ran dry, and my head pounded. When I drew closer to the cab, strange grunting noises were coming from inside. It took me a moment to figure out the guy was jacking off inside.

Gross.

I opened the truck's door and asked, "Do you need a hand?" I puked in my mouth, swallowing the nasty bile.

Marc sprang up, covering his penis with his hand. His face flushed red as he stammered, "You're..... you're not supposed to be here."

"I thought you'd be glad to see me." I moved my hand behind my back, right next to the unlocking mechanism, and my tone turned sultry. "You don't want a hand?"

"Ah, what about your man? I mean, sure."

Idiot. What guy is dumb enough to mention a husband when a pretty girl is propositioning him?

"My husband's back at our cabin. He doesn't like me out this late, even though I want to play. What he doesn't know can't hurt him." My voice rose an octave as I pressed the unlock button. The locks clicked, and I let myself inside the cab, hoping Marc heard nothing. I wasn't touching him yet. If I did, I'd have to use acid to wash myself off.

"You can play with me all you want." Marc's eyes heated. He removed his hand and relaxed, leaning back further. He held his cigarette close to the plush leather seat.

Come on, Bob. I never wanted to see my man more than ever.

Corrie appeared.

I coughed to keep my shocked sound from being overly audible.

"Can't you handle the ugly guy yourself, Jolene? What did I teach you?" Corrie asked.

Not a damn thing, I thought to her.

"I'm pretty sure I taught you something." Corrie winked at me. Yeah, she could hear my thoughts. Lucky for me.

Buzz off.

She did the whole zip her lip thing.

"You can play with me all you want," Marc repeated.

"Sorry. What about your woman?" I bought myself a little time. His truck was an extended cab, and it had the fancy dashboard and computer display. Was he overcompensating for something? I glanced at his dick. Four inches and hard.

Yep, he is overcompensating.

"This will be our little secret. Besides, I'm falling out of love with her. This little guy wants you to suck him dry." Marc touched his dick, and he was right by calling it small. I had never seen one so tiny before. I didn't know they came that way.

I bent. If I had to stick his penis in my mouth, I'd kill Bob. Why should I wait for him, like Corrie said? I slid my knife out as my mouth drew closer.

The driver's side door to the truck squeaked as it opened.

"Hey!" Marc shouted at the same time I sprang up.

"You shouldn't cheat." I stabbed the knife into his neck, aiming for his trachea. I pulled it back out, and blood came. Practicing had helped. This was my first time hitting my mark.

What a jackass. Soon a dead jackass.

"That's my girl!" Corrie said and then held out her hand for a high five after.

I attempted to hit her hand like a dumbass. I hoped Bob hadn't noticed my stupidity.

Bob watched the man dying in front of us. Good, he didn't see. Even in death, Corrie had made me look like an idiot.

Marc opened his mouth, but he couldn't scream with his breathing tube severed. I'd cut him as deep as I could. He covered his wound with his hand, but no amount of pressure he applied could stop him from suffocating.

He moved, or rather tried to move. He leaned against me, going unconscious and dying shortly after.

I pushed him away from me, and he slumped to the side. I wanted to cut off his penis. The way he treated his girlfriend pissed me off. No man should ever let his family be cruel to his woman. If Bob hadn't murdered his mom and she continued to say and do hurtful things to me, he would've killed her.

"One down," I said to Bob with a smile plastered across my face. The victim barely made a noise. I shifted in the seat and slid out of the truck.

Bob pressed the button to turn off the interior light, and the night encased us. He repositioned Marc to sitting up in the truck. The guy would look like he was alive from a distance. Until someone drew closer, they wouldn't realize the fog on the windows wasn't from moisture.

I shut my door, and Bob did the same on his side. We walked back to the end of the truck, heading into the woods.

"Great job, not a lot of mess," Bob said after we were far enough away to talk.

"I could've done something far worse," I said.

"Like what?"

"Cut off his pecker."

Bob covered his junk, and he shifted his weight between his feet. He must not like that idea one bit, but he added, "We can go back, and you can remove his dick."

"Hard pass. I'm not touching him ever again. The guy was a fuckin' creep. We did the world a favor by killing him."

"Man, I love you." Bob wrapped his arms around me, pulling me closer and giving me a kiss.

"What do we do now?" I asked.

"We'll have to draw the family out." Bob frowned.

"How?"

"Make a noise, maybe?"

An idea popped into my head, and I told him, "A fire would most definitely make someone come running. We have a truck and evidence to destroy."

Chapter 5

B ob nodded. "Pop the hood," he said as he made his way to the front of the truck.

I did what he asked me, memorized by his quick decision-making skills. I'd still decide how to plan everything out. My guy was a man of action. Impressive, really.

"Sweetie, the hood," Bob said when I didn't respond.

"Sorry." I opened the driver's door, hiding the smile that had to be plastered across my face. I searched for the latch and pulled up to unlatch the hood.

Bob secured the hood before I got to him. He cut a tube off somewhere and put the hood back down. He walked to the gasoline tank, inserting the plastic. "Please find something to hold the gas," he told me.

I searched around the truck cabin and found a few empty beers on the floor and two unopened ones. I took several to Bob, asking him, "Will this do?"

"That's more than enough." Bob pressed his lips against mine for a second before sticking his mouth onto the pipe. He sucked in and coughed out some gasoline onto the ground. The stench overpowered his body wash and filled my nose.

I held the bottles underneath the flow of gas until they were full, filling up the empties. I flipped the top on an unopened beer.

"Let me see that before you dump it out, please." Bob took the beer from me, taking a swig before handing it back.

"Will these four bottles be enough?" After taking a sip of the nasty beverage, I dumped the contents onto the ground. I needed some liquid courage for what we were doing tonight. The gas stopped flowing once the remaining two containers were full.

"If not, we'll make do. You take the passenger side." Bob took two of the bottles and went to the driver's side door, opening it. "Pour everything across the seat and floorboards, but soak nothing."

I wanted to thank Bob. He didn't force me to get close to the guy I had killed, and he trusted me to help him instead of doing everything himself. To tell him to thank him without saying it, I did as he instructed. I'd been camping enough to know drenching a piece of wood in flammable fluid was never a good idea. The flame would flicker and die fast. We needed a blaze and maybe an explosion to get the attention of those in the cabin.

Once my side was done, I joined Bob on his. No one could see us from the lodge because the truck blocked us. We couldn't make a trail to the gas tank to cause an explosion because of the snow. Did that even work in real life? Movies and television exaggerated a lot of things, like staying in a cabin in the middle of the woods in winter. The actors would freeze to death unless they knew how to keep a fire lit or a generator running. Electricity didn't reach where we stayed.

"I'll set the fire and get the truck to blow. Can you set up in line of sight in the woods? My plan is to pick off those that come out once everyone is outside," Bob said.

"What if they call for help?" I asked.

"This will prevent them. Thanks, I almost forgot to turn it on." Bob took out a black box with five antennas and flipped on the switch before sticking it back in his pocket.

"What am I supposed to do, exactly?" I rubbed my chin.

"Go in the tree line, hunker down, and once everyone has come outside, start shooting at them. Use your rifle. Unless you want to do what I'm doing. I don't want you in the line of fire or anywhere dangerous, but I doubt we can avoid it tonight."

"I'll do what you suggested," I said without taking a moment to think. I didn't know how to blow up a truck. Bob would have to teach me later.

"Signal me when you're ready." He kissed my forehead before I left him. He smelled of gas.

I walked a few good feet away from the clearing and into the trees. Snow crunched underneath my boots, despite my trying my best not to make a sound. I kept glancing back in the direction I had come, in order to see Bob. He'd let me know if anyone else reacted to my sound.

Eventually, I had to turn to go to the front. A few minutes later, I found a log on the ground. I took my rifle and set myself up. I glanced through the scope but couldn't see my man. He'd be there no matter what. He'd never leave me. I breathed in through my nose and out through my mouth to ease the empty feeling in the pit of my stomach. I touched the button to the laser I'd taped on the side of the gun. Ready or not, here we come.

Silence filled the air. Not even the wind howled. It was as if even the wind was holding its breath, waiting for something big to happen. A fire roared to life inside the truck. The blaze grew bigger, and the stench of it and burned leather filled the air. I saw a shadowy figure dart away. Bob would be safe in time for the explosion.

Boom.

The cabin door flew open a few seconds later. A man ran out, pulling on his coat. He went toward the burning truck. His hair was gray, so I assumed he was Glen.

My finger hovered over the trigger. I couldn't pick him off yet. He deserved a bullet in the back or the head.

Another guy followed Glen outside, and behind him ran the young boy.

I quickly changed my crosshairs to the other man. He hadn't been in the cabin when we visited last. Who was he? Could he be the kid's dad?

Bridgette walked out into the snow. She pulled her robe around her, and her hair was in curlers. She glanced around the area. Was she searching for her man? She would be easy to pick off.

The grandma, Betsy, stayed by the door. The light from the place illuminated her face. Her eyes widened with horror, and her hand flew to her mouth. Did she know her son was inside the fire? He was dead, but did she think he was being burned alive?

I saved her for last. Which was a good thing because she went back inside the cabin. I scoped the tree line for Bob's signal. Two small red dots flashed, signaling me to wait for a moment.

What did he see? I placed Glen in my crosshairs. He disappeared around the side of the cabin. The younger man with him followed, speaking to the boy first. What were the guys doing? Did they think they could put the fire out? Bob and I never checked the back of the cabin. They could have a hose, but I doubted it. They might have a well. Why would they run to it? The water from the well would have turned to ice.

The child returned to the cabin. He ran out with another man at the same time the two guys returned. Everyone held buckets of water. Bob should've had the fire going good enough that they couldn't do anything about it with their measly attempts.

Bridgette joined the guys, carrying one container. She wouldn't be much use.

A red beam shone across my vision. Crud, I missed the signal. I searched for Bob again, and he showed me he was ready. I tapped the laser once to let him know I understood. He'd take the guys in his line of sight while I picked off the rest.

Bob's shot rang out.

I couldn't tell if he had killed someone or not. My focus was entirely on finding my target.

My dad's words echoed through my head, *'Breathe through each shot.'* I took a deep breath and squeezed the trigger. My first shot went a little high with the wind. *'Try again. Don't rush. Line up the shot.'* I recalculated, tapping again.

Bang.

Bridgette dropped to the ground. Her brains splattered across the snow.

'Good girl.'

I seriously doubted my dad would've congratulated me for killing someone.

The guy and boy scattered, running zig-zag patterns toward the back of the cabin.

Crack.

The man fell because of Bob, but he still moved and climbed to his feet.

I lined up my shot, accounting for the wind. One breath in, one out, I aimed at the boy instead of the man; Bob could get him. I fired off to the side. The bullet slammed into the side of the cabin, splintering the wood. The child was out of my sight before I could try again. Hopefully, Bob wouldn't shoot him, too.

My shoulders tightened as I waited for Bob to fire. When nothing came, I sighed heavily. The boy should be alive for now.

I checked the entrance to the cabin, but no one came out. The occupants could make their way out the back. Bob and I hadn't discussed our next option, but we should breach, smoking everyone out, or chasing after them.

I stood, stuffing the bullet casings into my pocket and zipping it before taking off toward the back of the cabin. Bob and I had worn gloves before we put ammo into the barrel or magazines. One thing I knew for sure: I couldn't stay in my spot. If anyone ever returned fire, they would aim for me. Was Bob following me? Did I make the right decision?

What if someone other than my man was waiting for me? I wouldn't be an idiot and burst through the tree line, but I could take proper precautions. When I'd fired the gun, I'd taken off my night vision goggles. I donned them again.

A person ran in front of me.

My nerves were as raw as the wind that burned my face. Who could be there? They were moving away from me as if I were giving chase. I could only see their backs. They wore a camo coat and was about Bob's height.

Should I stop and aim my rifle? What if I hit Bob instead? I wasn't sure if there had been enough time for him to run in front of me. He had the speed. Why would he come around to my side of the cabin, though?

My mind spun with even more questions than answers. I needed to decide now before it was too late. To shoot or not to shoot? That was the question.

Screw it.

I stopped and positioned my rifle, aiming at the person's back. I pressed the trigger. The bullet went off course, slamming into a tree. The person stumbled and fell to the ground.

Please don't be Bob, I prayed inside my head repeatedly. I rushed forward to see who was there, but they'd rolled onto their back. I halted, sliding on the snow.

They raised their heads. The face of a man I'd never seen before stared at me. In his hand, he held a gun.

Bob's one word screamed in my head, '*Run!*' He always told me to do so whenever someone tried to use a weapon against me.

I dove to the side before the shot rang out and scrambled to hide behind a tree. The guy missed me. He fired again, missing me once more.

Count the shots and wait to return fire.

What kind of gun did he have? I hadn't gotten a good look at it before my instincts kicked in. He could have five, six, nine, or even more shots left.

Bullets three and four hit the tree I hid behind.

I unzipped a pocket in my coat, pulling out a blue laser. If I shone it toward his eyes, he'd be blind for a few seconds. I could make my move then.

Bang. Bang. He still had three shots left, or he could be reloading.

A sudden calmness washed over me. My heart pounded faster than a hummingbird's, and I should have been about ready to pee my pants, but I had complete tranquility. I removed a gun and waited for the next shot. After it came, I stepped out of my hiding spot, shining the laser at him.

The guy cried out, not in pain like I'd dumped hot water on him, but more in the tone of shock. He covered his face. His other hand trembled as he pulled the trigger.

I hadn't been fast enough. I aimed at the middle of his forehead, and the end of my barrel flashed. Another gunshot fired.

He dropped dead. At least I'd killed him before he killed me. Bob could finish the rest of them off.

I'd been running on pure adrenaline, but the pain should come soon enough. I didn't have a wound. My arms and legs moved just fine. Wait, I wasn't bleeding. He had a clear shot.

Footsteps crunched in the snow. Bob ran toward me. When he got close, he wrapped me in a big hug before saying, "I thought I had lost you. I saw you run toward the back entrance, and when I didn't see you, I thought the worst. Never scare me like that again."

"I can't breathe," I said. He held me so tightly.

"I'm sorry, babe. I didn't mean to squeeze you so hard." He let me go, and tears flashed into his eyes.

"Did you shoot the guy?"

"Yeah, thanks to you. I saw a blue light." If Bob hadn't seen my signal, I'd be dead right now. How stupid could I be?

My legs gave out, and I felt like I'd run a mile in less than thirty seconds. I couldn't catch my breath. What were we doing? We couldn't end this without one of us dying.

"Are you okay?" Bob asked. He sounded concerned. He bent down next to me.

"We need to flee," I said once I could speak.

Chapter 6

"Why? We got this," Bob said. He took his hat off, smoothed his hair, and then put his hat back on.

"No, we don't. We could die. You could die." Tears burned my eyes, and the cold weather made the sensation worse. I feared the water would turn to ice. I knew how ridiculous that sounded since I lived my whole life where it was cold for over half the year. The drops would freeze on my cheeks after they fell. The temperature dipped below freezing at night.

"Take a deep breath. I think you're having a panic attack."

I did what Bob instructed. After breathing in and out, I still didn't feel any better. No matter what we did, I had a strange feeling one of us would die or worse, we'd go to jail.

"Listen to me, Jolene. We've taken out five people. With three vehicles, they could hold twelve, max fifteen. We got this." Bob sat on the ground and pulled me into his arms. We were in the woods far away from anyone, but if they came looking for us, they could see us. "Take another deep breath."

He said five. The boy wasn't dead yet.

I snuggled into Bob, relaxing into his embrace. We could take out the rest, and we killed almost half of them unless two people sat in the back of the extended cab. I doubted it. No one could stomach being with Marc.

After a few minutes of holding me close and rubbing my back, Bob asked, "Are you feeling any better?" His voice was gentle.

I nodded and hiccupped.

"Can you stand?" he asked.

I nodded again.

"You're not talking, so I'm assuming you're good or you'll be soon. How's your knee?" Bob asked.

"It's okay," I answered. My voice cracked.

"Good, you can speak." Bob tilted my head and pressed his lips against mine. "For every person we kill, I'll kiss you, like this." He kissed me deeply, making my toes curl.

I touched the zipper on his coat, but he stopped me from unzipping it. I couldn't help myself. Whenever I got close to him, I wanted to tear his clothes off.

"We'll go further once the Jagers are dead, and we're safe. Until then, just a kiss." Bob touched our mouths together passionately and counted between each one. "Two. Three. Four. Five."

"Don't stop," I said. After every kiss, a jolt spread from there down my body. I wanted him so badly.

"Sorry, babe. I want to do a lot more to you, too, but until then we'll have to kiss only. Let me know if you feel another panic attack coming on. Flip on the blue light three times." His tone was husky, and his eyes went dark with need.

"What are we doing next? I think knowing the plan will help me, along with making out with you."

"We need to either breach the cabin or get those inside to come out."

"What if they're not in there?" I asked.

"We need to find that out too." Bob's eyebrows drew together. He stood and helped me to my feet. He brushed the snow off the back of my legs and butt. "I'm not sure how to get anyone out yet."

"How do the police breach?"

"By breaking down a door with protective gear. We don't have the resources, but we can do something else." His gray eyes danced, and he smiled. He never wore contacts, no matter how much we changed our looks. I was glad he didn't. I loved the color of his eyes.

"What can we do?"

"Follow me. I think the roof has a crawl space," he answered.

"What if they know what you're doing, and they shoot at you through the ceiling?" Another panic attack brewed, and I took another deep breath. The thought of losing Bob made me crazy with fear.

"I'll get to the crawl space before they realize I'm there. You'll have to distract them to make sure, though. Okay?" Bob rubbed my upper arms.

"Are you sure everyone didn't leave?"

"Only six sets of tracks are at the back of the house, leading inside; one from the boy going inside, four from Glen and whoever grabbed the buckets and returned, and the final prints came from the guy you killed. He probably tried to run to get help. Nice headshot, by the way."

The snowfall from last night helped us. A few flakes floated down now, and I stuck my tongue out, catching a few more. I said a silent prayer for the blizzard not to come yet. Didn't the radio say it would hold out until early morning?

"And the man we killed didn't go to the vehicles because?" I found our runaway neighbor's logic lacking. Bob had shot him first, and I'd ended him.

"I was shooting in that direction," Bob answered.

"Where are you climbing on the roof at?"

"Follow me." Bob led us through the woods and to the side of the cabin with no windows. He pointed to a balcony on the second floor.

"I think there's more than a crawl space." The front looked big, but now that I was closer, I didn't realize how huge this place was. We should've walked around and checked the cabin out more. "How can I cover everywhere?"

"You only have two exits to worry about. I'll make my way to the back, and you set up in the front, not where you were last time. Hide well, sweetie. If they find you, move. Give me ten minutes and then shoot out the windows. Space your shots."

I set a timer on my phone at the same time he did. My cell would vibrate in my pocket, not making a noise. Wouldn't that be stupid of me to announce my location?

Bob gave me a quick hug and slung his rifle over his shoulder before grabbing the railing. Using his upper body strength, he lifted himself all the way up. After a last wave at me, he disappeared over the rail.

I ran back to the woods and headed toward the front of the cabin. I found a bush to use as cover, hiding behind it and lying on the snow. After looking through the scope at the front door, I waited for the time to expire.

The truck had burned itself out with only a shell remaining, and it did some damage to the SUV parked right next to it. I was worried about a tree catching fire. The whole wood would burn. Bob should've put the blaze out to make sure that didn't happen. How much of Marc remained?

I wasn't curious enough to find out. I kept checking my cell, putting it back in my pocket after I was done. Dropping it might damage it when the snow melts. I also didn't want the light to give me away. My phone vibrated. Our time was up.

I took a deep breath and aimed.

Bang.

The bullet went wide and hit nothing.

Calm down. You got this. You've done it many times before. The little pep talk I gave myself helped. I squeezed the trigger after aiming and accounting for the slight wind.

Bam.

The bullet slammed into the window, making a hole, but not quite shattering it.

Oh, crap. What if I hit Bob? My stomach felt rock hard, like I was lying on a boulder and not the soft snow that blanketed the ground.

I counted for thirty seconds and fired again. Same damage.

Please be okay, Bob. Please, I prayed. We should've realized this before I started shooting, but I had to stick with the plan. Bob needed me.

My vision blurred, and I blinked away the tears. This time I waited a full minute and aimed at the door, so I wouldn't hit my man by mistake. The wood above the door splintered. This was a much better plan. At this height, no way I could hit Bob unless he was dropping.

"Shit!" I cursed.

Corrie appeared next to me. "This is the dumbest plan ever," she told me.

Who asked you?

"Keep shooting and hitting your man, then."

Can you go look for me?

"No, and you know why."

I didn't, really. I didn't even understand why she always came to haunt me. After I ignored her, I kept my gaze fixed through the scope. Should I shoot again? Corrie's words echoed in my mind. I better not. Another unsettling thought made me worry even more. Did Bob and I make the right choice? Maybe we should've waited until our neighbors tried to escape. They had enough food to last the weekend, but after that, who knew? Bob and I couldn't stay outside forever, not when temperatures dropped tonight. Why wasn't he coming out? Or them?

Was Bob hurt? I listened for some sign. The wind howled, and my heartbeat thrashed loud enough that I could hear it in my ears. No other sounds came, though. He could've gotten into a fistfight inside, and I wouldn't hear it this far away. How long should I wait? Another thing we needed to decide later.

The door opened, and I steadied myself. The old lady, Betsy, walked out with her hands in the air? What the hell?

Her grandson followed her. At least I assumed that was their relationship, and then three other people I didn't recognize, two women and one man. They had the same facial features, turned-up nose and tanned skin. They had to be related. Which one was the kid's mom? Or the dad? With two guys dead, Bob or I could've killed the father already. The boy could even have same-sex parents or just a single parent. There was simply no way of knowing at this point.

When Bob exited the cabin, he directed the people to stand in a line facing him. He motioned for them to get lower, possibly kneeling.

Should I come out? Bob wouldn't like me in any danger, but he could be in a lot more trouble right now. Handling five people alone wouldn't be easy.

Screw it.

I stood and took out a handgun like my man, shifting my rifle to across my back. I left the safety of the trees, and a twig snapped underneath my boot.

Everyone turned to glance at me, even Bob.

He shifted to stand taller. Did he stiffen? Did he not want me to reveal myself?

Well, I couldn't undo what I had done, so I just walked closer to the group.

"As you can see, I have a partner," Bob said to our captives. He must've been talking to them before I got there.

I missed hearing him because of the distance or because I was so relieved he was still alive that I hadn't paid attention.

Was there anyone else inside the cabin? I did the quick math. The trucks would've had room for four or five people each, along with the SUV. If they squished together like my friends and I used to do, they could have held even more. Someone could've ridden in the back of the sports vehicle. No one would've ridden in the back of the trucks because they didn't have a top.

"Why are you doing this?" one lady I didn't know asked. She kept her short hair underneath her hunting cap. She shivered but didn't lower her hands, even though she wore a coat like the rest of the hostages. How had Bob managed this?

"Does it matter?" I asked. They'd be dead soon.

"Please don't do this. Not to my son." She stared at me. She must think I was the softest of her attackers. Fresh tears filled her eyes and flowed down her cheeks. Her makeup had smudged. At least she wouldn't try to fix it like Bridgette would've if she were alive. Little did Bridgette know, a true good man wouldn't care what his lady looked like, concealer or no concealer.

"Take our money and jewelry, but please don't hurt us," Betsy whimpered after she spoke.

"Do you think begging for your life will save you? What do you think, babe?" Bob asked me.

The guy moved, and I rushed over and hit him in the back of his head with the butt of my gun.

One woman cried out, burying her face in her hands.

"My man says to stay on your knees. If you try anything stupid again, I'll kill you." My gaze shifted to Bob for a moment. I had a plan, and I hoped he went along with it. "Honey, we should end this. Let me take the boy inside to check for valuables." I winked.

"Good idea," Bob said.

"Come on, kid." When he didn't move, I nudged him with my foot.

The boy stood and walked toward Bob, actually the cabin, but my man was right in front of the door.

"Please don't take my son," the mother begged.

I ignored her and motioned with my gun for the boy to continue.

Bob shifted out of the way. He moved fast next and kicked the guy, who had tried to go after me, in the face. I never realized the idiot had tried to grab me as I followed the kid.

I aimed my gun and fired, shooting the guy in the back of his neck.

He tried to scream but could only gurgle. His blood poured from his wound and from his mouth. He placed his hand on the wound.

"Don't move," Bob said to the lady, who wasn't the boy's mother.

She blubbered and chewed on her lip. Her husband, her brother, her boyfriend, or whoever I shot bled out, and she was powerless to save him. She could try, but she valued her life more for now. I might have fun messing with her later. Letting her decide who lived or who died. How much did she care about the people she was with?

"My girl warned you all." Bob grinned, and his eyes lit up. Killing excited him. "Don't anyone else get any more ideas."

"Come on, kid. Let's go," I said.

"You...you killed my uncle," the boy stammered.

"What are you going to do about it?" I asked the kid.

"Just listen to them, Logan. Please don't hurt my boy," his mom pleaded to me.

"Will you be a good boy and listen to your mom?" My skin itched like tiny spiders were crawling their eight hairy legs all over it. I wanted to scratch myself, but I knew the feeling was out of guilt. The kid's name wasn't one I wanted to remember. I didn't want to put a name to what I was about to do.

Poor, Logan.

He nodded and headed into the cabin, with me trailing behind him.

The heat hit my face like a furnace was blowing hot air directly at me. My shots didn't break the door completely. If I'd been wearing glasses, they would've fogged up. Logan could've used the distraction to his advantage. Did this place have a heating system or just a fireplace like ours?

Logan stopped in the middle of the combo living room and kitchen.

Someone had spilled a beer bottle; the rug soaked up the contents. The air smelled of burned popcorn. Someone must've used the microwave since the stove was empty. Would the popcorn continue to burn and start a fire? I'd forgotten a bag or two and doused the kernels as soon as I remembered. The bag had smoked. Well, if a blaze started in the cabin, it wouldn't matter.

"Show me the nearest bedroom," I said. The space should have everything I needed for what I had in mind.

The boy directed us toward a door near the back. On our left was a hallway. I could see stairs to the next floor when I glanced down the hall. Muddy footprints led this way. Bob must've come down the stairs and surprised everyone here.

Once we were inside the room, I asked the boy, "How many people are with you?"

"My mom says I shouldn't talk to strangers."

"Did she teach you to listen to those with a gun?" I waved it and repositioned it to point at him again.

He crossed his arms over his chest.

Stubborn little bastard.

If I ever had a kid, I hoped he or she wouldn't act like this. Getting Logan to speak was like shoveling snow with an ice cream scoop: pointless and difficult. I pointed the gun at him and cocked it.

"Nine before you killed them," he finally answered.

"Is that all?"

"No, ten." He used his fingers as he said, "My mom, my dad, my grandpa, my grandma, my uncle, his girlfriend, my uncle Pat, who you just killed, his wife, my other uncle, and me. Yes, ten."

"Get on your knees," I instructed.

"Are you going to kill me?" Logan asked. His voice trembled. Despite his fear, he did what I told him.

"Turn around." I couldn't see his face. If I did, it would haunt me for the rest of my life. Why did I decide to kill him? Bob wouldn't be nice like me. He might torture Logan to make his family behave, or Bob might do it just for fun.

A gun sounded from outside, making Logan and me jump.

Logan moved.

"Don't," I warned.

My one word stopped him.

"Get back on your knees with your hands in the air, facing the other direction," I said. The second gunshot going off didn't surprise me. I wasn't killing Logan. I was killing just a boy. Someone I didn't know.

After the kid returned to his position, I brought the gun up and squeezed the trigger.

Bang.

Chapter 7

I shut the door and hurried out of the room. As long as I didn't think about what I'd done, I'd be fine. I also had something more important to worry about. Bob had shot twice, killing his hostages. I hoped. He could've missed every single one, or worse, someone could've tried to take him down. If what Logan—no, the kid—had said was true, everyone who remained was under our control. Three women wouldn't be able to take my man, or could they?

Bile rose into my mouth as I ran to the front door. The cold air shocked me as I burst through it, but nothing could stop me. I shook the panicky feeling off as I skidded to a halt.

One woman lay face down in the snow, right in the line that Bob had forced his captives to form. Was she the mother or the aunt? I could at least mark off the grandma, no white hair. Where was Betsy? A better question: where was Bob?

Frantically, I searched the tree line for any sign of my man or anyone else. With our footprints coming and going, I couldn't tell what direction Bob had gone. Panic rose in my chest, gripping my heart. I shoved it down and took out my night vision goggles. *Idiot.* I'd forgotten.

A heat residue lay in the snow twenty feet away between some trees. I watched as the degrees slowly dropped. The shape appeared to be human. It could've been an animal, too, though. I stepped forward and stopped myself, poised. What if Betsy or the other woman got a hold of a gun? I'd be a sitting duck. I glanced around with the goggles. No one was in sight before I ran to see if Bob was on the ground.

With each pump of my arms, a sickness washed over me. I didn't know how I'd go on without him. Bob was my anchor, my everything. I ripped off the goggles once I was close, and a sob flowed through my mouth. I covered it with my hand.

Bob wasn't dead; Betsy was. He had shot her in the back. A trail of her blood led to her, and the snow pooled red around her. Her chest didn't rise, and no puffs of air formed. She was gone.

How long had she been dead, though? I thought I heard the first shot about five minutes ago. Time didn't hold any meaning when panicking, and I hadn't glanced at my phone or the clock next to the bed to confirm. I'd been more focused on finding my man. Now that I could think and plan, I checked Betsy's minor wound on her back. She must've run and Bob shot her from a distance until she fell here. Did he come after her, though?

No other footprints but hers and mine were in the snow by her. My guy must be after the last woman, right? I hated this. Why couldn't people just sit down and die, making it easier on us? Why force us to hunt them down like animals?

At least I could tell Bob that Betsy bled to death. I toed her with my boot to make sure. She might've been holding her breath when I first approached. I had been standing over her for a few minutes now. She couldn't hold her breath for that long.

My man and I had one more person left to kill before we could leave. I glanced around further in the snow, trying to see if Bob had come close to check on Betsy. The dim light from the stars and moon didn't give me much light to see by, though. The cabin was too far away to be of any help.

Where had Bob gone? He must've followed the mother or the aunt.

Dang it.

I should've checked to see which one had died by the door. For now, I'll call her WWNTD, the Woman Who Needed to Die, especially if she messed with my man.

WWNTD come out, come out wherever you are?

I shoved my night vision goggles back on and hunkered down. After my eyesight adjusted, I scanned the area, but couldn't see anyone. The box that came with the goggles said they were good for a hundred and twenty yards.

Bob and the WWNTD must be on another side of the cabin, or they could've entered the back entrance. No one went inside through the front when I was there. I hadn't been dealing with the boy for long before the first gunshot rang out. Someone could've made it to the back by now.

An overwhelming sense of dread filled my entire body, even my cells. I needed to find my Bob fast. I shoved the panic down and ran in the cabin's direction. Once I neared the front, I lifted my goggles and checked the snow for prints. The ground was full of them. I couldn't tell which ones were Bob's and WWNTD's, mine, or from before.

Should I continue this way or try the other side? The vehicles were over there. Someone smart would go for them, but that would've been the obvious choice. I couldn't go that way without doubling back.

I pressed on and ambled to the rear end of the cabin, using the trees as cover. WWNTD shouldn't have night vision goggles like me. The annoying voice in the back of my head spoke; the one that doubted everything.

"Unless she stole the goggles from Bob," Corrie said. She'd been by my side off and on. And frankly, I was getting sick of her.

I shook my head. *Not possible.* My man knew how to handle himself.

After hiding behind a tree, I peeked out but couldn't see anybody. *Great.* They must've gone the other way. Should I double back and circle around? By the time I did, they could be too far away for me to see. And what if they were over there?

What's with all these damn questions?

I needed to stop and continue my search. What should I do in a situation like this? Finding Bob should be my top priority. He might've gotten injured or worse. I couldn't bring myself to say the one word, and I didn't hear another gunshot, just the two.

Bang.

Shit! Why did I have to think those words? Tears sprang into my eyes. *Don't cry now. It's too cold to cry.*

"He'll be alright," Corrie said.

I grunted. When was she ever on my side?

Another shot rang out.

My heart stopped beating. I shifted my night vision goggles to the top of my head and ran toward the gunfire. My boots crouched on the ground until I reached the other side of the cabin.

Please let it be Bob firing the gun and not the other woman. Please.

I flattened my back against the wood. Swallowing the anxiety building inside of me, I dared to peek around the corner. My eyes took a moment to adjust, and all the air escaped from my lungs.

A trail led a few feet from the vehicles, and I felt faint. Blood. It had to be blood. The light attached to the roof of the cabin didn't shine enough for me to confirm, however.

I searched for someone, something. Maybe Bob shot WWNTD or a deer. I could only hope.

A shadowy figure shifted by the truck, not damaged by the fire. From my distance and the outdoor light, I couldn't see much, just black movements. I'd give anything for some light pollution right now, and then I remembered my goggles and donned them. Twice in the past half hour, I'd been stupid to forget. This had to stop.

Two people were on either side of the hood, and from this distance, I couldn't tell which one was bigger. At least I assumed they were both human. Bears were hibernating, and apes didn't live in this forest or this country. The popular color from the one on the passenger side flashed between the colder metal of the truck as they made their way to the front. The others followed and stopped as the first did, like they were playing a game of cat and mouse.

I had little doubt that my man was the feline, but I didn't dare shoot just in case. I wouldn't risk him for anything. My mind raced over what I should do next. Without deciding, I edged closer. Maybe I'd figure it out once I got there.

Yeah, right? Sarcasm filled my thoughts.

When I got to the end of the cargo bed, I shifted my feet. So far, neither person reacted to my presence, or at least I didn't think they did. Hard to tell with these stupid goggles covering my eyes and only seeing through the front, side, and back windows of the truck. The damn headrests were in the way, too. I ripped the night vision goggles off and shoved them into my pocket. Should I go left, or right? No way to tell who was on which side.

I should let Bob handle WWNTD, but what if he couldn't? He might not be shooting at her for a reason like he was out of bullets. I dismissed that idea, knowing full well we'd stocked up more than enough before coming here to start our own mini war.

I was more nervous than I had ever been in my life. Bile rose in my mouth, but I choked it back down. Killing Marc or the police officer or anyone else was easy compared to this.

Of course, as soon as I got to the passenger side, the person there had to move around to the front. Crunching noises sounded until they faded away as Bob and WWNTD ran from my sight toward the front door to the cabin.

I chased after them, and my lungs burned from the frigid air. After I rounded the corner, no one was there. I stopped, skidding to a halt and catching myself before I fell.

Damn snow and ice.

No light flashed from the cabin door closing. They must've run to the other side. I had chosen Bob's path earlier, since he'd be pursuing her. I spun around and ran toward the back of the cabin. WWNTD was going down. My man and I would corner her if she went around the cabin. What was with these negative thoughts? Corrie was getting to me. I just needed to see Bob, and I'd be okay.

I pumped my arms, hoping it would give me more speed. Runners did it during a race. They must know what they were doing. I concentrated on my hands moving opposite and what was in front of me. My knee hurt like a motherfucker. I didn't bother to look down at the snow and ice beneath me. The second my gaze shifted, I knew I'd fall.

The end of the cabin was only a few more feet in front of me. Should I stop or round the corner and keep going? Too late. I went past the end, colliding with someone. We fell, and I landed hard on my messed-up knee.

My heart slammed into its cage as I scrambled to my feet.

Whoever I collided with rose, too.

I lifted my gun and pointed it at the person, choking out, "Turn around or I'll shoot you."

Chapter 8

The person stopped moving and slowly raised their hands, but they didn't do what I instructed. They kept their faces away from me. The hood of their camouflage jacket covered their head. This could've been Bob since it didn't have all the girly colors thrown in.

My finger hovered over the triggered, but I didn't dare shoot until I knew for sure that the person in front of me wasn't my man. "I said turn around." I bared my teeth and glared, waiting for them to listen to me. Bob would've answered me by now, right? He would've at least done as I instructed if he couldn't speak. "For the last time, turn around!"

The person shifted to their side.

I held my breath and gripped the gun harder, most likely turning my knuckles white.

"Shoot, babe, shoot," Bob said as he rounded the corner of the cabin.

WWNTD finally did what she should've done earlier.

I pulled the trigger three times, aiming for the vital spots my dad and my man had taught me. Once in the head, and two in the heart area. Two shots to the heart were just in case it was more on the right side instead of the usual left. Bob told me less than one percent of the population had their heart on the opposite side. My man was smart.

We planned for everything and made sure our kills counted. Dead people couldn't speak.

"We did it, babe," Bob said once he could breathe. He wrapped his arms around me, pulling me into him. "We're safe. We're home free."

I hugged him back, and relief washed over me. Tears stung my eyes for an additional reason. He was okay; he was safe. I pressed my lips against his, and he kissed me back.

As soon as we finished, I asked, "Are you okay?" Had his blood been on the trail I'd seen earlier? I glanced down at the boy's mother, and she had torn her pant leg. If she were still alive, she'd be bleeding.

"I'm good. Are you?" Bob placed his hands on my cheeks and his forehead against mine.

"Were you shot or hurt?" My throat thickened. I'd been running on pure adrenaline and didn't want to come off the high yet. My knee couldn't take it.

"I'm okay, sweetie. I don't want to worry you," Bob answered.

"Are you really? You know I will worry more if you don't tell me the truth," I said.

"I'm just tired, sweetie, and my stomach is acting up because of stress, or I might have an ulcer."

"You talk like an old man." A bubble of laughter flowed from my mouth to hide the cry from the sudden sharpness of pain shooting through my leg. I shifted my weight to get the pressure off the injured knee and stumbled.

Bob caught me.

My dumbass tripped way more than that vampire chick in all the novels and movies from years ago. My friends, my old friends, were totally into it. Well, the girls were. I shook my head and fought back the tears. They were dead. They didn't deserve my sadness, not after everything they did to my man.

"Who deserved what?" Corrie had her hands on her hips, her favorite pose.

I ignored her.

"How are you doing? Quit avoiding my question, honey. How's the knee?" Bob asked.

"I fucked it up after this bitch ran into me. Can you look? I'm afraid to." I would've kicked the dead mother for emphasis, but in my current condition, I couldn't do so without injuring myself further.

"Let's get you inside to check your leg and warm up before we head back home." Bob wrapped an arm around my waist so I could lean on him.

"Is that a good idea? We...we usually take off right away after a killing spree," I said nervously.

"With your knee, walking is not a good idea until I at least check and wrap it. We might have to steal the truck here before we go to our place to get our car." Taking a stolen vehicle and moving it wasn't a good idea. At least the sedan we drove had a name attached to it, a fake name, but still a name. Bob stopped us in front of the cabin. "Unless there is a reason you don't want to go inside."

"The boy." I held back a sob. I could barely face the truth and buried my head in Bob's chest, letting the tears fall. The cold air took only a moment to freeze the tears on my face.

"I'm sorry, sweetie. Don't cry. If I knew killing him would've been this hard on you, I would've done it myself." Bob wrapped me in a hug.

"That's not—" I said, but cut myself off as a light appeared in the corner of my eye.

Bob must've seen something too or sensed me because he let me go and turned around. Dim headlights appeared in front of us.

Whoever drove must've parked further away. Why weren't they coming any closer? Wouldn't the driver park behind the other three vehicles?

My man grabbed my hand and pulled us toward the front of the cabin.

I winced as I walked with him, but just kept going despite the pain. He'd be so mad at himself if he knew he'd caused me any agony. No way would I tell him.

Bob placed his finger on his lips.

I must've made a noise, but I didn't plan on breathing until we knew who we dealt with. Whoever was here couldn't see us without getting out of their vehicle and coming this way. Why weren't they? We guessed more people could come by the size of the cabin. The Jagers mentioned more people.

Had Bob asked them for more details? He'd been alone with the group for a short time before he killed the woman, the aunt. Maybe, or did he shoot the grandma first? People's faces blurred inside my head after I'd slain so many.

"What the hell?" some guy said. He must've gotten out of the vehicle and seen the burned-out truck. I doubted he'd stick his head out the window.

"Lindsay!" a lady yelled. Loud thumping sounds filled the air as she and probably her companion ran to the mother. By the noise they made, I couldn't tell if over two people were with her.

Oops. I forgot about the dead body. That would've been way more important than a burned truck. No wonder they stopped sooner.

I didn't stop the smirk from forming on my face. Marc's death was one of my best. Like I would ever want a man like him. I remembered the killing, just not the who most of the time. Eventually, his name would fade from my memory. I didn't feel guilty about what I did to him.

"We should try to take them out from this side before they scatter. You can set yourself up in the tree line using it as cover over there," Bob whispered after a few seconds. He pointed toward the woods near the vehicles, his face scrunched up, and he glanced down at my leg. "Ah, shit, sorry, honey. I forgot about your injury."

"Yeah, I don't think I can walk that far." I'd have to head more to the left so no one could see me first before going straight and then circling around to position myself. Even the thought of that much moving around made my knee ache even more.

"Crap. What will we do?" Bob took off his hat and ran a hand through his hair. He did that motion whenever he needed time to think. He would come up with a plan that wouldn't involve me getting hurt more, but that could take a lot of time. Time that we simply did not have.

I couldn't leave fast right now, so I'd have to suggest something to him, but what? A lot of walking was out. I could set myself up on the end of the cabin, taking my shots as soon as Bob was on the other side, but then he'd be in harm's way. I wouldn't shoot with him there. If he was at the back of the cabin and we shot at most halfway, we should be fine.

"You know what we have to do," I said after deciding. If I needed to leave my spot fast, I could manage a few feet. My best option would be inside the cabin if someone came after me. I could lock the door to keep them out while I found the way to the back.

"Are you sure?" Bob asked. He sounded unsure.

"Do we have any other choice?"

"Not really." Bob frowned. Being so close to him, I could see his facial expressions, which I loved, every one of them. Even his frown when he was upset over something made him even more adorable in my eyes.

"I'll hunker close to the edge here and wait for you to get set up in back. If they come near me or get too close, I can run inside the cabin and meet you where you are. We left WWNTD on what side?"

"WWNTD?" Bob's eyebrows scrunched together.

"Sorry. I didn't know who you killed, so I called her WWNTD, Woman Who Needed to Die, inside my head. She's the mother, Lindsey."

He smiled at me before saying, "You're so cute." Normally he would've laughed at my antics, but I got why he didn't right now. We were trying to be quiet so as not to alert anyone to our presence.

At least two people were talking about something, and the howling wind muffled their voices. They could check on Lindsay or try calling for help. Bob's little box was still working. Eventually, the people would check out the truck or the cabin.

"You need to go." I gave Bob a little shove.

"Stay safe," he said.

"Always."

"Please don't come on the killing side," I said.

"I won't," he said.

"Don't you dare either. Promise me you won't. Don't even signal me you will. If we kill them all, come back to me," I told him.

"I promise I won't. Don't worry, we got this, sweetie." Bob pressed our lips together for a brief second before running away. At least he could run. His stomach must not be upsetting him too much. What would cause the pain? We ate the same thing, so he shouldn't have food poisoning.

The most likely scenario came to me, and my eyes grew large. Bob might've gotten hurt. He said he wasn't, but he liked to do that macho-man bullshit thing. I needed to check his abdomen to see for myself.

I shook my head to clear my thoughts. Bob would have to wait. What if someone had shot him? I would've noticed the blood. I might not have, though. Why hadn't I insisted he show me his abs after he said his stomach hurt?

Stupid. Stupid. Stupid.

I hobbled over to the end and hunkered near Bridgette. She wouldn't mind me being near her since she was dead. Snow from the blowing wind covered her body some. The bucket of water she had carried had tipped over and frozen to the ground.

From here, I could army crawl into my position once Bob fired. His shots should force those to come toward me unless they had already made their way here. The hair on the back of my neck lifted. They couldn't be inside. Bob and I didn't take that long to plan our next move. They might've gotten close, though.

Someone ran in front of me, heading toward the SUV and cursing, "Shit, man."

I buried my face in the snow. Did they notice me?

Bang.

Someone screamed.

I shifted my rifle off my back. The snow melting on my face clouded my vision. I wiped off the water. Through the scope, a dark shadow stopped and then moved. It was looking at something, or most likely someone, on the ground. Glen, maybe, or someone else. Didn't matter. I took aim and squeezed the trigger, shattering the window on the SUV. Missed. With the next shot, I got them.

They fell to the ground.

Please don't be Bob. He promised me he wouldn't be here. His words and reassurance never stopped me from worrying about him, though, whenever I couldn't confirm his position.

After taking a deep breath, I shot the person on the ground again. If the first bullet wound didn't kill them, they'd at least bleed to death with the second. They couldn't have been Bob. He didn't have enough time to run past everyone and get by the vehicles.

I dragged myself twelve inches with my forearms, set the rifle in front of me, and lined up my next target. This time, I considered the wind before firing.

Bam.

Headshot.

Two down, I didn't know how many more I had left to kill or how many Bob had killed. I wasn't counting. We needed to keep on massacring until they were all dead. Afterward, we'd meet and tell each other how many victims remained. Well, we would if I wasn't hurt. My guy would most likely go after any stragglers, which meant I needed to be out of his way.

Retreating inside the cabin wasn't the best idea. I didn't just want to avoid it because of the boy. What if someone had made it inside?

I continued to scan with the scope, not seeing any shadows.

Crap.

This wasn't working. Morning was hours away, and when dawn came, I'd be just as vulnerable as my targets where I lay. I shifted my head to the side and pulled out my night-vision goggles.

My vision flashed with red and yellow from the light behind me until my gaze adjusted. No one was out here, but the dead body by the SUV was causing a hit with my goggles. The other body was in the tree line, my last kill. I didn't see any other signatures. I wished I knew what type of vehicle they drove. How many people could be here?

Snow crunched behind me.

My heart jumped into my throat, and I took out my gun before rolling onto my back.

Chapter 9

"**B**ob, you idiot, I could've shot you." A half-whimper and half-frustrated sigh escaped my lips.

He walked closer with his hands up, frowned at me, and then held out his hand.

I didn't mean to call him names. I was just so mad at him. He should've signaled me he was returning. I could've killed him. Despite being mad at him, I took his hand.

Bob helped me to stand.

"I'm sorry, you're not an idiot. But damnit! I could've shot you." Tears gathered in my eyes, and I wiped them away. He had scared me so much that I cried.

"I know. I'm sorry. I tried to signal to you that everyone was dead, but you must not have seen it. I killed two. How many did you?"

"The same as you."

"Can you forgive me? I couldn't come to you on the side you were shooting because I promised you I wouldn't." His gaze searched for something in mine.

"Thank you." I set my head on my chest and hiccupped. Our nightmare was over. We could leave.

"You're not mad at me?"

"No." I could never stay angry at him for long, even when I had a legitimate reason. We only had each other. "Is everyone dead?"

"They drove an SUV so four or five people could fit in it max if they were legal," Bob answered.

"So, no one else then?" I asked.

"Can't say yes for sure, you know me," Bob answered.

"Always cautious." Sometimes too cautious, but I didn't tell him that.

"They were still trying to save NNTWB or whatever you called her when I got around back."

"WWNTD."

"Yeah, WWNTD." Bob smiled. He looked so handsome when he did. "We should keep that name. A guy who needed to die had headed into the cabin, but I got him before he could enter. Let's get your knee looked at."

"Can't we go? You can look at my injury at our place." I didn't want to stay here any longer. What if we didn't get everyone?

Yeah, that is the real reason I want to leave.

"Sure, it is," Corrie said.

"We'll go in a minute, then. We need cash and a set of keys first. I'll be right back, then we can go," Bob said.

"Wait, I'll get the money from inside and near here. You deal with the others around back," I said before he could take off.

"Are you sure?" Bob raised an eyebrow.

"I can manage that much movement." I skipped Betsy in the woods. She didn't have a purse on her. Most women didn't keep cash in their pockets, unlike me.

Bob kissed me on the forehead before letting me go. He turned to leave.

"Hold on," I said to him after remembering something important. I waited for him to face me again. "Are you hurt?"

"Not really." Bob shifted his weight between his feet.

"Answer the question: yes or no? Are you hurt?" Why did men do that? My dad was the same way. I literally asked a yes or no question. I folded my arms and drummed my fingers on my biceps.

"You're so cute when you're mad."

"I'm not mad, but I'm about to be. Are you hurt?" I breathed heavily through my nose to calm the rage building inside of me.

"Yes, and no." Bob let out a short laugh.

"How are you hurt and not hurt, exactly?" I asked.

"I ran into a limb when I was running after WWNTD. It got me in the stomach. I'll be fine after some rest," he answered.

"Let me see."

"Let me see your knee," he countered.

"Fine. After we're back at our cabin, but before we're on the road. Deal?" I held out my hand for him to shake.

"You got it, babe." He laughed again and took my hand in his, giving it one good, solid tug before bringing it up to his lips, glove and all. "Get as much cash as you can from these people."

"And the truck keys?" I asked.

"No, the SUV will be easier unless it dies. The moron driver left the lights on, but I shut them off."

"We'll have to use the truck then. I shot the window out on the SUV, and it burned some in the fire. I can't wait to have the heat on," I said. A nice cup of hot cocoa would also be good, too.

"Go inside, sweetie. I'll get everything and then we can go." Bob placed his hands on my hips.

"No, we need to get the cash and valuables and leave. You've been telling me that, remember?"

"Oh, I remember alright. I do want to stop for one thing?"

"What?"

His eyes heated. "You know."

"Me too, honey. Me too. So, get going." Nothing made Bob hornier than a night of killing. He'd be making love to me until dawn. Seeing him wanting me so badly made my engines rev. I couldn't wait to get out of here now.

With one final peck, Bob took off, running toward the back. He always kissed me before he left. He said it could be our last.

I brushed the nasty thought away and hobbled the couple of steps to Bridgette's body. Bob and I would always be together, always. We even made a plan for when we were caught—no, if we were caught.

I rummaged through Bridgette's coat pockets and then her pants, only finding a few dollar bills and some condoms. I shoved the cash into my jeans. Marc didn't seem like the type of guy to wear the plastic. He probably had several kids out there he didn't know about, or did and didn't care.

Once I finished searching Bridgette, I stood and winced, not from the pain. Thinking about my next move made my knee ache. I had a couple of options. Hit the two in front of the house or head to the vehicles. Neither of the dead bodies close by would give me the keys to the SUV, so I decided on the latter.

Walking the few steps to the SUV was a pain. I must've messed up my leg a hell of a lot worse than I had thought.

When we're backing out of here, I'll ask Bob to run the bitch over for making me hurt myself more.

I used the vehicle as I shuffled around the front. Glen's body was about as covered with snow as Bridgette's. They died about the same time, and they both were out more in the open than the others.

Eureka! I removed Glen's wallet, and he had hundreds of dollar bills. This money would certainly come in handy, and so would his watch. I checked his last pocket and found nothing else.

After rolling the old man onto his back, his blue eyes stared blankly into the sky. I once heard that in order to close a dead person's eyes, they needed to be gone for a few hours. Bob and I had never stuck around to test that theory.

Inside his jacket pocket, I found the keys to either the SUV or the truck. This family bought its vehicles from the same company. They must like this brand, and anyone who didn't buy it, they ousted it. They seemed the type. My parents didn't care. They wouldn't even buy me a vehicle. Maybe Bob and I should pay them a visit. Didn't police shows have the criminal always get caught when they returned home? Yeah, we weren't going there soon.

As soon as I finished with Glen, I moved to an unknown man. This guy I shot between the vehicles was an idiot. He didn't bother ducking or running away once I shattered the SUV's window. He deserved a quick death. We didn't need his genes adding to the gene pool. I took out the cash, valuables, and keys. Shocker, he had the same make as the other three in this lot. At least he had a remote-control start. I pressed the unlock button.

Beep.

The headlights on the SUV at the back of the cabin flashed off and on, and a shadowed figure moved near that SUV.

I shifted my gun out of my pocket and waited until whoever was there came into the beam from the light on the cabin. A sigh of relief escaped my lips.

Bob headed toward me, and once he got to me, he said, "Good job, sweetie."

I handed him the keys, and he helped me to stand.

"Did you check everyone for cash?" Bob asked.

"I have Betsy left and the two in front of the cabin. I came this way first after checking the cabin," I answered.

"Okay, I'll search the remaining three."

"Why are you so concerned with money? How much do we have left?" I narrowed my eyes on Bob. Something was up with him. He usually wanted to go right after a killing, and I would have to persuade him to stay a minute or two more.

"We're completely out of cash. We can't even put gas in our car." Bob lowered his head and wouldn't look at me.

"We can't get work when we need a social security number. We'll figure something out, sweetie."

Bob raised his head and offered me the crook of his elbow to take. Once we got to the other side of the SUV, he let me go, telling me, "I'll be right back."

He kissed me on the forehead before taking off to the two dead people. He stopped in front of Bridgette and pointed at her.

I shooed him away with my hand. I doubt she had any hidden pockets that held cash. She probably made Marc pay for everything. By the new truck he used to drive, he could afford to take her out a few times. Well, he couldn't anymore now since he was dead.

Bob bent in front of the first body. I couldn't remember if it was the man or the woman. Snow covered them a little, but not as much as Bridgette. They and everyone else here would be well-covered in snow by mid-morning or afternoon. My man checked the weather before we left our cabin. We should start getting some flurries soon.

Bob shook his head once he finished searching. He must not have found much. He moved onto the next body and pulled out a wallet.

We needed a few hundred bucks to live for a few weeks. We could stretch it for a month if need be. Eating canned beans got annoying fast, but I didn't want to complain and make Bob think I was un-grateful. He offered more than once to return me home, but I didn't plan on going anywhere. I loved being with him.

Bob stuffed the cash and something else into his pocket. A credit card, perhaps? Using the plastic card more than once was stupid.

I sighed and made my way over to my man. I hated waiting. My knee ached, and I wanted a hot bath and to be snuggled next to him sleeping.

After I arrived, I asked, "Need help?"

"No, sweetie, I'm almost done. You should've stayed by the vehicle with your knee. I got this." Bob patted down the guy's jacket. When he found something, he pulled it out and tossed a package of chewing gum into the snow. He removed the guy's watch next.

We kept some valuables to sell at smaller pawn shops before we left a town if we needed quick cash. I didn't remember how much we had left or where they came from.

"Ready to go?" I asked once he finished and stood.

Before Bob could answer, something crashed inside the cabin.

Chapter 10

Bob and I looked at the cabin, and then he turned to me and asked, "You didn't kill the boy?" Anger flashed across his face.

"That's not—" I answered.

"Later." After cutting me off, Bob ran inside. I had never seen him so pissed off at me before. Well, I did at my old friends, but that wasn't me. Yeah, he got mad whenever I mentioned his dead sister. I always dropped the conversation right away once he was upset. I didn't blame him. My old friends and I had a part in her killing herself. What if he never forgave me for this?

More noise sounded through the open door until it settled into the frame. I sighed and wished I'd stayed against the SUV. At least I had something to help hold me upright.

A better idea would be to move away. I needed to be out of the way. I couldn't help Bob with what was going on inside. After I hobbled to the SUV, I leaned against it. Getting the weight off my knee felt so good.

How much damage did I do? Did I sprain my knee? Was that even possible? Not like I could look up what to do for a sore knee with the little box running. We were a little way from town and well out of signal range.

As I pondered my predicament, someone ran out the front door. I opened my mouth to yell at my man, but he came barreling out after them.

They ran across the clearing, heading toward the trees.

Why wasn't Bob shooting? I glanced around and spotted my rifle where I'd left it, propped up in the snow. My dumbass had forgotten to place it on my back. If I shuffled to it, I might get a shot in before the person Bob chased escaped.

I took aim, but my man blocked my view. Saliva filled my mouth, and my heart ached. I didn't dare press the trigger yet.

"Down!" I yelled.

Bob dived to the ground, or fell, or tripped. It didn't matter; he was out of the line of fire and safe.

I realigned the shot, considering the little wind.

Bang.

The guy fell forward into the snow just before the trees. Lucky shot. It had gone a little wide, hitting him in the shoulder blade.

Bob climbed to his feet and hurried to the guy on the ground. Something in his hand glinted, a knife most likely. Once he got to the other man, he lifted the guy's head.

I didn't have to see to know what happened next. Bob killed the guy—not the guy—the kid. Pain filled everywhere inside of me, or maybe it was sadness. I wouldn't be mad at my man for doing what needed to be done. *Stupid child.* I shook my head.

After I stood, I set the rifle on my back.

Bob checked the pockets of the dead boy. Why? Kids didn't carry any money on them. Never mind. I remembered Monte Jackson and how much cash he always had on him. He had a lot of money, despite never working a day in his life. His brother, Conrad, probably carried the same amount of money, if not more.

How was Conrad doing? He was the only one to survive the massacre besides me. I should look at his social media profile to check on him. I didn't dare reach out to him. He wouldn't understand that I wanted to stay with Bob.

My man finished his search and headed back to me.

I couldn't wait to put this nightmare behind us. We needed to get into the SUV and go. No matter how much Bob wanted to stay, I'd insist we leave. All I had to do was tell him I'd be leaving him, and he'd listen to me. Why hadn't I done that earlier? I silently cursed myself. My leg felt so much better propped up or out with the seat slid back.

Something moved in the woods behind my house. The more I stared, the more shadows I saw. What the hell?

Before I could tell Bob, several heavily armed police officers emerged from the woods, and one of them yelled, "Freeze! Drop your weapon or we'll shoot."

Bob held his knife in the air and stopped in his tracks. The guy he had just killed was now several feet behind him. My man could easily take the one person standing a little closer than the rest, but then he'd die too, with over ten cops pointing their guns at him. He would never survive that many bullets. The nearest hospital with surgery capability was well over an hour away. I couldn't lose him.

I shifted my rifle to my side. Bob would be in danger if I started shooting. Our trick earlier, with him ducking to the ground, wouldn't work. Cops were trained to shoot first and ask questions later. Tears prickled my eyes. What the hell could I do?

"Drop your gun," some guy said from behind me. Something hit my back, most likely his weapon.

Bob and I couldn't do anything now. The cops had caught us. Time for Plan B, or was it Plan C? I'd lost track.

I opened my palm, shook my shoulder, and the rifle fell to the ground. Police officers surrounded me. One of them forced my hands behind my back, and they shoved me to the ground, pinning me. I struggled against those holding me as they searched me, pulling out weapon after weapon.

They buried my face in the snow. I tried to lift my head to see Bob, but when I couldn't, I settled on at least facing him. He hadn't dropped his knife yet.

"Drop your weapon. I'll not repeat," an armed officer yelled. I couldn't tell if he was the same guy who had spoken earlier or not.

"Bob, please stop!" I screamed as I struggled harder against the cops holding me down. Some officer moved and shifted his knee to my back, holding my chest down. I started coughing. My vision blurred, and I couldn't see my man's next move. If he knew I was in danger, he'd strike. Ten, a hundred, a thousand police officers be damned.

"Let her up. We can't kill her. She needs to pay for what she did," a cop said. No wonder suspects died in their custody.

Once whoever shifted, I could breathe, but that truly didn't matter to me. I needed to see Bob. See my man.

Please still be alive.

Bob turned to me, and the next words out of his mouth broke my heart. "We promised forever if we got caught."

No, not Plan B! Tears streamed down my face, hitting the snow. I couldn't lose my man, I couldn't.

"No, don't!" I yelled. "Bob, I'm pregnant!"

Bob's mouth opened into a wide O.

"We can still have forever someday," I told him.

He looked at the knife and then at me. The police weren't even there for him. When Bob let the knife go, I breathed a sigh of relief.

The gnats swarmed him, and I couldn't see him anymore because of the damned bugs being in my line of sight.

"Secure," an officer said about me.

They hauled me to my feet and frog-marched me to a squad car. I barely touched the ground. Once I was close, a cop opened the door and shoved me inside.

"Stay here," some other officer said, maybe the one in charge.

I shifted my feet to the floor and rotated my body around to sit up, using the seat as leverage. The police had secured my legs with chains and my hands with handcuffs. They were probably afraid of me kicking them if I had the chance. I would next time for sure.

After sitting upright, I stared out the window at some fat ass. The damned cop blocked my view. I'd tell him to move, but I couldn't see anything. They had parked the sedan further back than the cabin.

Where was my Bob? Where was he? He had to be okay. I didn't hear a gunshot.

I couldn't escape with my limbs tied up. I was secure.

The police would stick Bob inside another cop car soon. They might take a while. My guy had way more knives and guns on him than I did. We used little ammo for this family.

"Is the other suspect secure?" someone said as they moved closer.

"Yes, sir. Getting him into another vehicle as we speak," the person answered.

"Good. We'll march them into the police station one at a time. The cameras will be waiting. The FBI should be on their way here to take them into custody."

"Who would imagine the notorious serial killers Bob Ghul and Jolene Argall would be in our woods?"

"It's something, isn't it?"

"Yeah, and the feds will get all the credit. She has to have Stockholm syndrome."

"Doesn't excuse what she did." Their voices grew fainter as they moved away.

I have Stockholm syndrome? Yeah, right? Bob mentioned I should use that as my defense if we were ever caught. I dismissed that idea. For how many lives we ended, he'd get the needle for sure, and I couldn't live with that decision at all. We were in this together forever.

At least I knew the police's plan for us. They'd bring my man by me one last time before court. If I looked now, I might spot him. My position didn't give me much of a view.

A mob of officers walked past the car. I couldn't see anything through them or the fat-assed cop in front of my window. They had to be carrying my man to the other vehicle. Someone would whisk us away in short order.

"Take them to the police station. We'll follow right behind," some man said. The head honcho for this department, maybe?

A police officer climbed into the front seat and buckled up.

Safety first.

Wouldn't he be safer with two cops in the vehicle with me? The police might not think I was the dangerous one.

The cop turned on the lights and maneuvered out of the parking spot without saying a word. About ten minutes in, he slowed the car and pulled along the side of the road.

My stomach twisted into a huge knot. I heard stories of men in authority stopping and forcing women to do sexual acts on them, but we weren't on an isolated road. Anyone could drive by and see us, like the police car Bob was in. I doubted the officer would let me go.

"I shouldn't be telling you this, but you and your lawyer will find out eventually," the officer said. His tone sounded calm. His gaze stared at me through the rearview mirror. I opened my mouth to say something, but he spoke again. "That family you killed. They weren't good people. They did bad things to the boy. You saved him."

Logan was alive? I cheered on the inside. The guy Bob killed last must've been the last passenger in the SUV that arrived not too long ago.

"What bad things?" I asked the officer, curious.

"The family used the boy for—" The officer's voice broke, and he covered his face with his hands. He didn't need to finish his sentence for me to know what the officer wanted to say. "I have kids at home his age."

Everything clicked together in my brain. When I got Logan to kneel by the bed, I had paid little attention to the place's appearance, but the image burned and buried itself in my mind until now. A camera sat on a tripod in front of the enormous bed. Why would someone need to videotape a mattress unless they were making a sex tape? I didn't want to imagine what they did with it. I shook my head. Logan was safe. Not me. Not my man. Bob and I would be, though. We had Plan C.

Christmas Day Massacre

The Holiday Killing Spree Book 3

K.A. Meng

Chapter 1

B lood oozed from Shelly Nicholson's neck. It ran down her body, soaking her big blue chair.

I'd taken her notebook from our session and slashed her with the hard cardboard edge. Her heart did most of the work, pumping her blood out. All I had to do was sit back and watch.

She took five minutes to bleed out. I should've cut her deeper.

Now I had less than thirty to escape. Her office was on the second floor and bars were on the only window. My guards stood by the sole entrance. My lawyer had planned for me and her to talk, like I needed any help. I was perfectly fine. Didn't normal people massacre others?

"Ms. Argall?" Shelly snapped me out of my daydream.

I hadn't been paying any attention to her since we started our session. Instead, I'd been imagining all the different ways I could kill her. Her pen, her notebook, her books, her awards on the shelf, her glasses, her coffee table, and even her hair tie could be weapons.

"Ms. Argall?" Shelly said again. Her tone sounded like nails on a chalkboard.

If I didn't say something soon, she'd give up or worse, she'd tell my parents. After rolling my eyes, I answered, "What?"

"I asked you a question."

"So what?" I shrugged my shoulders. She'd been trying to convince me since we met that my relationship with Bob Ghul wasn't normal.

I didn't care what she thought. What he and I had in words couldn't describe. We belonged together, together forever.

Shelly took a deep breath and let it out. She tapped her pen against the notebook she always carried. When I asked about what she wrote, she always said, 'just minor notes to remind myself of our session.' She didn't realize I could read what she wrote by following the movement of her ballpoint. She'd written two words multiple times.

Stockholm Syndrome?

Minor notes, my ass, I thought.

My lawyer paid her to figure out if I was crazy or not. If I suffered from being held hostage by my man, which I didn't. She added the question mark every time she wrote the condition because she wasn't sure.

She's such a dumbass.

I was sane. I wanted to do nothing more than take that pen and shove it into her, but not her neck because that'd cause way too much spray back. Her side maybe, and afterward, I'd watch her slowly bleed out for all the mean things she said about my Bob.

"Jolene!" Shelly pressed. She liked me to call her by her first name too, not Ms. Nicholson, shrink, or bitch. She said it made our meetings more personal.

"What?" I grunted. The image of her blood pooling on her gray carpet flipped into my mind. Maybe I should get her to stand first and then take her down, causing less commotion. One quick jab and my hand over her mouth should do it. The armed guards, who waited in the hall, wouldn't hear it.

"Jolene, what you've been through isn't your fault. What he did—"

"Excuse me, don't mention my Bob again. He did nothing wrong."

"A lot of prisoners empathize with their capturer, but—" Shelly said before I cut her off again.

"Here's the thing: I wasn't a prisoner. What Bob and I did, we did together." I pulled my sleeve down on my right arm after the bandage showed. Bob would be mad at me if he found out what I had attempted. Everyone told me too many lies about him. I couldn't take their deceit anymore and the stress of everything. I glanced out the window as my throat thickened. My bad angle on the couch and the bars blocked most of my view.

"Please let me finish." Shelly tucked a strand of her curly red hair behind her ear that had gotten loose from her Santa hat. How lame could she be? Why did she bother to tame her wild mane? She'd look way better letting it loose with some product; she could actually be pretty. "You have positive feelings for Bob. You didn't have a previous relationship with him until the Friday before Labor Day this year, right?"

"I met him years ago. He's Kaylee's twin. Well, he was her twin. Would he still be if she were dead? I think so. Death doesn't change who you are." Kaylee had killed herself. I took a deep breath to calm myself. Bob wouldn't hate me; he'd understand why I attempted to harm myself. I felt so alone.

"But that wasn't a relationship. You talked to him how much? A handful of times?"

"So what?" I folded my arms and leaned back. I kicked myself for not giving Bobby the time of day back then. Everyone called him Bobby then. To me, he was Bob, my sweet, sexy, muscular, and handsome man now.

"You didn't have an actual relationship with him at this time, though," Shelly said.

"I was a jerk to him when we were younger, and I regret that now. What's your point?" I didn't get where she was going with this.

"Let's move on. You're refusing to cooperate with the police and the FBI?"

"I don't like cops." No one did unless they needed them, and from what I hear in bigger cities, they didn't want to call them.

"Everyone in law enforcement is trying to help you, even me."

"You're not a cop," I pointed out. If she were, I wouldn't be talking to her. Bad enough, she had a PhD in psychology.

"I'm here for you, Jolene. Do you think Bob is dangerous?" Shelly asked as she leaned in closer to me. Her voice sounded sweeter than molasses.

"That's where you're wrong. Bob *is* dangerous, and I know it. He is not to me." I honestly believed wholeheartedly that he would never lay a finger on me. I was the one who stopped him from doing worse things; his rock. "When he isn't around me, you can't stop him."

"What do you mean?"

Shit! I shouldn't have said that.

"What do you mean?" Shelly asked again. Her red eyebrows rose to her hairline. Her hair and eyebrow colors matched when they shouldn't have.

Is her hair fake too, or does she dye her eyebrows to match her hair? Either way, she was a weirdo. From what I've seen in my old classmates, redheads had either light brown brows or red brows that weren't the same color as their hair.

"Jolene, tell me what you mean, please," Shelly said.

I pressed my lips together into a tight line. I hadn't gotten to see Bob since the day I told him I was pregnant, and I absentmindedly touched my belly. The police marched me into the station, followed by him. I assumed the latter since I didn't get to see him. I didn't have access to the news or a phone. Except if I made a phone call, the jail monitored it. Any contact I had with anyone was bare minimum, even before the accident where I hurt myself. This could be my chance to see him, or I could make the situation worse.

"Jolene?" Shelly asked. Her tone softened.

"Never mind." I waved my hand in front of me, and afterward I pulled my sleeve back down.

"Okay, we'll drop this conversation for now. You'd tell me if Bob would hurt anyone, wouldn't you?"

No, I won't. I blinked at her instead of answering. I didn't want him to be in solitary confinement like me. Being alone with my own thoughts all day was driving me a little crazy.

I had scratched myself deeply. I never did before. Ever since I hurt myself, I had to show the guards my nails, and if they were too long, I had to bite them down or they would forcefully cut them. Talk about a sick, perverse justice system.

"Of course," I muttered, a complete lie.

Shelly wrote something that I worked to figure out before she said, "With the time remaining, let's talk about your friends."

"They're dead. Why do we have to talk about them?" I shrugged my shoulders, and I didn't care if I had no one left. I had Bob.

"How did your friends die?"

"I wasn't there for most of their deaths." I rattled off how I thought each died, but I never mentioned who killed them. When I got to Bob's sister, his twin, I took a deep breath. "Kaylee killed herself."

Out of everyone's death, she brought tears to my eyes. I brushed them away. I hated myself for not knowing what was happening at her home. Why wasn't I a better friend?

"What do all their deaths have in common?" Shelly asked gently.

"They deserved to die except for Kaylee," I answered after taking a moment to think. She had done nothing, and her sick stepfather used her. My fists tightened at my sides.

"Here, use this." Shelly handed me a tissue from the coffee table in front of me.

I dabbed at the corners of my eyes. I didn't realize I'd been crying. Yeah, a few tears here and there, but nothing like this. Whenever I was at the damn shrink's office, I bawled like a baby. Who wouldn't with everything going on? I started pretrial on Monday, the day after tomorrow. I'd have to give my plea. My lawyer advised me to plead insanity. If I did, I'd spend years in a psych ward. What would happen to my baby then?

On top of my drama, I had to talk about my feelings with Shelly. She and my lawyer also tried to get me to relive the things that I'd done. I had killed people, big deal.

She glanced at her notes after I blew my nose. "Do you think Corrie deserved to be tortured and gutted?" Shelly asked.

"Yeah! She was the worst of my old friends," I answered without hesitation.

"Why are you saying old? Your friends are dead, Jolene. Killed by your boyfriend. They are still your friends, even if they're gone."

"My dead friends deserved to die, especially Corrie."

"You can't believe that. What could a seventeen-year-old teenage girl do to deserve death?"

"She's the reason everything happened. If that bossy bitch Corrie hadn't forced us to ignore Kaylee, Kaylee would still be alive." I ground my teeth together, and heat flushed through my body.

"You didn't have to ignore Kaylee," Shelly pointed out.

"Have you ever dealt with a queen bee, or should I say a queen bitch? If you don't listen to her, you're ousted, too."

"I was in high school once. I know what it's like."

"What, a million years ago? Time has changed everything."

Shelly's lips twitched before she said wistfully, "No, only ten, but I know what it was like to want to be popular." Her cheeks turned a little pink.

"I didn't know 'what it was like' because I was, and if you didn't follow the queen bee, you were out. Corrie liked to make the lives of any girls who crossed her miserable," I said. Like what she did to Molly Bremer. Molly had turned the corner and bumped into Corrie by accident. The harassment had gotten so bad that Molly switched schools. I didn't stand up for the other girl even when Corrie should've been paying attention to where she walked. I didn't bother telling my shrink this story, since she wouldn't understand.

"We're getting off topic here. With Kaylee, you also had a choice not to ignore her, but you did," Shelly pointed out.

"High school must've changed in the decade since you've been there. You either listen to the queen and king or you're..." My voice trailed off, and I made the motion of getting a throat slit.

"You have to be kidding." Shelly's hand flew to her chest.

"Corrie's dead, isn't she?" I asked.

Shelly paused and then said, "Yeah, Corrie was murdered." My shrink had to stop and think. If she mentioned Bob in any negative light, I shut down and refused to speak to her. She was like a kid. I gave her one warning, and if she continued, I was done. One session we didn't speak for fifty-five minutes. She spoke to my lawyer and offered to try again the next day.

"Corrie deserved to die because she wasn't a good person."

Again, Shelly looked at her notes before speaking, "If you say so. What about Abby Miller? Did she deserve to be stabbed?"

Amateur.

"Yes, Abby wasn't great at anything." I smiled at my own private joke. Abby loved the five-letter word 'great'. After Bob gave her justice for her part in his sister's death, he'd written it on the wall above her bed. I'd been horrified. Now I found it quite amusing.

"I don't get why you're smiling. Why are you suddenly happy?" Shelly narrowed her eyes at me.

"Everything is just great." A bubble of laughter burst through my mouth, and I covered it. I fought against the giggling fit that was building up inside me. If I didn't stop chuckling, the shrink would sign off on me as being crazy. At least that would make my parents and my lawyer happy.

Think of the baby.

Those words sobered me fast, and I explained, "Inside joke. I'm thinking the stress of the trial is getting to me."

"Yeah, stress affects people in different ways. Do you feel stressed a lot?" Shelly asked.

"I didn't until the police kidnapped me. I was fine before then. Everything's been...been a blur these last few weeks." After refusing to speak to the cops the night they took me, I was in their custody for a few hours and then whisked away the next morning by the FBI to another, much bigger jail for a week. From there, I spent the rest of the time in a state prison until these last seven days, when I was back in the smaller jail to await my court date. Wasn't I supposed to have had an arraignment a long time ago?

I'd seen my lawyer and FBI or other police agency members many times, so many that I forgot their names. My parents visited once, but after they spoke badly about Bob, I refused to see them.

"How do you feel when you're stressed?" Shelly asked.

"Like my life is out of control." I held up my arm as evidence.

"How do you feel about your attempted suicide?"

"I didn't attempt to kill myself. I kept on scratching until it didn't hurt anymore, and then I was tired and exhausted. Before the stress and the lies, I never scratched myself."

"I'm glad you can admit to the suicide attempt, Jolene. That's progress. Let's use the time we have left to discuss some ways for you to deal with stress. Since you have limited access to the outside world, we can go over a few things you can do. Taking care of yourself is essential. You need to sleep and eat all of your meals. Are you getting to go outside?" Shelly asked.

I shook my head. The only time I'd seen the sun was the few times I'd come here between transportations, so for five minutes.

"Since you can't go in the yard, I can teach you some exercise routines you can do in your cell." Shelly stood and asked me to do the same. Once I did, she continued. "Walk in place to warm up. Once you feel your heart pumping, you can do some jumping jacks, squats, sit-ups, and burpees. Do you have access to any weights?"

"No," I said with a laugh. I had a bed with a thin ass mattress, a sheet, and a rock-hard pillow. The rest of my sleeping arrangement contained another sleeping spot and a toilet. I had to go easy on the TP because of a shortage. At least I didn't have to share the tiny cell with anyone.

"Do you have a bar?"

"I'm not staying at a fancy hotel."

"I'll look up some exercises for you to do for your next visit. Getting into a routine will help you deal with stress." The timer Shelly set buzzed. "Our session is over. I think we made some actual progress here."

"Can you show me what a burpee is before I go?" I asked, even though I knew full well how to do one. Monte Jackson and Hank Pratt used to do them as a competition. Hank had won every single time.

Now they would never do it again because they were dead, unless they were doing it in hell. I could see them having adjoining cells.

Shelly paled a little, but said, "Of course. You start on the ground and place your hands shoulder-width apart." She kicked off her stilettos and slid them underneath her chair.

Now those shoes would make a killer weapon. A couple of stabs and she'd be bleeding on the carpet. Her death would be a little faster and more painful after our talk. Or should I let her die slowly?

Decisions. Decisions.

Shelly continued with her instructions, being oblivious to my plan, and then said, "That's how you do a burpee. Do you have questions?" She had winded herself after the one.

"No, I'm good. Thank you." I swore I heard her sigh with relief.

"Before you go, Jolene. Someone has reached out to me to talk to you. I think it would do you some good to speak to them."

"Someone? Not my mom or dad, right?" I wouldn't talk to either of them, not until they apologized. They never would.

"Conrad Jackson. Should I arrange a meeting with the three of us for tomorrow?" Shelly asked.

"Conrad wants to see me?" I asked, surprised. I thought he'd hate me for his brother, Monte, dying. Yeah, they didn't get along like most siblings. I was an only child, so I didn't know, but I saw it enough with my dead friends and classmates.

"Yes."

"Okay, then." What did Conrad want to say to me or yell at me? I deserved whatever he wanted to do. Hopefully, after he did, he'd get some peace. I couldn't change his brother's death. Monte had his junk cut off and his innards pulled out. He shouldn't have slept with Kaylee while he dated Corrie.

Shelly glanced at the clock on the wall and said, "Looks like your lawyer is running late, but your guards can take you to jail without him."

"I can see myself out then," I said.

"No, the rule for you to come here is that your lawyer or an adult must accompany you in and out of this room. I guess me doing it will be fine."

I didn't point out that I was an adult, and if I walked the few feet to the door, it wouldn't kill me. Not like I could disappear without her noticing.

Someone knocked on the door. Before Shelly could answer it, my lawyer, Roger Dangers, entered the room, saying, "Sorry, traffic. Did everything go well?"

"Yes, Jolene and I made actual progress. I still want to see her tomorrow for a longer appointment, Mr. Dangers," Shelly said.

"Call me Roger, Shelly," my lawyer said. He turned to me. "Jolene, please sit and wait for your therapist and I to finish speaking."

Why did old people do this? They clearly wanted to talk about me. I grumbled and sat on the couch. At least I'd get a few more minutes to look out the window despite the bars.

I asked Shelly once did she normally saw such dangerous people. She answered me after taking a moment to think, 'Not normally,' and didn't say another word about it, so I didn't ask again. She'd gotten special arrangements for me to come here. I guessed the extra protection was part of the deal.

Snow had fallen the previous night. It lined the roof of the building next door. The sun shone off the white stuff, making everything much brighter. How I missed standing in the rays or shoveling the nasty white stuff away from the cabin door. Bob would be outside cutting down a tree.

"Have you…" my lawyer said before his voice quieted down. He glanced over at me.

"Doctor patient confidentiality," Shelly said.

I heard that loud and clear.

"Give me something to work with, I'm trying to…" Dangers whispered next, and I missed the rest of his words.

To what? Save my life? He has to be kidding me. What Bob and I did was out of necessity. People wouldn't just let us live our lives. We would've been fine if everyone left us alone.

"I need more…" Shelly said.

More what?

"Will ask you…" my lawyer said.

The rest of their words I couldn't make out because they whispered even lower.

I sighed and stood, having had enough before saying, "I need to go. I got plans."

"Yeah, we'll talk later," my lawyer said to my psychologist.

"Tomorrow, I got other clients to see," Shelly said. "You have a good day, Jolene."

My lawyer escorted me to the guard who shackled me before we headed outside.

At least tomorrow I'd get to see Conrad. What was I going to wear? Ah, my normal tan shirt and pants the jail provided.

Maybe I can steal or make some makeup before tomorrow.

Chapter 2

I couldn't get makeup, do my hair, or do anything to make myself look even remotely presentable. Being locked in solitary confinement definitely had its downsides. The upside was that I didn't have to deal with other prisoners.

Bile rose in my mouth, and I choked it back down. I'd been a nervous wreck the entire drive to see Conrad. I didn't know what he would do when he saw me.

The van halted, and a guard climbed out. He shuffled to the side door and tugged it open. It screeched in protest. They needed to oil it to stop the noise. He bent and undid the lock that bolted my chains to the floor.

I imagined taking the cuffs attached to my wrists and wrapping the links around his neck. How long could I strangle him until the other guard got out? Would I kill him in time? Who was I kidding? I only wanted to kill him so I didn't have to face Conrad. What would he say to me? Would he blame me?

The guard stood before I could kill him and told me, "Get out." He tugged on the chain.

I slid out of my seat and exited the van. The sun blinded me for a moment until my eyes adjusted. The fresh snow yesterday made everything so much brighter. I wished I could stand here and enjoy the warmth, but I didn't get to stop for long.

My guards marched me into the two-story building. My shrink's room was on the second floor. I marveled at how no one was around. The giant Christmas tree in the corner looked lonely. Everyone in the building must've cleared out when they heard I was coming. Who would leave a receptionist's desk empty in the middle of the day?

The driver pushed the button for the elevator, and the doors slid open. We entered, and the other guard pressed the button for the second floor. With no one around, going up and down was so much easier. I didn't understand why Shelly didn't come see me at the prison. I wouldn't have to waste time being driven into the city and then back.

The guards and I walked the twenty-five steps to her office. She had hung a Christmas wreath on the door sometime yesterday or this morning. It hadn't been there at my previous visit.

One of my guards knocked, and she opened the door for us.

"Please take off Ms. Argall's shackles," Shelly said, like always. Today she wore an elf hat that clashed with her hair. If she would've gone with more green than red instead of red with green trim, she would've matched better.

"About that..." the guard said. His voice trailed off. He glanced at his partner.

"Let's get inside and talk." Shelly moved out of the way.

My heart plummeted to the floor, and I couldn't move.

Standing inside the room with his back toward us was someone I would recognize anywhere. The broad shoulders had to be Monte Jackson, but he was dead. Monte turned, and for a split second, I saw him. Then his face shifted to that of his brother.

Conrad had a lighter shade of hair and the same dark brown eyes. In three months, he'd grown two inches or more. He also lost his usual dark skater or emo boy clothes. He replaced them with baggy khakis over a brown shirt with a collar and a tan jacket. No wonder I'd gotten him confused with his dead brother.

"Jolene," Conrad said. His voice sounded older. He had been through a lot, and death made people grow up faster.

My mouth went dry, and I couldn't speak. What should I say to him? What could I say to him? Sorry, didn't sound good enough. I hadn't killed Monte.

"Jolene?" Conrad asked. His tone sounded unsure and more like himself.

Once I found my voice, I asked, "Conrad, how are you?"

"I've been…I've been good." He shook his head. "How have you been?"

"I'm good, I guess."

"You guess?" Conrad asked.

"Let's come into the room more and take off Jolene's handcuffs," Shelly said.

"We're not removing the cuffs today, following orders," the guard who drove said.

"I don't see why not," Shelly said.

"You have a guest," the same guard said.

"Jolene won't hurt me," Conrad said.

They glanced at him and then back at me.

"We'll leave the handcuffs on for now. Let's get inside and sit down." Shelly touched my elbow, but her hand dropped to her side.

I walked into the room some more.

Conrad shifted closer to me, raising his arms.

My heart jumped into my throat, and the desire to flee swept through me. I couldn't go out the window with the bars on it. I couldn't turn around and run back down the hall, not with two guards behind me and my wrists shackled. Why couldn't they remove the handcuffs? Didn't they know hooking my arms around their neck would make a much better weapon?

Conrad glanced at my guards and my shrink, asking, "Can we hug?"

"Not allowed," the driver guard said.

"Why not?" Conrad lowered his hands.

"We'll allow hugging this one time," Shelly said.

Conrad moved to me and wrapped his arms around me.

I stiffened under his embrace. Bob wouldn't like me hugging another man, but this was Conrad. He was still a boy. He didn't count, right? I patted his back with one hand, attempting to appear as if I wanted to hug him back.

Conrad stepped away and his dark eyes darkened. Something crossed his face that I couldn't read.

"Please take a seat." Shelly glanced at everyone, even my guards.

I sat on the couch.

Conrad took the spot next to me, taking my hand in his and giving it a squeeze. He leaned back. He was so like his brother.

My guards moved to the ends of the couch, still standing. Their hands were at their sides.

Shelly positioned herself on the chair, saying, "Isn't this nice?" She shifted in her spot and waited for a response. When no one answered, she continued. "Conrad has been asking to see you every day, Jolene. He would like to visit you in jail, but he can't until you're out of solitary confinement."

"Why is she in there?" Conrad asked.

"Jolene had an incident." Shelly stepped aside the answer with ease, like a pro.

"What type of incident?"

"I'm not at liberty to say because of HIPPA," Shelly answered.

"Whatever," Conrad shook his head.

"Let's move on and talk about why you want to see Jolene," Shelly said.

"I want to tell you," Conrad said to me, but stopped.

I shifted to stare at him. *Tell me what?* He was glad I wasn't dead?

"Thank you," Conrad said.

"For what?" I asked, confused.

"For saving me and going with that monster. I...I can't imagine what you've been through."

"Bob's not a monster."

"He killed my brother. Your friends. His mother. His stepfather. What else would you call him but a killer?" Conrad asked. His nostrils flared, and sweat beaded his brow.

I moved my hand, forcing him to drop his hold on me. Annoyance built inside me. I did not like it when anyone talked badly about my Bob. No one had the right to, not even Bob.

"Let's not call anyone names," Shelly told Conrad.

"Fine. You saved me by going with...with Bob. I can't imagine what you've been through." Conrad traced my skin where the handcuff had dug in and ripped off the bandage. "What the hell did you do, Jolene?"

"Nothing." I tucked my arm away after checking to make sure the scratches didn't bleed again. Getting a bandage in prison was a pain. The guards wouldn't just hand me one. They had to take me to the clinic, and the nurse gave me one after cleaning the wound. Way too much work for something that should take a few minutes.

"Your arm has marks on it. What did you do?" Conrad asked.

"I scratched myself, no big deal," I said.

"It's a big deal. Did you try to kill yourself?" Conrad's eyes widened and his mouth popped open.

"No!" My face heated, despite my words.

"What is this, then?" Conrad grabbed my arm and forced it down, revealing the marks.

"I scratched myself. I was—" I said, but the right words escaped me.

"You were what, Jolene?" Conrad asked. When I didn't respond, he repeated his question.

"Give her some time to answer," Shelly said.

"I was upset. Everyone was talking badly about Bob. He was there for me when no one else was. He isn't bad, and then the stress of the coming trial. I scratched myself and then just kept scratching myself." I sighed. No one would understand.

"No one is all bad, Jolene. Everyone is trying to help you. We want to understand what you went through," Shelly said.

"Why? Mine and Bob's relationship is no one's business. We're both consenting adults."

Shelly glanced at Conrad, and a look passed between them.

"Your psychologist is trying to say we're here for you. Not for Bob. For you. Your mom told me you're pregnant," Conrad said.

"She did?" I asked, skeptical.

"Yes, she did. She also wants to know how you're doing? How's your baby?"

I snorted. No way would my mom want anyone to know I was pregnant. She planned on giving away the baby as soon as it was born. As soon as her grandbaby was born. My child. She must've asked Conrad for help. He was in cahoots with her and my damn shrink.

"How are you? How's the baby?" Conrad asked again. He sounded like he cared, but he didn't fool me.

"We're fine. I'm only two months along. I've had no complications and no morning sickness," I answered.

"Can they give you anything while in jail?" Conrad asked.

"I'm not sure," I answered.

"My mom said she took *6 Down* and crackers to help her upset stomach," Conrad said. I wasn't a fan of the pop Conrad mentioned.

"Why did you talk to your mom?" I asked.

"I was curious about babies. My friend is having one." Conrad smiled at me.

"Unless the state drops the charges, or I'm found not guilty, I don't get to keep the baby."

"What? Is there anything we can do?" Conrad's gaze shifted to my shrink. "Ms. Nicholson, how can we help?"

"I'm not sure. Jolene's parents are declining to keep the baby, and she's refusing to talk to them. Maybe if she did, she could convince them to watch her baby until she is out of jail," Shelly answered. Did she just violate a hundred patient and psychiatrist laws?

"Why won't you see your parents?" Conrad asked me.

"They talked badly about Bob." If Conrad was on a first-name basis with my mom and dad, it wouldn't surprise me. He wasn't like his dead brother. Parents would want to meet him and not hide their daughters.

"Jolene doesn't like anyone to speak badly about Bob. We try not to here," Shelly said. When did that start?

"Why not? Bob killed," Conrad said. Maybe he was more like his brother than I thought.

"Bob did what he thought was right." I shifted away from Conrad, and my handcuffs bit into me until I put them in my lap.

"How was killing my brother right?" Conrad pounded his fist on his thigh. Monte would've done that, knocked over a table, or broken something.

"He slept with Kaylee."

"My brother slept with a lot of women, even you," Conrad said.

"No way. We've only kissed once before Corrie started dating him. Monte's not my type." Our relationship ended because she liked him. I would not tell Conrad that.

"What did Corrie do to get gutted?" Conrad asked.

"Hello? She called you a name. She was a bitch." I tried to run a hand through my hair, but my handcuffs made it difficult. My wounds hurt again. "Corrie got jealous of Kaylee sleeping with her slutty boyfriend."

"Don't call my brother slutty," Conrad said. His voice rose.

"A whore then? Sucks when women are called that. Why can't men be called that, too?" I asked.

"What's wrong with you, Jolene? You weren't like this before you left with the psychotic serial killer," Conrad said.

"What was I like? Timid? Quiet? Not willing to stand up for my-self?" I asked. Conrad disgusted me.

"Kind. You were kind. You were the only friend of Monte's who knew I existed. I saw you save that girl at a party once," Conrad said.

"What girl?" I asked.

"The drunk one. I don't know her name. Monte and his boys kept feeding her shots. She was about to pass out. You went over there and yelled at everyone, including those within ten feet of her. You were my hero every day, until today," Conrad said.

I shrugged. What could I say? Meeting Bob had changed my life for the better. Okay, I was in jail, but I'd get out, eventually. No one messed with me while I was in prison and not in solitary confinement. If they tried, I would give them a look, and they would run away. Being the queen bee in prison was kind of cool.

"I just can't." Conrad stood and said to my shrink, "I don't know if I can help Jolene. She's too far gone. She doesn't know what she's saying. Bob cast a spell on her. I doubt she sees killing is wrong."

"Is it?" I asked.

"I want to meet with Jolene again in a month or more. When she's on trial for murder, she'll come to her senses." Conrad turned to me. "Merry Christmas, Jolene, if I don't see you. Please accept my visit when I schedule it." He left without looking back.

Where had the Conrad that I used to know gone? He was so much like his brother: arrogant and a know-it-all. If I had a chance, I would kill him. The world had one Monte for a short time. It didn't need another.

Chapter 3

"Jolene, how do you feel about Conrad leaving?" Shelly asked once she got my handcuffs off and forced the guards out of the room. My shrink and I were alone now.

I want to kill him. Instead, I answered, "I don't know how to feel. Conrad doesn't know me. People change. I changed."

"Let's go back. Conrad said he admired you."

"I heard."

"How does that make you feel?"

I shrugged. "He doesn't anymore, so does it matter?"

"How does that make you feel?" Shelly asked.

"Well, I don't care either way. Conrad isn't a friend. I hung out with his brother, not him. I didn't know he admired me."

"I think Conrad more than admired you."

"What?" I asked. He did not like me.

Gross!

"I'm not sure if I should tell you this. Conrad is not my patient. He has a crush on you," Shelly said.

"You're kidding me, right?" I half laughed.

"Have you ever liked Conrad?"

"No, I have Bob."

"Have you spoken to Bob since your arrest?"

I shook my head. I'd asked my lawyer, and he said he would try. He hadn't told me anything since then. I was too afraid to ask him, fearing he'd say any conversations between Bob and me were impossible.

Shelly scribbled in her notebook before shutting it.

I could make out the words she'd written.

Ask Roger about Bob.

When did she and my lawyer use their first names? I heard him tell her every time they met to call him Roger, but she never did. I didn't know if another Roger was with my case. He could be with the FBI, the police, or the DA.

"I must apologize to you, Jolene. I'm sorry," Shelly said.

"For what?" I asked, confused.

"I've been trying to get you to understand that your relationship with Bob isn't good. What he did and forced you to do." She shook her head.

I opened my mouth to yell at her, but she held her hand up.

"Let me finish." Shelly swiped at a strand of hair and tucked it behind her ear. "I should listen to you. I should understand your experience. I should tell you, or help you rather, understand it's okay to be sympathetic toward Bob. You had to be in order to survive. I'm sorry, Jolene."

"Wait, hold on. Why would I be sympathetic toward Bob? We're together. We're dating," I said.

"I understand you were."

"We are." I grunted. This new turn in our sessions sucked. I could shut down on purpose when she said something stupid. Now, what would I do?

"Tell me more about yours and Bob's relationship," Shelly said.

"You know a lot." I kept an edge in my voice.

"Tell me how you met?"

"The first time?" When she didn't stop me, I answered her stupid question. "I met Kaylee in middle school after she moved to town. We walked home together since we lived in the same direction. Bob walked with us. He said little and kept his distance. We re-met the Friday before Labor Day this year." I smiled as the memory flashed through my brain. I'd made a horrible attempt at flirting with him when we reconnected.

"Tell me more," Shelly said.

I told her our jokes and everything that led up to finding Abby's dead body.

"How do you feel about Bob killing your friend?" Shelly asked.

An idea popped into my head. "Bob didn't," I answered.

"I thought you said he killed your friends." Shelly flipped open her notebook and scanned through her notes.

"I never said that. If you wrote that down, it's wrong. I said my friend was murdered, and she deserved to die. Actually, you asked me, 'Did she deserve to be stabbed?' I said, 'yes'."

"Did Bob kill her?"

"No. The police are wrong. That's why I'm so confused and hurt myself." I held up my hand, and tears flashed into my eyes. I could put on a show for anyone, including the jury and her.

"Hold on. You've never told me you thought Bob was innocent. Who killed all your friends?" Shelly asked.

"Not all are dead. Bob's alive." Another idea popped into my head. If the police and the FBI wanted a suspect, I would give them one.

"Yes." Shelly pressed her lips together in a tight line, and a crease formed in her brow. She had to be thinking, going over everything I had told her. Not once had I said to her Bob had killed my friends.

I couldn't let her figure out my plan. It was something that I needed to talk to my lawyer about. "Do you have those exercises you wanted to show me? Our session is almost done."

"Okay." Shelly closed her notebook, stood, and snapped the top back on her pen before setting her items on the chair. She kicked off her killer high heels. "I consulted a doctor on some exercises I'm going to show you."

"Will these exercises be safe for the baby?" I asked, horrified.

"Yes. The first thing I want you to do is warm up and stretch." Shelly started jogging in place. We ran through a version I learned in high school. "Are you feeling limber?"

"I guess."

"Okay." Shelly clapped her hands together and sounded like a cheerleader. "You want to stay away from lying on your back now that you are in your second trimester. Sit-ups are out. Any yoga forms that require lying down as well."

"Why yoga?" I asked.

"Yoga is a good way to reduce stress. You'll be under a lot of pressure once your trial begins tomorrow," Shelly said.

"I thought I had arraignment only." A massive bubble of nerves rose in my throat, high enough that I felt like I was choking on it. I was fine until a moment ago. This was another reason Shelly had to die.

"Everything will move faster after your hearing. I want you to be prepared. Let's work on exercises and then ways you can relax. Move your left foot to the side like me."

I did what she told me.

"Great. Move it back. Great. Do ten or twenty more. Do it however many times you feel like. The point is to get your body moving. This is safe for the baby. Once you're done with your left leg, you can switch to your right. Great, Jolene," Shelly said.

Maybe she should die for saying the word great too many times, like Abby.

"Now shake out your hands. That's good." Shelly changed her stance so her legs were shoulder-width apart. "Now we're going to make a fist and hit the air above your head. Follow me. Perfect. Keep doing that, and if you feel tired, stop. Give your body a break. Your body will tell you what you can handle more than anything." She stopped in order to give herself a breather. Her shoulders heaved.

The good thing about being on the run for so long was that I was always moving. I didn't work up a sweat as fast as my shrink. I always did something like sleeping with Bob, walking into town for supplies, chopping wood, sleeping with Bob, cooking, etc.

Shelly showed me six other things I could do. A few wouldn't be good for the baby. I wanted to keep my feet on the ground and not have the unborn child I carried jiggle around so much.

"Now that we've gotten a workout, let's cool down." Shelly had taken her jacket off. Sweat dotted her brow, and she breathed heavily between the words she had said. She waved her hand in the air and exclaimed. "We'll start off with the sukhasana pose. I think that is how you pronounce it. SOOkas-ana."

I shrugged. Like I knew anything about yoga. Corrie had tried to get me to take a class with her more than once. I couldn't afford to waste my money on such useless things.

"Anyway, sukhasana is an easy pose. You've probably seen this in yoga. Sit cross-legged. You want to sit up straight; imagine a pole pulling the top of your head and straightening your back out. Close your eyes. I've seen two ways to hold your hands. The first is like you're praying. For the second, put your hands on your knees and make the okay sign with your thumb and pointer fingers." Shelly opened one eye to make sure I was following her.

I did what I was told, using the OK sign. I didn't feel like praying so much right now. What kind of God would take my Bob away from me?

"Breathe in and breathe out. Deep breathing is also a good way to calm yourself down. Whenever you have negative thoughts, breathe in and then breathe the negative thoughts out," Shelly said.

I refrained from rolling my eyes, but I followed her instructions. The panic I had felt when we first started exercising had subsided until now. So, I asked her, "What else can I do?"

"For what?" Shelly breathed in and then out; her nose whistled when she did. She was one of those people.

"To help with stress." Why was she always such an idiot?

"We went over a few things, like exercising and deep breathing. Talking to me about what happened will also help you. Really talking, Jolene. I'm here for you and not to judge you. I'm sorry if it sounded like I was." Shelly rubbed her chin. "You need to relax your muscles by stretching, rubbing the muscles that hurt, and sleeping for at least seven hours at night. Another good way is to take a hot shower or a warm bath. A little hard to do in prison."

I nodded and kept my snide remark to myself.

"Other ways I'd tell you is to eat well. The jail provides your meals, though. I'd tell you to leave earlier for where you're going and take your time getting there, but you can't do that," Shelly said.

"Is jail a massive place where stress lives and breeds?" I interrupted her next unhelpful tip.

"Jail can be. We'll find a way, though. Can you get books?"

"I think so."

"Do you like reading?"

"Some books," I answered.

"You can read, watch TV, or listen to music to relax. I'm not sure if the prison system will let you do anything else," Shelly said.

"You make it sound like I'm never getting out of jail."

"Are you? The state has charged you with how many counts of murder?"

I shrugged. I didn't know, but my lawyer should.

"Jolene, this is important. You need to speak to Mr. Dangers and know all your charges. The state can put you to death," Shelly said. Her tone filled with disappointment.

"Does this state have a death penalty?" Suddenly, I felt too hot and the next second too cold.

"I don't know." Shelly sighed.

"Wasn't my arraignment pushed back because the FBI had to figure out all the charges?"

"I don't know."

"What are more things I can do to relax?" I would need every single tip that Shelly could provide me with. What was the point of getting upset over something she was clueless about?

"I...I need a second."

I frowned at her. She was the person who was supposed to help me. My lawyer hired her to decide if I was sane or insane.

"Okay, I'll tell you two things at the same time. You need to go easy on yourself while eliminating your triggers. If the court stresses you out, avoid thinking about it. Mr. Dangers is your attorney. I've worked with him many times before. He's a damn good one. Follow his advice and let him help you. Don't put yourself down. You went through a traumatic incident and fell in love with a guy that the state has charged with some rather serious crimes. I don't know which ones," Shelly said.

"Your advice is to not freak out or think about what causes me to freak out?" I asked in disbelief.

"Yes, doing so will only cause you more stress. Do the breathing techniques when you feel overwhelmed. I'm not telling you to avoid anything, just take court one day at a time. You do not know what the judge or jury will decide. Talk to your lawyer and ask lots of questions."

"What are you going to say at my arraignment?"

"I'm not sure if I'll be there. I'll talk to your lawyer. Usually, I'll come later if Mr. Dangers wants me to. My testimony can either help your case or harm it."

"Are you a witness?" I asked.

"You'll have to ask your lawyer. Oh yeah, I remembered another thing you can do. If you're getting stressed about your case, think about something else," Shelly answered.

"Like what?"

"Whatever puts your mind at ease. Let's do that. We'll do some visual exercises with the rest of our time here." We did exactly that. Pretending to be on an island would help me stop thinking about being locked in a jail cell or in a courtroom. She was a fucking idiot.

Roger Dangers knocked on the door and entered without waiting for Shelly to tell him he could, saying, "Sorry, I'm late."

"We're used to it." Shelly winked at me.

I actually smiled at her.

"Jolene let Shelly and me talk. Come with me and wait in the hall." Dangers led me out the door. "I'll be right out," he told the guards.

They placed me in handcuffs.

I should take my shrink's advice and speak to my lawyer about my case. Her advice wasn't completely worthless.

Dangers didn't make me wait too long. Was he talking about me or asking Shelly out?

"We'll talk in the prison about your case. I have all the charges, and I want to talk to you about them," Dangers said. I did like him because he had a no-nonsense attitude like my dad. But he was not my father.

The drive to the jail was always too long. My legs and neck were always sore by the time we arrived, and I couldn't get any stretching in since my attorney wanted to talk to me. Were my parents still footing his bill? I'd have to ask him.

After we halted outside, I used the couple of free seconds alone in the van to stretch before I climbed out. The air was bitter cold, and my breath left clouds in the air until they disappeared seconds later.

"Let's get inside. I booked us a room for an hour." Dangers shivered.

My guards led me by a chain to the detention center and then into a little room. The FBI had interviewed me in a similar room. Dangers had been there and objected to almost all of their questions. My lawyer would be the top in the world if I judged him on how many protests he had done.

"Please remove Ms. Argall's shackles. We have paperwork for her to look over," Dangers told the guards.

"We were told not to," one of my guards said. They didn't wear the typical tan or dark blue shirt over gray slacks. Instead, they wore a black t-shirt underneath a bulletproof camouflage vest. They had pinned their badges to their protective gear. Did who they were matter? Not really. They got me to point B from point A, even when I didn't want to go, like visiting my psychologist or court.

"Ms. Argall is a third of my size and is pregnant. Take off the damn shackles so we can work."

"She murdered."

"Allegedly," Dangers said.

The guards did what Dangers told them and left the room.

"Please sit, Ms. Argall." Dangers was always formal with me. Once I sat in front of him, he opened his briefcase and brought out several sheets of paper. "The state has charged you with thirteen counts of first-degree murder, one charge of attempted murder, multiple weapon possession charges, domestic terrorism, and a slew of other crimes."

"Terrorism?" I asked.

"Yes, mass murder is domestic terrorism. I still have the plea deal on the table. It will remain there until the start of your arraignment. I believe this plea deal is pretty good, and I'd like to discuss it."

"What about Bob?"

"What about Mr. Ghul?"

"What is he charged with? Did he get the same plea deal?" I asked.

"His charges are the same as yours and a hell of a lot more. The most I've ever seen. He has his own lawyer. I'm not sure if he got a plea deal or not. I haven't spoken to his attorney yet. He might have. You should take the deal," Dangers said.

"What does mine say?"

"You'll have to testify against Mr. Ghul and receive twenty-six years in prison. Two years for every death."

"I have to testify against Bob?" Anger rose inside of me, and I could never do that.

"He might be against you. How much can you trust Mr. Ghul?" Dangers asked.

"With my life," I said without hesitating.

"This is real, and the young puppy love you have for each other might not survive a trial or a court sentence. Are you sure you won't accept the deal? I'm not even sure how I can help your defense. Your psychologist may or may not help us if we want to plea insanity."

"I'm not insane." Bob and I were ride or die. At least, I thought we were. I'd find out tomorrow for sure. Bile rose in my mouth, and I pushed it back down.

Trust Bob.

Chapter 4

The court wasn't at all what I expected. The judge was absent, and I kept my head down, only glancing up as necessary. I waited off to the side, where I assumed the jury would go once we started the trial. A row of seats was behind me, but my guards stood in front of them.

Today, they wore their vests and either a dark or light green shirt with the same-colored cargo pants. Written across their chests was the word 'sheriff'. Two of them brought me to the courthouse, but we met over a dozen of them. They scattered throughout the room, hovering near me and the important points of entry. They folded their hands across their chests, or they touched their belts or their guns.

Press and loved ones filled the rest of the room. I assumed the latter because they were crying. Where was Bob?

When the door opened, my breath caught in my throat.

Bob entered, being escorted by two guards, and behind him his attorney, his lady attorney. Following them were another dozen police officers. They led my man up to the front and forced him to sit in the chair furthest from me. He didn't even glance at me. What was going on?

He'd lost weight, and a bruise darkened his right eye. Had he been in a fight? With whom? Why wasn't he looking at me?

My mouth went dry. Did he take the plea deal? Was that why he wasn't acknowledging me?

"All rise. Court is now in session. Honorable Judge Katherine Hayes presiding. Please be seated," the bailiff said.

I snapped my attention to the judge as she walked inside. I climbed to my feet like everyone else, daring a glance at my Bob.

His guard chained his wrists together, and the links connected his wrists to his ankles, just like mine. He didn't even look at me. He wore a dark red, almost orange, jail jumpsuit.

The courtroom sat again, and the Judge said, "Okay, we're here for the arraignment of Jolene Argall and Robert Ghul. Will the attorneys please present themselves for the record?"

My lawyer and Bob's hot one, who barely looked old enough to practice law, dashed to the table in front. They almost knocked each other over.

"Roger Dangers for the defense of Jolene Argall, Your Honor," my attorney, the first to speak, said.

I wiped my mouth to hide my grin.

"Eleanor York for the defense of Roger 'Bob' Ghul, Your Honor," York said.

"Alex Turnbuckle for the state of..." the first state attorney said. His voice fading as I mentally tuned him out.

My head swarmed with all the fresh faces. Eleanor's stood out the most. I bet a lot of men would find her pretty, my Bob included. I shook the thought away, missing the name of the second state attorney. Two against one didn't seem fair.

"Alright, let's start with Ms. Argall." Judge Hayes shuffled through her paperwork before continuing on. "You've been charged by indictment. The count one indictment is for murder in the first degree of Bridgette Hornsby, a first-degree felony punishable by death. The state has sought the death penalty in this case. Count two indictment is for murder in the first degree of Glen Jager, a first-degree—"

"Your Honor, we waive formal reading of the indictments as this time. Ms. Argall is aware of the charges," Dangers, my lawyer, said.

"Do you have a standing?" the Judge asked.

"Yes, to enter a plea, we do, Your Honor," Dangers said.

"Are there any objections?"

"No, Your Honor," the state attorney Turnbuckle said.

"What is the standing if you're waving a formal reading?" the Judge asked.

"Not guilty on all charges," Dangers said.

Murmurs filled the courtroom. Were people surprised I didn't plead insanity? The radio DJs were speculating until a guard shut it off. Was Bob bewildered? Did he have any reaction at all to my plea? Everyone else had distracted me.

Judge Hayes acted as if nothing had happened and said, "Mr. Ghul has been charged by indictment, and count one indictment is for murder in the first degree of Corey Irving, a first-degree felony punishable by death." Corey had been Bob's and Kaylee's stepfather. Judge Hayes rattled off the next charge.

"Your Honor, we waive formal reading of the indictments. Mr. Ghul has had his charges read and is ready to enter a plea," York said before the Judge could say the third charge.

My stomach would've dropped to my knees if it were possible. Vomit did rise in my throat, though, and I choked it back down.

Corrie appeared next to me, crossing her legs.

I jumped. Her sudden appearance was always surprising, not just by the way she looked. She appeared like the last time I saw her dead, but I could see through her.

"Let's be honest. How much do you trust Bobby? I mean Bob?" she asked.

Completely, I thought.

"Really? I never knew you could be one of those girls."

What girls?

"The ones that lose themselves in any man that looks at them for a second. I thought I taught you better than that." Corrie tsked.

"Are there any objections?" the Judge asked.

"No, Your Honor," the other state attorney, besides Turnbuckle, said. I should learn her name and made a mental note to ask my lawyer about it later, but right now I had far more important things to worry about.

"What is the standing of Mr. Ghul if you are waving a formal reading?" Judge Hayes asked.

How does Bob stand?

"We enter a plea of not guilty on all charges, Your Honor," York said.

I let go of a breath of air that I didn't realize I'd been holding onto. Someone knocked near me.

I turned my head to Bob.

He held three fingers on the railing and then placed his pinky up there, too. Those fingers stood for 'I love you', our own little gesture. The fourth meant 'forever'.

I cleared my throat and blinked back tears. I'd been right to put my faith in him.

"Don't gloat, yet," the bitch Corrie said. "Court isn't over."

Before I could think or ask her what she meant by that, she was gone.

Good riddance. I didn't need her in my life, creating issues. I had enough to deal with.

Bob removed his hands from the rail.

After shifting back, I returned the gesture in my lap for only him and those behind me to see. I loved him forever.

"The only other matter we need to address today is to set the date of the calendar trial, which is December 12th, next Monday. Is that alright?" the Judge asked.

All lawyers agreed.

"One matter, Your Honor. We want to advise the court that if Ms. Argall wants to enter a plea of guilty on all thirteen accounts for life sentences, we'll waive the death penalty," the other state attorney, not Turnbuckle, said. I didn't want to learn her name now.

"Is there anything else?" Judge Hayes shuffled through her paperwork.

"We have to figure out whether or not Mr. Ghul is indigent." York took out some paperwork and handed it to the state attorneys and the judge. "These are documents from the estate of Alison Irving."

I racked my brain as I tried to figure out what indigent meant. I did well in high school, but the word escaped me. What was the bitch trying to say my guy was?

"Alison Irving, Mr. Ghul's mother, and her husband, Corey Irving, have an estate and a substantial life insurance, with Mr. Ghul being the only beneficiary," York said.

Would Bob receiving the policy from both his mom and step-asshole after he killed them be funny? York and the Judge debated this information for the next half an hour. Court was boring. No wonder the justice system was so slow.

I received two-million-dollar bail. My parents could never afford to pay it, or even one percent of that to a bondsman. I doubted anyone would ever go that low. Dangers said he could swing ten percent, but my parents weren't at my court hearing. They weren't happy with me.

Bob didn't get the option. The court decided he was too dangerous. If only they knew the truth.

"I've decided on something important," my attorney said when he walked into the room the next day. He glanced at the guards. "Unlock her cuffs. I need her to sign some documents."

My guard grumbled, but did what he was told.

"Please wait in the hall. What my *client* and I have to discuss needs to be done in private. No video." Dangers stared at the camera in the corner until the light flashed and then went out. Once the guards strolled out of the room, my lawyer set to work. Whatever money he made didn't get wasted. "I've been going over your defense. Do you remember what the state said about you taking a plea deal?"

"Yeah, and I'm not taking it." My arraignment was only yesterday. I wouldn't forget so fast.

"Why not?" Dangers sighed and sat next to me. He set his briefcase with the initials R.A.D. on it.

"Because I can go free."

"You can also die, too. You have thirteen charges against you. Any of those can get you the death penalty."

"The state never offered Bob the deal," I said.

"They want him dead. He killed way more people than you. I doubt anyone believes you actually killed the thirteen. You're charged because you were there, and you're an accomplice. We don't have a defense," Dangers said.

"You don't. I do."

"Fill me in then." He sat back and steepled his fingers, smug as hell.

"What does the state need to prove?" I knew the answer. TV was good for something.

"Beyond a reasonable doubt that you killed all these people." Dangers tapped the stack of court paperwork. The top of the first page listed the state vs. me and a bunch of other legal crap.

"We can go about doing so by pinning the crime on another or self-defense or..." I let my voice trail off, hoping he'd fill in the dots for me.

Dangers rubbed his clean-shaven chin. "We could do the self-defense route, but the state has a lot of evidence. A ton. We can only go down this path if you trust me explicitly."

"I will. Will Bob and his attorney do the same?"

"I'm not sure what they're going to do. They might even try to pin the murders on us, on you."

"They won't," I said without hesitation.

"How do you know? Can you bet your life on Mr. Ghul and Eleanor York?" Dangers asked.

"Not on York, but on Bob I would. Why did she pull the weird money stuff yesterday?"

"Mrs. York made a smart move. She forced the court to keep her appointed. You will trust Mr. Ghul with your life. Let's start with the first pieces of evidence against you. This is the knife you carried and then dropped in front of the police. The state has over a dozen witnesses to testify, and your fingerprints are all over the handle." Dangers pulled out a photograph of the weapon in the snow. "The blood in the guard belonged to Marc Jager."

"Marc Jager was a puke. He came onto me even in front of Bob and his girlfriend, Bridgette. He even tried to get me to suck his dick in his truck. I almost cut it off. Instead, I—"

"I know you're guilty. I need to hear the whole truth," Dangers said after I stopped myself.

"I slit his throat," I said. Did my words hold any remorse? I sure didn't feel any.

"Who burned the truck?"

"Both Bob and I. We poured gasoline on it and then lit it on fire to draw those in the cabin out."

"We know what your defense can be against Marc Jager. If you're claiming anything, make sure your story doesn't change." Did Dangers just suggest for me to commit perjury? He did, but he also saved himself from getting into trouble if the police ever asked him.

I liked him more. I still wasn't one hundred percent sure about him, though, so I said, "I hope my parents are paying you well for your time."

"They're not." Dangers didn't glance at me, and he had his attention on some more paperwork instead.

"Are you working pro bono, then? I can't afford you."

"I am."

Why is he helping me? Whenever a man or guy did, they always wanted something from me. Only Bob didn't. I wanted to ask him why, but he had moved on.

"What can you tell me about Pat Jager?" Dangers asked.

"Who?" My mind drew a blank.

Dangers set an image in front of me.

"Oh, that guy. He tried to get away, so I killed him," I said.

Dangers studied me for a moment before saying, "We'll come back to him. How did you kill Betsy Jager?"

I shrugged. I didn't remember everyone I killed. Would anyone after dropping so many bodies? The Judge had stated Bridgette's name yesterday, and Marc was hard to forget for now.

"Let's move on. This is the rifle you carried and then dropped in front of the police." Dangers pulled out a photograph of a gun in the snow. "The bullets matched the victims in multiple shootings. Your prints are on the hilt."

"Not smart of me, huh?" I asked.

"I've had dumber clients."

"I shot Bridgette in the head. She was annoying."

"Bridgette Hornsby?"

"What does she look like before the head wound?" I asked.

Dangers pulled out a file and shuffled through the items inside, pulling out a photograph of her and her man. He set it in front of me.

"That's her." She had her brown hair styled big and wore bright lipstick. She looked happy, but her man, Marc, did not. Yeah, I didn't feel bad for killing her. The world needed one less woman who begged for a man's attention. They should be even, like me and Bob.

"Our defense will not be that she's annoying," Dangers said.

I laughed at his joke and stopped myself. This wasn't the time to be amused or anytime during my case.

Dangers and I worked for over an hour before an officer interrupted us, saying, "Mr. Dangers, your time is up."

My attorney glanced at his watch, saying, "Time for lunch already. We'll pick this up tomorrow, same time and place." He had kept his paperwork neatly in place, so the cleanup was fast for him.

"Why are you taking my case?" I asked before he left.

"What do you mean?"

"Why are you representing me if you..." I glanced over at the officer.

"Give us a minute, Officer Timmons."

Timmons nodded and left the room. He had shackled me already. If I were the president, I'd make sure the police didn't chain people like animals.

"Why are you representing me if you know I killed people?" I asked my lawyer.

"You murdered bad people. People I've wanted to," Dangers answered. He sounded honest.

"Why do you want to kill?" I doubted he could handle it.

"I don't give out too many details of my personal life, but for you I will, only this once. We need to trust each other. My sister was kidnapped and taken into the sex trade. I never saw her again. Seeing and hearing the details of what you did to those child molesters, I can't help but wonder what if someone had stopped her? Would she be home?"

"Is your sister dead?"

"Oh, God, I hope so," Dangers said emphatically. Then he left the room without saying another word.

Chapter 5

C ourt started on Monday. Every day, Dangers and I met, and we got a little closer to a more believable defense. I was itching to tell him my plan for my man. Dangers had reached out to Eleanor York, but she didn't return his call until Friday, since the state proceeded with a trial against Bob and me as scheduled. York tried to get our cases separated several times and failed.

"Like I told you on Sunday, we have to select twelve members of the jury and six alternates. We'll be working with Mrs. York. We're splitting the number of challenges to four each, and then for the final two, we'll decide together. I've gotten us a jury consultant," Dangers whispered to me. He nodded at the person behind him.

His associate sat between me and Bob. She opened her computer and then a program with eighteen empty boxes for writing in information about the jury; I assumed. I hoped once the trial began, she would be gone so I could sit next to my guy. The four of us, including Bob's lawyer, sat at a long table on the right of the court facing the Judge, who hadn't arrived yet.

"You also should not be smiling. Look glum," Dangers said before the jury arrived.

"All rise, the Honorable Judge Hayes presiding," the bailiff said.

"Please be seated," the Judge said before taking her seat. "Please bring in the first eighteen for the voir dire."

The jury shuffled in and settled into the chairs. Bob and I had taken up two of them last Monday. We could've been in this courtroom then. I wasn't sure. Wasn't every room supposed to be the same?

"I'll be asking you questions, so will the prosecutor and the defense lawyers, too. You have taken an oath to tell the truth. You'll not be giving out any personal information because of the high-profile case. If you do, you'll be excused," Judge Hayes said before taking a breath. She went into a long rant about how the jury was there to uphold the law and a lot more.

Blah. Blah. Blah. Court is so boring.

My attorney jotted something on the white, wide-ruled tablet in front of him and showed me what he wrote.

There's always one.

I didn't dare ask him what he meant because everything was moving too fast. The Judge had already started asking basic information from the jury pool. One man got excused because he said his name.

Dangers circled his first saying and then wrote another, showing me it.

Told you so.

I stopped myself from smiling. I get what he meant now.

"I'm Mrs. Jones. I work in realty and I live—" the potential juror said.

"Juror number 18 is excused," the Judge cut her off.

I expected Dangers to comment on the second person, but he didn't.

He shrugged instead.

Did she say her last name on purpose? I would like to get out of jury duty since the court paid very little, from what I overheard my parents say.

Dangers had explained to me that the goal for choosing the jury was to decide who would most likely vote not guilty for Bob and me. The lawyers battled it out, hoping not to use all of their ten challenges. A challenge was the right to remove the juror if they believed the juror wouldn't vote guilty or not guilty. The lawyers could claim the juror had a bias toward something instead of using a challenge, but the judge decided on bias or not bias. This sounded like a game to me. I didn't like anyone playing with my life or my man's.

"The prosecution, please stand and introduce yourself," Judge Hayes said. After they did, she did the same for the defense. "Does anyone know the defendants or any of the lawyers?"

None of the jurors raised their hands.

"Does anyone know anyone who works for the attorney general's office? Other attorneys from there could be introduced during this trial." The Judge read off a list.

No one again.

"The prosecution may proceed," Judge Hayes said.

Turnbuckle stood and said, "Good morning, I am Alex Turnbuckle, and I'm with the prosecution. My associate, Sharon Sullivan, and I will ask you several questions today. Has anyone had a family member or a friend commit suicide?"

Over a third of the jury raised their hands.

Why are they asking about suicide? I figured out Turnbuckle restated his name because he had stated a lot, and with so many statements, some of the jury might not know his name.

"You know why," Corrie said.

I didn't need to turn around to see her sitting behind me. She hadn't been there when I arrived at court.

Go away. I don't need people to think I'm crazy.

"You already are," Corrie said.

"This case involves suicide. Was anyone the cause of their friends or family member's suicide?" Turnbuckle asked.

Only unlucky juror thirteen kept his hand raised.

"I'd like to excuse juror number thirteen," Turnbuckle said. The state sought to remove anyone blamed for another's death, like my dead friends.

A new juror member replaced number thirteen, and the Judge asked them to state their occupation and where they lived.

Mrs. York stood, and my lawyer's assistant scooted her chair closer to me.

I saw Bob for all of two seconds.

He looked good in a suit. The dark material hugged his shape, showing off every muscular part of him. When his gaze shifted to me, his dark brown eyes sparkled at me. He had makeup covering his black eye. The next moment, he was stoic.

York walked to the front of the room, introduced herself and Bob, and the situation with me as the other defendant. She and my lawyer let her be the first voice to appear less like the overbearing male attorney defending the murderers. Would their ploy work? I honestly didn't know.

"Have you ever been a victim of a crime?" York asked.

Jurors numbers two, ten, and twelve raised their hands.

"Were you harmed in the crime?" York asked.

The second juror kept his hand up, and the rest lowered theirs.

York glanced back at my attorney, who nodded at her.

Dangers cleared his throat and situated himself in his chair.

"I'll excuse juror number two," York said.

The prosecution stood and asked three questions. They excused two more jurors. My lawyer was next and didn't ask anyone to leave. The state's attorney took their turn after and then Bob's lawyer went again. Whittling down the jury pool happened again and again as the lawyers excused more or made them out as biased for the next two days. Once my attorney used his last challenge, the Judge scheduled our trial to start on Thursday.

Chapter 6

I was exhausted by the time court was called for the night. I wanted to just go to my cell and sleep for a week, but I couldn't. The actual trial would begin tomorrow.

"How are you doing?" Dangers asked me.

"Okay. Tired, I guess." I rubbed my belly.

Bob stared at me now. He had to want to speak to me.

I wanted to speak with him as well. I needed to tell Bob my idea that could help him, that could save him. Shaking my head, I couldn't do it here. I should use my lawyer to contact him.

A guard placed chains on my wrists yet again.

"Have you been able to see your psychologist?" Dangers asked.

"Not since jury selection started. Why?" I asked.

"I'll schedule a meeting tonight after we talk," Dangers answered.

I sighed heavily. I didn't want to share my feelings with Shelly today or any day.

"We need to leave, Mr. Dangers," a guard said once he finished.

"Hold on a second. Why don't you want to see Ms. Nicholson?" Dangers asked me.

"I'm exhausted. I need to sleep. The baby needs sleep," I lied. Since I was pregnant, I might as well use it.

"If Ms. Nicholson came to the jail, will that help? You should see her."

"If you insist, I guess I can," I said. Why did he want me to speak to her? Was this another ploy?

"I'll plan right now." Dangers glanced at his watch. "I'll see you in an hour. Officer, please make sure Ms. Argall has something to eat. She looks pale."

The officer nodded and went to my side. His partner joined him, along with six others, and marched me out of the courthouse.

The ride to the jail was long because of the lunch rush. At least we weren't heading out after five pm like we had been for the rest of the week. I settled into my spot and closed my eyes.

Is Bob in the same jailhouse as me? I had never seen the van his guards escorted him to and from. We went separate ways. I didn't even know if the police, guards, or whatever they were called used a van. They could've driven my man to the court in an SUV or an armored truck, for all I knew.

The van screeched to a halt, and I opened my eyes. I glanced around. Just the police were here to take me to jail. Someday, I hoped Bob would be there and we would escape.

Dangers rushed into the prison visiting room right on schedule and set his briefcase on the table in front of me. He pulled out more paperwork, possibly evidence for us to go through. I never knew what he would bring. "Did you eat?" he asked.

"Yeah." If what the jail served could be called food, I had something. The rice was dry and mixed with peas and some type of meat I couldn't identify, which made it even drier. I would have never thought that was possible. The pork and beans with cornbread and butter went together. The juice was the only fruit I received. I craved actual produce so much that I'd gladly kill for some.

My guards left the room without being told.

Dangers glanced at the camera in the corner and left the room before coming back once the light had gone out, saying, "Tomorrow starts with opening statements. The state goes first, and I think Turnbuckle will speak. He's known for his opening statements. Sullivan isn't as experienced, and the prosecution will want to use the more experienced attorney. York, Bob's lawyer, and I spoke, and we've split up our parts. She'll go after me."

"Why?"

"My going first will benefit our case."

"I want her to," I said. Did I like her? Absolutely not, but she was Bob's best chance to go free.

"I'm going to advise against York speaking first," Dangers said.

"Bob has more charges. He needs more help than I do."

"You're pregnant with a child." Dangers sat in the chair across from me.

"Wouldn't that help me more?" I knew little about the law and never wanted to learn. I should gain some sympathy.

"Sometimes." Dangers rubbed the back of his neck. "You're making my job more difficult than it needs to be. Didn't we discuss you trusting me and letting me do what I do best?"

"Look, either Bob and I go free or we go to prison together." I couldn't imagine my life without him.

"I guess I can start working with York more if she'll let me."

Why aren't they in the first place? I asked him that question.

"She's doing what is best for her client. She believes distancing herself from you will help Mr. Ghul more," Dangers said.

"Does Bob believe what his lawyer does?" My heart squeezed as I waited for an answer.

"I don't know. Since she isn't playing ball, it makes me think she's up to something, and whatever it is will not be good for us."

"Bob won't let her use me."

Dangers stared at me with his piercing blue eyes.

I didn't dare blink or look away.

"You have a lot of faith in a man you met not that long ago," Dangers finally said.

"Bob and I are soulmates," I said. At least we told each other that more than once. I couldn't think or believe anything else, so I told Dangers my plan.

"That could work for Mr. Ghul. Are you sure you want to go down that route? I can't advise you to lie in court."

"I'll do anything for my man."

"He's a killer," Dangers said. His tone held an edge to it.

"Bob will stop when he's with me."

"Are you sure?" Corrie asked as she appeared next to me. She hovered as if she sat, but she didn't have a chair.

I ignored her.

"Are you sure?" Dangers asked the same thing.

Can Corrie be manipulating him? I shook the thought away, saying, "Bob never killed me. I was to blame for his sister's death as much as everyone else." Guilt rose into my throat, almost choking me, and I barely got the next words out before I sobbed. "I killed the family, not him. He wanted to leave. Do you still want to represent an actual murderer?"

"Your lawyer does not," Corrie said before she disappeared. A lot of help she ever was.

"Nope. I'm representing a hero. You saved the little boy," Dangers answered.

I didn't dare tell Dangers I'd killed others between Labor Day and the cabin. He should worry more about me than my man.

Dangers and I worked for the next hour, going over what he would say in his opening statement and then how the rest of the trial would go for the next few days. Each side would give its summary of its side of the case. After they finished, the first witness for the state would be called. Sounded like many long, freaking days. At least we'd get some breaks in there.

Someone knocked on the door right when Dangers and I were wrapping up.

I stood, hoping whoever was there wasn't a guard. I needed to stand and stretch without the cuffs on my wrists.

Shelly stepped into the room and asked, "Is Jolene ready to see me?" Her voice was too upbeat.

I groaned on the inside. No, I didn't want to see my shrink, but I didn't have a choice. Dangers must be up to something.

"Yeah, come on in. I wanted you two to talk," Dangers said to Shelly.

She smiled at him, her eyes sparkled, and she shook his hand. She must be smitten with him. I understood why. If he were a few years younger, he would've been hot, but not as good-looking as my man.

Dangers' hair had turned gray and didn't thin at the top. His dark blue suit hugged his trim, lean body. When he gripped Shelly's hand for a firm shake, he flexed the one biceps. He released his hold on her. Did he like her too? Was I just the ploy to get her here so he could see her?

"Thank you. I want to continue mine and Jolene's conversation from earlier," Shelly said.

"Please do." Dangers shoved the rest of his papers into the briefcase. I was right about the evidence. He turned to me. "I'll see you tomorrow morning, Ms. Argall. Shelly, I'll try to make your visits with my client at least weekly, if not twice a week."

"Usually, I see patients like Jolene three times, but her being in jail doesn't make it easy."

Dangers nodded but said nothing about my situation. "You ladies have a pleasant chat now." With those last words, he left.

"Do you need to stretch more?" Shelly asked me.

"Yeah, sitting for a few hours made me stiff," I answered.

"Let's work on a routine you can do during the breaks at your trial."

"How do you know about the breaks?" I didn't keep the shock out of my voice.

"I've testified before."

I wished the police had charged her with something that would make her more interesting. But no, she was as boring as ever.

"What part of you hurts?" Shelly asked.

"My lower back," I answered.

"During pregnancy, the lower back gets more strain on it. Follow me and I'll show you how to relieve some of it. I doubt the jail will give you anything for the pain." We worked through some stretches and added to my relaxation technique. "I've been studying some trial footage, and I've come up with a way for you to calm down when you're feeling overly pressured. The jury shouldn't notice too much."

"For real?"

"Yes, I'm here to help you. The fastest way is to take a deep breath and then let it out while you pay attention to your body. As long as you take a longer breath instead of short ones, few will notice."

I knew Bob would. "What else can I do?" I asked.

Shelly gave me a couple more techniques to try. I would have to ask my lawyer if they would be okay to do in court.

"How are you doing?" Shelly asked.

"I feel overwhelmed." My truthfulness surprised even me.

"Have you seen your parents?"

I shook my head. I tried not to care that they wanted nothing to do with me and even suggested I give up the baby. They were a big part of my life until my man came along.

"They've reached out," Shelly said carefully.

"I don't want to see them," I said.

"I'll let them know."

"You will not pressure me?"

"Why would I? I'm here for you."

I wasn't sure if I liked this overly understanding shrink.

Chapter 7

J udge Hayes entered the bench, shuffled her papers, and took her seat before saying, "This is an open court. If you need to speak, leave. I'll not allow any interruptions. If you do, I'll ask you to leave, or I'll confiscate the device that interrupted until this court is adjourned. All witnesses will wait outside the courtroom until they're called upon to testify. They should not discuss the case. Is there anything else?" She paused for a moment. When no one spoke, she continued. "Please bring the jurors out."

Everyone stood as the jurors entered the courtroom.

I recognized everyone from yesterday, and I still wasn't sure why any of them would vote not guilty. According to the reassurance from my lawyer, though, they all would.

My parents weren't here, but my dead friends' families were. They sat on the other side. I could guess what they thought about me. I couldn't care less.

"Sure, you do," Corrie said as she appeared behind me. I could feel her icy presence. "Go tell my mom hi, and you're sorry I'm dead."

I took a deep breath and let it out slowly, not enough to give myself away.

What else did my psychologist tell me to do? Oh, yeah, pay attention to something else, like what is going on around me.

The Judge swore the jury into court and told everyone to be seated before stating, "Ladies and gentlemen, you've been selected and sworn to render a true verdict for the state's case brought against Jolene Argall and Robert Ghul. This is a criminal indictment." She went over the charges brought against Bob and me, all of them. It took over ten minutes. "I will do my best to explain the law to you. You're tasked with deciding if the state has proven its accusations beyond a reasonable doubt. A reasonable doubt is exactly as the words state, a doubt beyond reason."

Judge Hayes went into further detail about what would happen in court. I knew the stages because of my attorney. She spent the next twenty minutes informing the jurors of what she expected of them. I could have summarized it in less than two.

Don't talk about the trial, don't discuss the trial, and if you find yourself in a predicament where someone is trying to talk to you about this trial, walk away and tell the court. I should've been a judge.

"With that, I will ask the state to start with its opening statement," Judge Hayes said.

Turnbuckle walked to the front, opened his stance, and said, "Good morning. On September 2nd, after 10:00 a.m. the bodies of Alison and Corey Irving were found by the police after Corey's work asked for a welfare check when he didn't show up that day. The evidence will show that Alison's son, Robert Ghul, ended her life and her husband's the night before. Robert Ghul is one defendant." Turnbuckle pointed at my man. "Robert Ghul tortured Alison and Corey before he killed them.

"Afterward, Mr. Ghul joined his dead twin sister's friends at a lake. There, he killed eight people and Detective Rebecca Gibson. He spared Jolene, the other defendant," Turnbuckle pointed at me now, "and one other person, Conrad Jackson." Wasn't that gesture rude?

"Mr. Ghul and Ms. Argall evaded police for over two months. Together they massacred thirteen people in the woods before the police apprehended them.

"All the evidence will show they killed these people. You'll hear from the first responders at each location. You'll hear from the coroners who autopsied the bodies. Twenty-five people died. Twenty-five." Turnbuckle raised two fingers on his left hand and five on his right, like he was a kid. He repeated the number one more time.

Turnbuckle pointed to two whiteboards next to him. I hadn't noticed them earlier, thanks to Corrie. He had separated the boards into three crime scenes. Lines marked those that were related, like he'd made a family tree. "This is a chart I made so you can keep track of these deaths," he said.

The prosecution went on and on. They had so much evidence against us, Bob and me, that I contemplated for a second taking the plea deal, but I would never testify against my man.

"First up for the defense, may proceed before we take a break," Judge Hayes said, once Turnbuckle finally finished.

York stood, and her perfect blonde hair swayed as she walked. Once she drew closer to the jury, she told them, "Good morning. My client is Robert Ghul, but he goes by Bob. Bob did not kill his mother or his stepfather on the night of September 1st. He wasn't home. He left when they were still alive to find his dead sister's friends so he could discuss the information he found in her diary. Kaylee Ghul, *his twin*, wrote about how their stepfather, Corey Irving, had repeatedly molested and raped her."

Gasps filled the courtroom.

The Judge gave everyone a stern look.

York must've gotten the exact reaction she wanted, and she said, "Corey Irving is a rapist and a child molester. Kaylee wrote about all that he did to her, and when she could not take any more, she took her own life on August 26th. They held her funeral five days later.

"Bob came home from being sent away at twelve years old. Why was he sent away? Because Corey Irving wanted to manipulate Kaylee and abuse his wife, Bob and Kaylee's mother, with no one there to stop him. The evidence will show this with multiple police reports and doctor visits.

"Mr. Irving couldn't hide what he did. When my client, Bob, confronted him, they fought. Bob left his stepfather alive, stating that he'd 'be back with the police'. Fearing what this would do to his reputation, Mr. Irving killed his wife and then took his own life."

Silence fell in the courtroom.

"Bob found Kaylee's friends, so he could see if they knew anything about what had happened to his sister before he went to the police. He found the lake they went to that she mentioned in her diary, and he met with them the next day. While there, Bob, Jolene, and Kaylee's friends were hunted. Nine people died that day, including a detective, but the police needed a scapegoat, so they blamed my client." York discussed the next massacre and how the evidence would prove what happened at the cabin in the woods.

Once she finished, York sat, but she didn't use my idea. Before I could ask my attorney why not, Judge Hayes called for a recess.

I stood and stretched.

Bob did the same next to me.

"We're taking you for a restroom break," one guard said once the jury had left the room.

"Together?" I asked, surprised, and then I felt foolish. They'd never leave Bob and me alone.

"Yeah, right?" The guard shackled me and took me down the hall first.

I did my business, returning to court after, where I was free of my cuffs once again. The police had stationed themselves around the room at the points of exit and entry. I hadn't noticed them until everyone had cleared out. They were discreet because the jury could determine Bob's or my guilt or innocence from them.

Bob nodded at me when he returned. He brought in his own personal entourage.

I wished he would speak to me, say something. I missed his voice.

Before Judge Hayes entered the room, the bailiff asked everyone to rise. "Please be seated. Is there anything we need to discuss before we start?" she asked.

No one spoke.

"Bring the jury in," the Judge said.

The twelve and six alternate jurors shuffled into the room. Seeing them angered me a little. How could they determine my innocence or guilt?

I might rush them and kill one or two. Bob would jump into the fray, doubling the amount of the dead, but we'd both die after with the police in the room. I placed a hand on my belly. I wouldn't risk my child, at least not yet. If anyone had to die, the first would have to be the police.

"Mr. Dangers for the defense may proceed with his opening statement," Judge Hayes said.

Dangers grew closer to the jury, he spoke, "Jolene Argall and her friends left to the lake on Labor Day Weekend to get away from their parents, responsibilities, and their lives so they could grieve over the death—no excuse me—the suicide of their friend. What they didn't know was that someone would stalk and kill them, try to kill them. The only three to make it out alive were Jolene Argall, Bob Ghul, and Conrad Jackson. Written testimony will show the first to die at the lake was Abigail 'Abby' Miller. Her killer wrote the word, 'Great', on the wall."

The door to the courtroom squeaked open, and I turned around.

My psychologist walked into the room. What was she doing here? According to Dangers, opening statements were to describe the case. She shouldn't be here for that. She wouldn't testify for a few days or weeks, if she testified at all. My lawyer hadn't decided if he wanted to use her. Wasn't she a witness? Shouldn't she stay and wait outside?

Corrie appeared in my attorney's chair and asked, "Worried she'll tell everyone you're nuts?" I was glad when she left me earlier for, I didn't know where. Like always, she returned at the worst times.

I knew I was crazy. After seeing Corrie, a dead person, I couldn't be sane. *Am I psychic?* I would know if I were.

"You're more of a psycho. Who dates the guy who killed her friends?" Corrie tossed her head back and cackled at her own joke.

I counted to ten over and over in my head. When that didn't work, I paid more attention to my lawyer. He could speak forever, not a bad thing. He was good-looking for an old guy.

"The only people who knew Abby liked to say the word 'great' were her friends and classmates." Dangers wore a black suit that went well with his blue and black striped tie. Corrie would've said, he looked slammin'. She would've hit on him, too, if she were still alive.

"The police didn't charge my client, Jolene, with her friend's murder. They charged Bob Ghul, the man she met there, and started to date. The other defendant." Dangers pointed at my man. He didn't notice someone had taken his spot, and he acted like nothing had happened, continuing on. "Bob couldn't have known about Abby's favorite word. He had spent the last five years in a boot camp so that his stepfather could abuse his twin sister and mother without Bob interfering.

"Witness testimony will prove that Abby's body disappeared, and the police did nothing to help the distraught teenagers. Seven more died because the cops didn't act. Eight more, if you include the detective, who finally helped.

"Jolene and Bob ran, fearing for their lives. Why should they trust the police? The detectives didn't believe them when they said someone had murdered Abby. One detective died in front of them. Who could they trust?

"On the first day of opening season, Jolene and Bob visited a cabin in the woods. They learned thirteen members of the Jager clan were child molesters. Jolene and Bob couldn't trust the police, so they tried to free little Logan Jager themselves. Instead, they had to fight for their own survival. The evidence will prove all of this. Thank you for your time." Dangers nodded and returned to his chair.

Corrie had moved behind me again.

A quiet mumble began behind me from those watching. Even my lawyer's words captivated me. Dangers spoke about how selecting the jury was a show, but what he did now for his opening must be the next act. The genuine drama would now begin. The air hummed with that knowledge. I found myself not minding this drama one bit.

Judge Hayes gave the courtroom a stern look. When everyone quieted down, she glanced at her watch before calling for lunch.

I looked at the clock on the wall that read 11:34 a.m. Holy crap, where had the time gone? Court might not be as boring as I thought.

Chapter 8

Never mind, court sucked. I ate my lunch alone beside the guards, who stood around me. Dangers had to do something.

"Court is running a little late," Dangers said after he hurried into the room.

"Why?" I asked.

"Not sure. Someone hasn't arrived, so the prosecution is asking for ten more minutes. We'll get another half an hour." He turned to my guards and said, "My client and I need to speak in private."

My guards left the room. One of them stood at the door, and I could see their silhouette through the frosted glass on the top part of the door.

"Do you have questions?" Dangers asked me once we were alone.

"Why is my shrink here?" The words popped out of my mouth before I could stop them.

"I haven't spoken to Ms. Nicholson at all. She's an expert and can be called anytime," Dangers answered.

"How could she be at my trial, then?"

"Was she?"

I thought back and didn't remember seeing her after the state's attorney made their opening statements. Not that I'd been paying much attention to anyone but Corrie and my lawyer.

"Does Ms. Nicholson being here bother you?" Dangers asked.

"I don't know," I lied.

"Well, you and Ms. Nicholson can discuss your issues tonight. Is there anything you want to ask me?"

On the inside, I groaned. Today was a long day, and having to speak to my shrink would make it that much longer. I opened my eyes, not realizing I had closed them. Dangers wanted me to answer his question.

"Nothing at the moment." Something nagged at my brain, as if I'd forgotten it, but I couldn't remember what. "How do you think my case is going?"

"About expected of a mass murder trial. Could I have done better? I'll always think that up to your verdict and even after." Dangers' face turned solemn.

"You want to help me?"

"I do. I told you I did. Are you ready to let me?" Dangers asked.

"Okay." I even nodded. What could him being on my side hurt? He'd been the only person besides Bob and now Shelly.

Dangers and I chatted for a few more minutes, and then someone let us know court had been called. I thought she was his assistant. I'd met so many people in these last few months that I lost track of who was who.

The Judge went over some matters before calling the jury.

I glanced at the clock. 2:09 p.m. Damn, court was slower than molasses in winter. When was everything supposed to move faster, like my shrink said?

"The state may call its first witness," Judge Hayes said.

"The state calls Detective Horner to the stand," Sharon Sullivan said for the prosecution. She and her partner must have some strategy, since this was the first time she spoke, besides stating her name during the start of the trial, not jury selection. After the Judge swore in the detective, Sullivan began her questions. "Please tell the court about yourself."

"My name is Detective Todd Horner. I have worked for the police department for fifteen years. Of those fifteen years, I spent the first five of them as an officer and the rest as a detective." Horner and Sullivan held a conversation about the day he was called to investigate the deaths of Bob's mother and stepfather.

When Sullivan finished her line of questioning, she said, "I have no further questions." She turned on her heel and took her seat.

I had learned nothing new, besides Detective Horner was the primary on the homicides.

"The defense may proceed," Judge Hayes said.

York went to the podium and said, "Thank you. How were Mr. and Mrs. Irving's deaths determined to be murders?"

"The county coroner, Ji-yong Kim, did the autopsies on Mr. and Mrs. Irving," Detective Horner answered.

"Did you find any evidence that Mr. Irving hurt his wife?"

"No," Detective Horner answered.

"You don't have any police records of Mr. Irving hitting his wife?" York asked.

Detective Horner shifted and cleared his throat before saying, "We found some afterward." He was clearly uncomfortable about being caught in his own lie.

York introduced the medical records of Alison Irving and police records into evidence. She also produced Kaylee Ghul's journal. According to York, Bob hid it from the police. She kept reading parts of it that pertained to the other documentation, asking the detective questions that only he would know how to answer.

"No further questions," York said.

Did Corey kill his wife and himself to not get arrested for sex with a minor? If I were asking, then the jury should be too. York was good. I was glad Bob had someone on his side.

Why is she helping my man? He can't afford her. The annoying voice nagged, not Corrie. I remembered the next second York was court-appointed.

"Does the defense have any more questions?" the Judge asked.

Dangers stood and said, "We have no further questions for this witness, Your Honor."

"You may step down," Judge Hayes told the witness.

The detective left the stand and the room.

"Any further witnesses for the state?" the Judge asked.

"The state calls the county coroner, Kim Ji-yong, to the stand," Turnbuckle said.

An older man walked to the front of the courtroom, where Judge Hayes swore him in. He raised his right hand, which was dotted with age spots, and replied, "Yes, Your Honor."

Turnbuckle asked Kim Ji-yong to introduce himself to the jury. Detective Horner had said the coroner's name wrong. Traditionally, the family name came first in Korea, which was where Kim said he was from. After graduating high school and surviving in the military for two years, he'd come to America and attended a prestigious college. He'd been working in his profession for longer than I'd been alive.

After Turnbuckle established the coroner's credentials, he questioned the other man about the death of Bob's mother and stepfather. Turnbuckle also presented several pictures into evidence. If this court were a TV show, this would be the third act. People know the characters, and now the writers set the scene for what would happen next.

Dangers yet again didn't need to ask questions. I assumed because this part of the hearing didn't apply to me. The state was apparently going in order of deaths.

York asked for her turn, "Mr. Kim, you ruled Alison Irving's death as a murder, correct?"

"Yes," the coroner answered.

"How?"

"She was shot in the head," the coroner answered.

"By a gun, correct?" York asked. For a second, I thought her question was stupid, but then I remembered I could shoot an arrow from a bow.

"Yes."

"Was the gun found on the scene?" York asked.

"Yes," Kim answered.

York kept on asking quick-fire questions to the coroner until she got to the next one. "How old was this bruise?" She pointed at the discoloration around Alison's neck.

"The coloring is green, so I'd say five to ten days," Kim answered.

"Before death?"

"Yes, blood settles in the lowest portion of the body, since the heart isn't working to pump it anymore," Kim answered.

"So, Alison had bruises from five to ten days *before* she died?"

"Yes," Kim answered again.

"Was there any other bruising that didn't happen at the time of death for Mrs. Irving?" York asked.

"She had several on her arms. Both arms."

They went into further detail.

I glanced at Bob.

He clenched his teeth. Only I could see this, since I sat so close to him.

The urge to reassure him swept through me, but I kept those feelings at bay. According to my lawyer, I had to not show any affection in front of the jury. Like I said, court was all an act. Call it a play, a TV show, or whatever.

York brought out the journal again, matching Kaylee's account of what happened with the documentation. Once she finished, she asked the same question she did of Detective Horner, "Would Mr. Irving be investigated with this diary as evidence?"

"I'm not sure. I just deal with dead bodies," Kim answered. Detective Horner responded the way Bob's lawyer wanted when asked the same question. If Corey were still alive, the police would investigate any claims.

"Did you autopsy Kaylee Ghul's body?" York asked.

I sucked in a breath, my heart jumped into my throat, and tears burned my eyes. I blinked them away, hoping no one noticed. Bob must be on the verge of crying himself or ready to kill someone. I didn't dare check on him to find out. If I did, I would start bawling. Being pregnant sucked.

Pregnancy jacked my emotions. I used to only cry over bad news or a dead animal, not spilled milk. I burst into tears this morning for not being able to bend and put on my sock.

"Objection," Turnbuckle said for the state.

"Overruled," Judge Hayes said after a few seconds.

My lawyer had told me at least seven common reasons for an objection to be allowed. None of them fit this circumstance except for irrelevant ones. What Mr. Irving did to Kaylee and what she did to herself most certainly applied to Bob's case.

"I'll repeat the question. Did you autopsy Kaylee Ghul's body?" York asked the coroner.

"I did," he answered. They went into detail about how she died and the suicide note. Bob hadn't destroyed it like I thought.

Hearing how Kaylee died made me sick. I wanted to kill her stepdad and my friends all over again.

"Did Mr. Irving kill himself to prevent his dirty secret from getting out?" York asked Kim.

Turnbuckle rose to his feet and called out, "Objection. Calls for speculation."

"Sustained. Move on, council," the Judge decided.

"You stated earlier that the gunshot to the head killed Mr. Irving, correct?" York asked.

"Yes," Kim answered.

"The gun had to be inside Mr. Irving's mouth, correct?"

"Yes," Kim answered. Did he ever not agree?

"In your experience, have you seen many homicides where someone else stuck a gun in the victim's mouth before killing them?" York asked.

"No." Finally, Kim said no.

"No further questions," York cut him off before he said anything else.

"Redirect, Your Honor?" Turnbuckle asked.

"Proceed." Judge Hayes stifled her own yawn and sat back in her chair.

"How did Mr. Irving die?" Turnbuckle asked the coroner.

"Irving was shot," Kim answered.

"In your professional opinion, do you think Mr. Irving shot himself?"

"No," Kim answered.

"No further questions, Your Honor," Turnbuckle said.

Judge Hayes glanced at her watch before saying, "We'll take a short, ten-minute recess to stretch our legs." Once we did, we returned, except for the jury. "We may have time for one or two more witnesses today, and then we will resume tomorrow at 8 am."

"Yes, Your Honor," the attorneys said. Could they even object to her wishes? I doubted it.

"Bring in the jury." They settled in, and Judge Hayes continued on as if she told no one else the plan. I guessed being part of the panel had limited knowledge of what would happen. "The state may call its next witness."

"The state calls Detective Willmar Morgenstern," Turnbuckle said.

In walked the smug asshole I met last September. Nothing about him had changed. He still wore a too-tight suit, and his charming face held a cocky grin on it.

"Please state your name for the record and tell us about yourself," Turnbuckle said.

"Is that the detective who let me die?" Corrie asked.

Yes, I thought. *Will you leave me alone and go haunt him instead?*

"I'm not going anywhere. At least not yet. Not until I get justice," Corrie said.

"For..." I said. My voice trailed off as I caught myself.

Dangers glanced at me.

I shook my head.

Stupid. Stupid. Stupid. Get out of my head and life.

"You're such an idiot. I'm not even here," Corrie said.

What? I can hear you, and most of the time I can see you. I didn't dare turn around to see if I could see her now.

Corrie didn't answer me, though.

Morgenstern had finished his introduction about himself and discussed the case with the prosecution. I was there, so I didn't need to pay attention.

Abby Miller was gutted. Bob wrote her favorite word, 'great', on the wall. My friends and I called the police, but he hid her body. Detective Morgenstern and his partner, Detective Rebecca Gibson, didn't believe us. They left. Lindsay and Tabby died next. I didn't remember if Ned got his head cut off, if Detective Gibson's assailant shot her, or if someone poisoned Brad after them. A bunch of my friends had died.

While York cross-examined Detective Morgenstern, I zoned out. Until she asked, "Why did you leave?"

"Because my partner and I thought the kids were playing a prank," Detective Morgenstern answered.

"Do kids normally play these types of pranks on the police?"

"They're always doing something to the police." Detective Morgenstern flashed a grin, and a few members of the jury laughed. He'd won those three women and a man over.

"Like what?" York asked.

"Make false phone calls. Egg our cars," Detective Morgenstern answered.

"Do kids report a dead body?" York asked.

"No."

"So, you left seven more kids to die?" York asked.

"I didn't kill them," Detective Morgenstern answered.

"Do you feel guilty for letting the kids die?" York asked.

"Objection!" Turnbuckle yelled.

Judge Hayes called the attorneys up to the bench, and they murmured at the sidebar. After they finished whispering, she said, "Sometimes we speak, letting no one else hear. The jury will disregard us coming together, but they will not disregard the question asked. I have overruled the objection. Detective, you may answer the question."

"What was the question again?" Detective Morgenstern asked.

"Do you feel guilty for letting the kids die?" York asked again.

"No." He shifted in his chair, and the smile on his face vanished. He had to be uncomfortable. Over what, though? I wished I could ask him some questions.

"Why not?" York asked.

"I was following my senior partner's advice," Detective Morgenstern answered.

"Which was?" York set her hands on the podium.

"Come back later and check on the kids, the teenagers," Detective Morgenstern answered.

York and Detective Morgenstern discussed police protocol and procedure next. It all led up to the fact that the detectives shouldn't have left.

"Why didn't you return with Detective Gibson?" York asked once they finished.

"I was at another scene." Detective Morgenstern rubbed his hands on his pants.

"Why did Detective Gibson get there so late?"

"She was also at the other scene with me." Detective Morgenstern rubbed next to his eye and then returned his hands to his lap.

"No further questions," York asked.

Dangers took his turn.

After he finished his line of questioning, I tapped him on the shoulder.

Dangers moved closer to me.

"Why didn't you ask questions about—?" I whispered before he cut me off.

"Because I'm not sharing your plan," Dangers said.

"Why not?" My idea was the best defense for Bob.

"I've called you as a witness instead. Can you handle the state's questions?" Dangers asked.

After all I've been through, I definitely could, so I said, "Yeah."

"We'll work on your interrogation tonight until it's your turn to testify."

Chapter 9

Court ended for the day. I was exhausted and chomped down my supper fast because I had to meet with my shrink. After we spoke, I had my first training session with my lawyer over my testimony. My goal was not to cry, but I failed miserably. I tried again and again for the next eleven days. I always bawled over something stupid. What did Dangers expect? I was pregnant. My hormones were out of whack.

"Are you ready for this?" Dangers asked the Tuesday before court started.

The prosecution took over a week to present its case. They still hadn't rested, aka stopped calling witnesses. Dangers had warned me they'd almost gone through their list of witnesses, so I needed to be prepared.

I nodded. I liked the idea of only him and me knowing what I would say soon.

"We can always give you more time," Dangers said.

"No, let's get this over with." What would more time do besides get me closer to giving birth? I still remembered the promise Bob and I made. Our timeline was drawing near. Christmas was less than a week away now. We needed to be done with the court before then.

"Okay." Dangers' voice didn't sound too sure.

I liked the fact that Dangers listened, unlike my parents. Shelly would let me know whenever they reached out, which was more often than I liked. I ignored them. They never came to my trial. Why would I talk to them if they couldn't accept me or Bob? Or our child?

The bailiff called, "All rise."

Everyone stood, including me, even though my feet ached. Shelly suggested I eat less sodium to help with the bloating, but I was in jail. I didn't get to decide what I ate. Every time we got up to show respect to the judge was a pain in the ass and killed my soles.

"Court is now in session. Honorable Judge Katherine Hayes presiding," the bailiff said.

Judge Hayes came into the room and said, "Please be seated."

Everyone sat.

I wanted to kick my shoes off and rub my feet. My breasts were sore. At least I didn't have to deal with nausea yet. I had to pee like every five minutes, so the brief breaks helped.

The Judge asked for any updates, and when no one had any, she called in the jury.

I tugged on Dangers' sleeve and whispered in his ear, "I need to go to the restroom."

"Now? Is the baby alright?" Dangers asked, like always.

"My baby is fine. I just need to pee."

"Hold on, Your Honor. Can we take a restroom break?" Dangers asked.

"Again?" Judge Hayes asked.

"Sorry, pregnant client, Your Honor," Dangers said.

She nodded. "I'll allow five minutes."

My guards handcuffed and escorted me out of the room. People whispered as I passed. They thought the excuse was another tactic my lawyer used because I didn't look pregnant. I carried myself well. How could those rude gawkers hold my size against me? If the court ran for another thirty weeks, it would see me give birth. Even then, they likely wouldn't believe me.

"You have three minutes," my guard said, unshackling me. He opened the door to the restroom.

Do my parents plan on keeping me locked up?

Corrie had followed me and asked, "Like they want everyone to know they raised a killer?"

She made an excellent point.

A guard, who was a woman, accompanied me into the lady's room. She let me do my business, hovering near the door. The windows had bars, so besides the entrance I couldn't go anywhere.

"Thank you," I mumbled to her as we left. Should I be thanking her? Probably not, but I didn't care. I wanted her to know I appreciated the fact that she gave me some space. I didn't need people watching me pee, but that was one of the many luxuries I gave up after getting arrested.

After I returned, Judge Hayes called in the jury. Once they settled, she said, "The state may call its next witness."

"The state calls Conrad Jackson to the stand," Turnbuckle's partner, Sharon Sullivan, said at the podium.

The doors to the courtroom opened and in Conrad walked. He looked so much like his brother that I wanted to puke. Conrad even had Monte's swagger down.

The Judge swore in Conrad and asked him to state his name, age, and occupation of student for the record, which he did.

"Conrad, what do you do outside of school?" Sullivan asked him.

"I volunteer at soup kitchens, ran a clothing drive this winter, and help my parents," Conrad answered.

"How are your grades?"

"I'm getting A's," Conrad answered.

Conrad and the state's attorney discussed what really happened at the lake. Bob had hunted our friends down. Finally, the state said, "I have no further questions."

"The defense may cross-examine the witness," Judge Hayes said.

"Thank you, Your Honor," my lawyer, Dangers, said. He walked the couple of steps to the podium and undid one of his buttons on his suit jacket. "Mr. Jackson, may I call you Conrad?"

"Sure," Conrad's gaze shifted to me.

I stared back at him, unwilling to blink.

"Conrad, when did you start volunteering?" Dangers asked.

"After school and on weekends," Conrad said.

"No, when did you start *volunteering,* as in date and time? When did you start running a clothing drive?"

"This year. About a month after my brother was murdered," Conrad answered.

"What did you do before then?" Dangers asked.

"What do you mean?" Conrad's handsome face scrunched up.

"Did you volunteer before your brother died?" Dangers asked.

"No," Conrad answered.

"Did you run a clothing drive before your brother died?"

"No," Conrad answered.

"Did you help your parents before your brother died?" Dangers opened his stance up wider and shifted his weight between his feet.

"Yeah."

"Really? How many times did your parents have to tell you to do something before you did it? This was before your brother died?" Dangers asked.

"A few times, like most kids," Conrad admitted.

"Yes, like most kids. Now you don't have to be told twice." Dangers cut him off and the sound of his tone wasn't like he asked a question.

"Yes," Conrad answered anyway.

"Did you get along with your brother?" Dangers asked Conrad.

Conrad hesitated before answering, "Most of the time."

"What do you mean?" Dangers asked.

"We fought a lot, but I didn't want my brother dead." Conrad's voice broke, and my heart squeezed. I hated seeing him in pain. At least, I thought I did. Wasn't he like Monte now? Monte certainly wasn't all bad. I mean, he would do some good things, but then he always bragged about it when he did.

"So did you like your brother?" Dangers asked Conrad.

"Most of the time, I didn't. I couldn't stand him. I...I hoped we'd start getting along the older we got." Conrad swiped at the tears at the corner of his eyes.

"Did you like any of Monte's friends?"

"Most of them were alright," Conrad said.

"Who wasn't?" Dangers asked.

"I don't want to speak ill of the dead."

"Why not? The dead can't hear you. They won't mind," Dangers said.

Two jurors laughed.

"I just don't want to say," Conrad answered.

"Did you get along with my client, Jolene Argall?" Dangers asked him.

"Yes, before my brother died. I admired. She was very kind," Conrad answered.

And now I'm not to him. Did I care? Not really. I had Bob.

"Did you get along with Abby Miller?" Dangers pointed at her on the state's whiteboard.

"Sometimes. She was annoying, very needy," Conrad answered.

Dangers circled his fingers around and stopped on Corrie. "Did you get along with Corrie Sommers?"

"Ah, no," Conrad snorted.

"Why not?"

Conrad took a big breath and said, "Corrie used to call me Con-Reject after a girl rejected me. I didn't even ask the girl out." He shifted in his chair.

"No further questions, Your Honor." Dangers stepped away from the podium and sat next to me in his chair.

"Does the state want to rebut?" the Judge asked.

"Yes, Your Honor." Turnbuckle stood and maneuvered between the tables. "Conrad, did you kill your brother?"

"No!" Conrad shouted. His face turned red, and he breathed heavily through his nose.

"Did you kill Abby or Corrie?"

"No and no," Conrad answered.

"No further questions, Your Honor," Turnbuckle said. "The state rests, Your Honor."

"The witness may step down," Judge Hayes said. We took a break, and I was more nervous now than I had ever been in my life.

When court was called back, the jury wasn't present. Instead, the Judge said, "Ms. Argall, we'll be placing you under oath." What was the big deal? Everyone who testified was sworn in.

"Yes, Your Honor," I said.

Bob sucked in a breath next to me. Did he not like my testimony? I wished we could talk, but we barely had any time between breaks.

The court stenographer said, "Please raise your right hand."

Do I need to stand up or go to the witness box? Since she didn't state for me to, I did a mental shrug and did what I was told.

She asked me the whole swearing to tell the truth, which I had already heard a bunch of times, and if I did, did I swear in front of God?

I agreed and put my hand down. If church and state were supposed to be separate, why did we always swear to God? I needed to ask my attorney about that later, or even my psychologist. The answer was bugging me.

"Ms. Argall, did you consider your constitutional right to remain silent in this case?" the Judge asked me.

"Yes, Your Honor," I answered.

"If you choose to remain silent, I would've instructed your jury that they're not to consider your silence in rendering a verdict. The decision for you to testify in this trial is yours and yours alone. Did you discuss this with your experienced trial attorney?"

"Yes, Your Honor."

"Do you need any additional time?" Judge Hayes asked me.

"No, Your Honor," I answered. Why did I feel like I was being scolded, or was this the worst decision I ever made? My heart plummeted. Oh well. It was too late now.

Think of Bob.

"You should think about Bob," Corrie said behind me.

Why now, of all times, do you have to bug me? I ignored Corrie's reply and shifted in my chair to hear the judge better.

"Your attorney has stated that you wish to testify in this trial. Is that correct?" Judge Hayes asked me.

"Yes, Your Honor." I shifted again. I hoped she and my lawyer thought I was uncomfortable because I was pregnant, and not because I was being haunted.

"When you take the stand, the state will cross-examine you just as they have with any other witness. Do you understand?" the Judge asked.

I nodded.

"I need the words," the Judge said before repeating the question.

"Yes, Your Honor," I answered.

"Is there anything else?" When no one answered, she said, "Thank you, let's bring in the jury, please."

"We got this," Dangers whispered to me before leaving to stand at the podium between our table and the state's.

The jury must've been returning because the bailiff said a minute later, "All rise for the jury."

The jury took its place.

The Judge said, "Please be seated."

We all sat.

"The defense may call its first witness," Judge Hayes said. The court went back to business as usual. Would it be less boring now that I was about to take the stand?

"The defense calls Jolene Argall to the stand," Dangers said.

I stood and my legs felt heavy, like I had strapped ankle weights to them. They shook as I walked across the small stand.

"Don't sit," the Judge instructed.

"Please raise your right hand. Do you solemnly swear that the testimony you're about to enter in the case is the truth, nothing but the truth, the whole truth, so help you God?" Judge Hayes asked.

"I do," I answered, a fib. My tongue felt thick, and a billion what-ifs filtered through my brain. What if the prosecution knew I lied? What if the evidence said otherwise?

"Sure, you do," Corrie said.

Please go away. I blinked at her and reached down next to me to adjust my chair.

"Why? I'm here to help."

Yeah, right? If I talked to her, the judge would rule me unfit to stand trial, which wouldn't help Bob.

"State your full name for the record," Dangers said once I finished.

"Jolene Candace Argall," I said.

"How old are you, Jolene?"

"I'm eighteen," I answered.

"When did you turn eighteen?" Dangers asked.

"On October 11th." Dangers told me to only answer the questions and not go into further detail. I assumed he meant for himself as well.

"What happened at the lake on September 2nd of this year?" Dangers asked.

"Objection, Your Honor," Sullivan, the state's attorney, said.

"Sustained," Judge Hayes agreed. I didn't know why. The question wasn't hearsay or the other 'rules' to object to.

"Where did you live on September 2nd of this year?" Dangers asked me.

I gave him the address and told him about my parents when he asked who I lived with. Did I still live there now? I didn't think so.

"When did you leave for the lake?" Dangers asked me.

"My friends and I left by eight a.m.," I answered.

"What time did you get to the lake?"

"The trip took about an hour so I'll say around 9 a.m.," I answered.

"What did you do first?" Dangers asked next.

"I grabbed my bags out of the back of Monte Jackson's SUV," I answered.

"After that?"

"I went inside." We went step by excruciatingly slow step for the events on September 2nd. I dropped off my bags, the argument with Monte and Corrie, and the decision to head out onto the lake. Yes, court was still boring even when I was on the stand.

"Hold on, what is a pontoon?" Dangers asked.

I turned to face the jury, like Dangers said to do, and answered, "It's a bigger, flatter boat that can seat many people. Usually, an oval or rectangle shape. Beyond that, I don't know. I can't afford one."

The jury chuckled.

"Who was with you on the pontoon?" Dangers asked.

"My friends and I." I listed off their names, and Dangers pointed to each one on the state's board.

"Who stayed behind?"

"Abby Miller and—" I answered, but Dangers interrupted me before I could say the second name.

"Why didn't Abby go with you all?" Dangers asked me.

"She had a headache."

"Who else stayed behind?" Dangers asked.

"Conrad Jackson." My gaze darted to him.

Conrad sat in the front row because he'd already testified. He clenched his jaw and pressed his lips together. Was he pissed that I had mentioned him?

"Why?" Dangers asked.

I shrugged, saying, "I don't know. No one asked him to join."

"What time did you go out onto the lake?"

"Shortly after we arrived. We stayed out on the lake until around 5 p.m. I wasn't exactly keeping track of the time. The sun was descending, but it was still light out for a few more hours."

"What time did Abby Miller die?" Dangers asked.

"I don't know. Corrie Sommers and I found her after we returned to the lake house. Abby was dead," I answered.

"I have the coroner's report on Abby Miller's death. Have you read it?"

"No." Pain settled in the back of my throat, and I resisted the urge to clear it. I'd glanced at it when Dangers brought it to build a timeline.

"This is state evidence number 112. It states here the approximate time of death. Can you read it?" Dangers showed me the sheet.

"The time of death is approximately 11 a.m. to 1 p.m.," I answered.

"Where were you from 11 a.m. to 1 p.m.?" Dangers asked.

"On the pontoon."

"Can anyone collaborate your location at the time of death?" Dangers asked.

"All my friends are dead except for Conrad Jackson and Bob Ghul, but Conrad stayed behind. Bob Ghul can, and the other teenagers we met in the middle of the lake. I didn't get their names," I answered.

"What time did Bob Ghul get on the pontoon?"

"After my friends and I tossed our anchor, so I'd say around 10 a.m.," I shaved off another half an hour.

"How long was he there?" Dangers asked.

"On the pontoon?" I asked for clarification.

"Yes," Dangers said.

"Until we got back to the lake house around 5 p.m.," I answered.

"So, the only person left at the lake house was Conrad Jackson?" Dangers asked.

Chapter 10

"Objection, Your Honor. Calls for speculation," Turnbuckle shouted.

Judge Hayes' forehead wrinkled before she said, "Sustained."

"To your knowledge, the only person left at the lake house was Conrad Jackson?" Dangers asked me after rewording the question.

"Yes," I answered. The jury must think only Conrad could've killed Abby just like I wanted them to.

"Good going. Blame the innocent. Your mom and dad must be so proud. Oh wait, they aren't. They won't even see you," Corrie said.

"Stop it," I spoke out loud. My face heated, and I tried to look less crazy. "Sorry. The baby's moving." I adjusted myself in my chair.

"Good recovery," Corrie said.

"Ms. Argall, are you able to continue?" the Judge asked.

"Yes, Your Honor," I answered.

"The jury will disregard Ms. Argall's outburst. Defense, please continue," Judge Hayes said.

"What did you do after finding Abby's body?" Dangers asked me, as if nothing had happened.

"Corrie screamed. My friends and Bob came to check on us. We argued until I called 911. Monte Jackson, Conrad's brother, took my phone and gave them the address," I answered. "We stopped the party afterward while we waited for the police. They came and ushered us into another room."

"What happened when the detectives arrived?" Dangers asked me.

"Detective Rebecca Gibson and Detective Willmar Morgenstern questioned us. They didn't believe my friends when we told them Abby was dead," I answered.

"Why not?" my lawyer asked.

"They didn't find her body."

"Where was Abby's body?" Dangers asked.

"Objection," Sullivan said.

"Sustained," the Judge said.

"Did you find Abby's body?" Dangers asked me.

"Yes," I answered. This was another reason I hated court. The earlier question was not leading and not hearsay. I wanted to groan in frustration. I was so glad not to be a lawyer and have to deal with this dumb shit.

"Where did you find Abby's body?" Dangers asked.

"Someone had sunk her body into the lake in the Jackson boathouse." Someone had hidden Abby, not Bob. This was the answer my lawyer and I were going for. We added to my man's innocence, and I wasn't done.

"What happened after the detectives questioned you?" Dangers asked.

"They left." If I had a nail, I would hammer it into the detectives' coffins, pounding away and creating doubt.

"Are you aware this was not police protocol?"

"No, I'm not a cop," I answered.

Dangers and I discussed how my dead friends and Conrad thought Abby and I were pulling a prank on them. I was not the type of person to do that. My lawyer proved it by asking me questions about what I did. I had volunteered to look good for college, but it worked here, too. We also mentioned that whenever I saw a dead animal, I buried it or tried to find the owner. I was an outstanding, law-abiding student and citizen.

"What happened after your friends couldn't find Abby?" Dangers asked me.

"Corrie screamed and came running downstairs," I answered.

"Why?"

"The killer attacked her," I said.

"What did you do?" Dangers asked.

"I went running upstairs with my friends to see what happened."

"Where was Conrad?" Dangers asked.

"Conrad was outside searching for Abby and came back inside once he heard the scream." Lying grew easier the more I did it. Bob was with me, so he couldn't have killed two of my friends upstairs. I ticked off two more deaths associated with Conrad and then two more with the next line of questioning. I had implicated him in four of the nine deaths.

Detective Gibson's death was easy to pin on Conrad. I switched places with him and my guy.

"So, Bob was with you when Detective Gibson died?" Dangers asked me to clarify since Conrad's descriptions and mine were not the same.

"Yes, Bob stayed with me. Conrad went with the detective to see Abby's body," I answered.

"What happened next?"

"My friends and I heard a gunshot, and we ran in that direction to save Conrad. He's Monte's brother," I answered.

Conrad had stated the opposite when questioned by the state. Bob had gone off with the detective, and then I ran to save him. What testimony made more sense? Who was I more worried about? The guy I had just met or someone I'd known for years?

"What happened next?" Dangers asked.

"Someone had shot Detective Gibson." I answered.

"Who?" Dangers asked.

I glanced at Conrad.

If looks could kill, I'd be so dead.

I contained my grin before saying, "I didn't know who shot the detective. I checked her pulse, but it was fading and she...she told me—" I couldn't finish the rest. I swiped at the tears in the corner of my eyes. Was I good or what?

"Take all the time you need," Dangers said.

Silence filled the courtroom, and I wiped away some more tears.

After a couple of seconds, I said, "I think I can continue now."

"What did Detective Gibson say?" Dangers said.

"She whispered to me Con-reject." My gaze shifted to each member of the jury to see his or her reaction. Conrad had told them his nickname from Corrie earlier when my lawyer cross-examined him. "I thought she wanted to make sure he was safe, but..." I let my voice trail off. Everyone had to know that I meant Detective Gibson had given me the killer's name.

"But what?" Dangers pressed.

"Detective Gibson said Conrad's nickname because he killed her," I said.

"Objection!" Turnbuckle roared.

"On what grounds?" Judge Hayes asked.

I didn't dare glance at Conrad again while the state searched for a reason. He had to be angry. He hadn't asked to visit me in jail again, and now he never would.

Turnbuckle must be just as mad. He couldn't use my being incompetent because I wasn't incompetent. He couldn't use the violation of the best evidence rule, since there was no evidence, only me. My statement wasn't hearsay, speculation, or repetitive.

Unease settled inside me. Who knew what reason a judge could agree with as the argument against my statement?

"Overruled," Judge Hayes said when the state couldn't find a reason.

"Tell us what happened next," Dangers said. Wasn't he worried about the ruling earlier? I guessed it didn't matter now that my comment could stay with the jury.

"My friends and I split up," I answered.

"Why?"

"Wouldn't you? Someone killed a detective, and we all realized it could be one of us, *any of us,*" I answered.

Five members of the jury nodded their heads.

"Where did you go?" Dangers asked me.

"To the woods. I wanted to walk to town or the next lake house, but I didn't get far since I wasn't wearing any shoes. I lost them in the lake." Inside my head, I scolded myself. I shouldn't have given more detail than my lawyer asked me. I needed to remind myself not to do that in the future. Court made me nervous, and I wanted to puke.

"Where did you go after the woods?" Dangers asked.

"I went around the back of the cabin using the woods as cover," I answered.

"Did anything happen?" Dangers asked.

"Yeah, I found Monte Jackson, Conrad's brother, dead." A single tear rolled down my cheek, and I swiped it away. I could feel upset over the loss of my friends, even though I believed they deserved to die. "Sorry."

"You've been through a lot. Tell us how Monte died and then what happened next," Dangers said.

I described how I noticed Monte's junk was missing, and then I stepped back, feeling the squish behind me and thinking I'd stepped on it. A few of the jury grimaced along with me. After I had checked underneath my foot. I went into some detail about how I had found Corrie.

Well-deserved death, I thought once I ended the description of intestines being pulled out.

"Why did I deserve to die?" Corrie asked once she reappeared beside me.

You were a bitch. Now go haunt someone else.

My lawyer asked me more questions about the lake and Hank's death, my last friend there to die. Once we finished there, we went into the cabin in the woods. I believed I did a great job telling everyone my defense story with Bob and me, trying to save a kid.

"No further questions," Dangers said after we finished.

"We'll take a lunch break, and when we return, the state will cross-examine the witness," the Judge said to everyone. Another thing I hated about court was that Judge Hayes decided everything. The state and my attorney knew their roles. Why did we have to wait to take our places?

The jury filed out of the room. By the time they left, most of the courtroom had cleared out.

"We need to talk," York, Bob's lawyer, said. She didn't sound too happy. She wasn't talking to me.

"Let's confer over lunch," Dangers said with ease.

"Fine, then." York huffed before storming out of the room. Why was she pissed? We gave her the perfect defense.

"I'll be back, but I doubt we'll get any time to discuss anything. You got this," Dangers whispered to me.

Bob cleared his throat, and a sour look crossed his face. Before I could ask him what his problem was, a guard was by his side and mine.

"Stand, Mr. Ghul," the guard said.

"Stand, Ms. Argall," another one told me.

I did what I was told, and the guard led me out of the courtroom for my lunch in another room. Bob probably went to another room where he'd eat, too. I went over my plan for the state's cross-examination. I hoped I didn't cry.

Court was called back. The Judge asked if there were any issues. When she didn't hear any, she announced the return of the jury. Like I said, these parts were a waste of freakin' time.

I liked the breaks. I needed the break, but I could do without the judge calling the jury into the room after checking with the lawyers. Bob and I were closing in on our deadline.

"Ms. Argall, how did you know the Jagers were sexual predators?" Sullivan, with the state, asked me as her first question.

"When Bob and I went inside for a beer, they closed the door to their back room. The boy's father sat close to him. I've seen these actions before with another abusive father I used to babysit," I answered.

"Did you tell anyone about this child?"

"Yes, my mother," I answered.

"She can collaborate on this story?" Sullivan asked.

"Yes." At least I hoped my mom would. I doubted she did anything with the information I had given her. She cared way too much about appearances. Who cared if a kid was getting hurt as long as she had the best chocolate chip cookies in the neighborhood?

"With this *other* family, you didn't save the child?" Sullivan asked.

Crap. She was doing what my lawyer warned me about. Any hint of my testimony being a lie, she'd grab onto it like a vet who suspected pet abuse.

"Good luck getting out of this," Corrie said. Her lips twisted into a smirk.

"No," I answered out loud.

"Why not? You went and saved Logan Jager? Why not the other child?" Sullivan asked.

"I wasn't the adult who was supposed to step in and help them," I answered.

Take that bitch.

Corrie sneered at me.

"So, you felt compelled to help Logan Jager?" Sullivan asked.

"I always feel compelled to help those in need. I just couldn't help the other family," I answered.

"Because you weren't an adult?"

"Yes," I answered. Was Sullivan an idiot? Was she related to my shrink?

"You couldn't go to the police?" Sullivan asked.

"Was I supposed to? I told my mom. I couldn't call the police about Logan Jager, since they blasted my image and Bob's all over the news."

Sullivan and I went back and forth. Each time she found some small bit, I said she dug into it. Like, why would a brother kill another brother? Jealousy? Inheritance? I didn't know I wasn't the police. They should figure out why Conrad murdered, not me.

By the time my cross-examination finished, even I believed Conrad had killed everyone. My attorney and Bob's called witnesses that collaborated my story with some facts and evidence. A Jager tried to take a gun from us, and we accidentally killed them for it. My man and I defended ourselves against the horrible family.

"Court will resume tomorrow with closing arguments," Judge Hayes said once the last witness left the stand two days later.

Chapter 11

Court started the next day with an issue. One of the jury members was too sick to continue. At first, I was nervous, fearing I would have to retell my side of the story all over again, and then the Judge called on the first alternate. I almost sighed with relief.

"Don't get too comfortable yet. You'll get the needle soon enough, or does this state have the chair?" Corrie asked. She'd been hanging around with me a lot more.

The more stress I was under, the more I saw her. My shrink told me to try relaxation techniques whenever the mental pressure was too high. I did every chance I got.

"All rise," the bailiff said as the new member of the jury took their position.

"Please be seated," Judge Hayes said. Once everyone had listened, she carried on. "Now that the defense is done with its witnesses, the state will start its closing statement. Afterward, the defense will take their turn, each of the lawyers. The state then has a chance for rebuttal. Let's proceed."

Turnbuckle stood and shifted over to the podium between the two desks, saying, "Good morning."

The jury said the same thing back.

"This has been a long couple of weeks," Turnbuckle said.

The jury chuckled.

"Did you believe the story Ms. Argall told? Boy, was that a whopper. She claims that Mr. Conrad Jackson killed his brother and their friends. I haven't heard of a crazier account in all my years as a prosecutor. The evidence shows that Abby Miller was stabbed. We never found a weapon." Turnbuckle listed off each death, pointing out the evidence that would go with it or if the police didn't find the weapon. "Conrad's an outstanding citizen. Ever since his brother was murdered, he's done a lot to help the community. He told everyone here how he helps organize fundraisers, gives back to the poor, and so much more. Does that sound like a killer to you?"

Turnbuckle paused for a second before saying, "The defense claims that Corey Irving killed himself and then his wife. We know the evidence does not point to a self-inflicted wound. The only person who stayed with the Irvings was the defendant, Robert Ghul.

"Well..." Turnbuckle wet his lips. "I take back my statement of the craziest story with the murders over Labor Day weekend. An even taller tale was the opening season massacre at the cabin in the woods. Ms. Argall claims that she and her man, Mr. Robert Ghul, killed to save little Logan Jager from his sex offender family. Yes, his family are all sex offenders. At least they would've been if Ms. Argall and Mr. Ghul had just reported what they witnessed to the proper authorities. The Jager clan would be on trial and not wiped out. This is not justice."

Turnbuckle took a deep breath, as if he was about to go on a long rant. He'd done that more than once during my trial. Usually, when he started, I tuned him out. I could tell two jury members did, too. Their eyes would glaze over.

"This was murder. First-degree murder in fact," Turnbuckle said before glancing down at a sheet in front of him. "The definition of first-degree murder is: the unlawful killing that is premeditated and willful. Premeditated means planning the murder in advance. Did Ms. Argall and Mr. Ghul plan out the murders of the Jager clan in advance? They brought these weapons with them to the Jager's cabin."

Turnbuckle went to his table and lifted a rifle that Bob had used to kill. The state's attorney selected the knife I had used on the pervert Marc Jager to slice his throat. Turnbuckle continued to select firearms and blades from his table, telling who each weapon had been responsible for killing.

"Why bring all these weapons if not to kill? Not only kill but maim, slaughter, and stab? Ms. Argall and Mr. Ghul willfully—deliberately, on purpose—annihilated the Jager family. Therefore, vote guilty on all charges. Thank you for your time." Turnbuckle wiped the spittle from the corners of his mouth before he left.

"We'll start with York for the defense of Mr. Ghul for her closing argument," the Judge said after glancing at her watch. Turnbuckle's long-winded statement took over an hour. I was ready to stretch my legs. My guess was we'd get a break right after Bob's lawyer spoke.

York whispered something to Bob before she stood and took her place at the podium.

I kept my annoyance in check.

"Look at the hottie lawyer your man scored. Is he still your man? Or did he replace you with this new woman? How often do you talk to him?" Corrie asked me.

I wanted to send letters, but my attorney advised against it, since the jail would read everything. The state could've taken copies and used them against Bob and me. I guessed that was why he never sent me anything either. He must want to know how his baby was doing, and how I was doing. I wished I could communicate with him. We were fine.

"One thing the state forgot is that the first-degree murder charge against my client, Robert 'Bob' Ghul, needs to prove beyond a reasonable doubt that he did the murders. That means if the state couldn't prove Bob killed his mother and stepfather beyond any doubt, you can't convict." York shuffled the notecards she had brought with her before she continued. "We've heard testimony from doctors that proves Corey Irving killed his wife, Alison Irving. Why did he? Because he was raping his stepdaughter, and a better man was about to prove it. Corey's world would've shattered. He would not do well in prison; no sex offender does. What did he do instead? He took the coward's way out. He killed himself, which was also proven by witness testimony.

"As the state said, if Bob went to the proper authorities, they would've investigated Corey. This diary." York held it up. "Would've been evidence against him. He killed himself so he didn't have to go to court. So he wouldn't have to go to trial and face what he did. The coroner testified that placing a gun in another man's mouth is difficult alone. Ms. Jolene Argall had already left with her friends to the lake. Bob was on his way there. The only person left was Corey.

"Jolene has testified that Bob did not kill her friends. She stated the fact that Conrad Jackson had murdered them. Why hasn't the state bothered looking into her claims? Because Conrad is rich. Don't let another poor boy, who has done the right thing all his life, go down for another rich kid's crimes."

York played up the story I told about how the Jager family attacked Bob and me first. How we had to defend ourselves from them. I actually liked her after her argument. Once the Judge called for a recess, she whispered to my man again. This time, she placed a hand on his arm.

I took the pen my lawyer left on the table, clicked the ballpoint pen out, and stabbed her with the end.

Blood gushed from her wound as she screamed in pain. She gripped her hand, pulling the wounded one close to her chest.

Everyone else was stunned and did nothing for a heartbeat before most of them screamed.

"Don't touch my man," I said with a smile on my face.

"What did you say?" Dangers asked me.

"Nothing." My face heated. I needed to stop fantasizing about someone getting hurt or dying.

"When was the last time you touched your guy?" Corrie asked, all smug. She knew damn well when the last time was.

York continued to whisper in Bob's ear, and her hand never left the top of his arm.

I contemplated stabbing her with a pen again. How much trouble would I get into? Would I care? Could I get away with the injury saying pregnancy hormones?

"Jolene, do you need a break?" Dangers whispered to me. He snapped me out of my daze.

"Oh, God, yes." I couldn't stand another moment of my man and her talking.

Dangers called over a guard, "Please take her to the restroom."

After the guard shackled me and brought me to the restroom, I relieved myself. I washed my hands and then splashed water on my face. Nausea swept through me.

Can I make the next few hours? My attorney still had to say his closing argument and then the state. I hoped Turnbuckle wouldn't drag the court into tomorrow. Didn't he believe in Christmas? An additional worry formed inside of me as the pending day approached.

"Let's get you back," my guard said.

I nodded and followed her out the door.

Court took another thirty minutes to get settled. At this rate, we'd be working past lunch. Judge Hayes directed Dangers to give his closing argument, and he took the podium. I had no clue what he would say. I trusted him. Did I just gamble my whole life away?

"Good morning. It's still morning, right?" Dangers asked.

The jury chuckled.

I had to give Dangers' credit. He was good at getting people to like him.

"Thank you for your time. I also want to thank my client, Jolene, and her boyfriend, Bob, for saving little Logan Jager. I rarely talk about my life, especially not in my closing argument, but I feel like I need to here." Dangers paused, and he clenched his fists at his side.

Is he nervous?

"Someone kidnapped my sister and sold her into the sex trade. I don't know what happened to her. If others like Ms. Argall and Mr. Ghul stepped in, she might be home today. Thank you, Jolene and Bob, for saving Logan." Dangers shook his head and sighed. "The state stated they could've called the police. My client testified to you why she didn't. She and her boyfriend didn't trust law enforcement. Can you blame them? The police had plastered their faces everywhere for crimes Bob didn't commit. Jolene went with him willingly. News reports said he kidnapped her. Her statement proved that was a lie.

"What else did the law lie about? When they told Detective Morgenstern what happened at the lake, he didn't believe them and left them. He testified that what he and his partner did was not protocol."

Dangers paused for a moment. Was he letting that information sink in? "I'll start with the Jager's cabin in the woods. Bob went into town, and a pawnbroker recognized him, calling the police," my lawyer said.

Bob and I were found out because of him? I always thought I had something to do with it. Why did my man go into town?

"He has some side chick there," Corrie answered my question with my worry.

I'll ask him later, and I'll ignore Corrie's comments, too.

"You know I can hear you?"

I contained my eye roll and did my best to shut her the fuck out. She was working on my last nerve, and I was about to lose my shit.

"Once the sighting came across, what did the police do? They went in full force to apprehend Jolene and Bob, all because of one testimony. One testimony Jolene proved was a lie 'Ever since his brother was murdered,' Conrad Jackson has been an outstanding citizen. Ever since his brother was murdered was what the state said. What about before then?" Dangers said, and then paused. He took a small breath and continued. "Conrad's grades were horrible. He was not the golden child like he pretends to be today. His brother, Monte, was. Conrad admitted he couldn't stand his brother. Siblings don't always love each other. They fight and argue. When money is involved, they murder.

"The police never investigated Jolene's statement. They decided, like Mrs. York said, Bob was guilty. Jolene did a lot for her community, unlike Conrad. She helped those who had lost animals. She volunteered and tried to make the world a better place. If you can't believe my client, believe the evidence."

Dangers shifted over to the table. He held up the gun I used to shoot Will Jager, an uncle. Dangers had told me his name. Did I care? Not really.

"Will Jager tried to murder Jolene. She shot him to save her own life. Self-defense is not first-degree murder. You heard the definition. The charge is intentionally killing a person willfully, with a plan, or deliberately. My client planned on protecting herself. That was why she and her man brought weapons with them. Would you go into a hunter's cabin unarmed?" Dangers placed the gun down and selected the next weapon. He went through each kill I did and claimed self-defense. If the jury bought it, I should go free. What about Bob?

After Dangers stated the jury couldn't convict me and stepped down, the Judge glanced at her watch again.

I was ready to use the restroom, but I wanted to get out of here more.

Judge Hayes asked, "Does the state want to redirect?"

"Yes, Your Honor," Turnbuckle said. He walked to the podium and addressed the jury. "A few things that the defense missed. Placing a gun into a man's mouth alone is not impossible. If someone told you to open your mouth or they would kill you, how many of you would oblige?

"The defense is also claiming that Jolene and Bob killed the Jager family in self-defense. They killed thirteen people in self-defense?" Turnbuckle asked. His voice rose in shock, and then he made it normal for the rest of his statement. "Do I need to say anything more? That is all I have. You have all the evidence to convict. Thank you for your time."

My stomach did flip-flops. The state had made excellent points. I waited for the Judge to release the jury, and then once they were gone, I asked, "Garbage? Please."

"Just wait," my lawyer said as he held a wastebasket close. "Hold on, the jury is almost gone. Here you go."

I tossed my cookies into the trash. "Morning sickness," I lied after thanking him.

"Here." Dangers handed me a handkerchief.

"Now what?" I wiped my mouth.

"We wait."

Chapter 12

I waited, I waited, and I waited. Twenty-four hours stretched on for a long time. I went to bed, and the next day, Christmas Eve, I waited some more. Before I went to sleep that night, I prayed for some resolution. Would the jury come back before noon on Christmas? Before the deadline?

A guard banged on my cell, startling me awake. "Get ready," she said.

"For what?" I asked. Planning to get myself into the hospital at a certain time was difficult in prison. How were Bob and I supposed to have known we wouldn't have a way to tell time? My breath caught in my throat. Was I about to be taken to lunch?

"Court," my guard answered.

A wave of relief washed over me, but the feeling didn't last long. I was such a dumbass. I'd forgotten for a second that I was about to be found guilty or not guilty for thirteen first-degree murders and some other dumb charges.

The drive to the court was agonizingly slow. I had to deal with all the what-ifs inside my head and Corrie's stupid commentary. I wished she'd go away. No matter what happened today, I needed to let my psychologist know so I could force her to disappear with some shrink skill or medication.

The closer I got to the courthouse, the worse I felt. My guards led me everywhere, like a dog on a chain. I had no choice. Not even the clothes my lawyer brought me were my choice.

"All rise," the bailiff said in court.

The Judge came in and set down her glasses before saying, "You may be seated. Are there any matters we need to discuss before I bring the jury in?"

"The offer for Ms. Argall still stands until the verdict is read," Turnbuckle said.

Everyone turned to me. How could I testify against Bob if the trial was over? Unless the jury couldn't decide.

I shook my head, and vomit flooded my mouth. I choked it back down.

"My client will not be taking the plea deal," Dangers said for me. He gave me a reassuring smile. Did he agree with my decision?

"I need to address the court before we begin. I do not know the verdict, but someone will not like what has been decided. If you need to react, leave. If you do not go, you'll be held in contempt," Judge Hayes said. "I want a record made that Jolene Argall and Robert Ghul, along with their councils, are in court. Bring the jury in."

"All rise," the bailiff said.

My feet felt like I had lead weights attached. I stood anyway and tried not to shift between them.

Once everyone settled, the Judge called, "Please be seated. Has the jury reached a verdict?"

"Yes, Your Honor," the jury foreman said. At least, I assumed he was. TV and movies got that part right. Everything else? Not so much.

"Please hand that verdict to the bailiff."

The bailiff handed the paperwork to Judge Hayes, who looked everything over. No emotion filtered across her face. If she could display such a poker face during a real poker game, she'd be a top player in a world tournament.

"I'll give this to the clerk to publish," the Judge said after she finished reading.

"Yes, Your Honor," the clerk said.

"Will Mr. Ghul, Ms. Argall, and their council please rise?" Judge Hayes asked, like we had a choice.

We rose to our feet.

"Post the verdict, please," the Judge said.

"The state vs. Robert Ghul, we, the jury, find the defendant not guilty of first-degree murder of Alison Irving with a firearm," the clerk read.

I bit back my scream of joy.

The clerk read on, "We, the jury, find Robert Ghul, the defendant, not guilty of the first-degree murder of Corey Irving with a firearm." Each charge for Bob was the same; he was not guilty.

Bob took my hand and squeezed it tight.

I fought back tears. Even if they found me guilty, Bob would at least be able to raise our baby. I would be okay with that. I would also have him promise not to kill again, at least until our child was eighteen.

"The state vs. Jolene Argall, we, the jury, find the defendant not guilty of the first-degree murder of Marc Jager with a sharp weapon," the clerk said.

I couldn't believe what I heard. I was not guilty. The clerk read the rest of my charges, and I had the same result. This time, when the tears sprang into my eyes, I let them fall. I brushed them away. With Bob holding my hand so tight, I wouldn't faint. He was my strength, my rock, my everything.

"Court is not done yet," the Judge said. "Members of the jury, is this your verdict?"

They said together, "Yes."

"Did anyone not agree with the verdicts as read?" Judge Hayes asked.

"No," the jury said.

"Thank you for your time." The Judge continued to praise the jury while I looked behind me.

Most of the court had cleared out. They must not have been able to handle the verdict. Well, fuck them. This was the way the court worked.

My gaze settled on Corric.

She waved to me.

I nodded at her, watching her fade away.

"What are you looking at?" Bob whispered to me.

"Nothing." I turned to him and smiled. Despite what I thought about Corrie, we were still friends. I could finally let the guilt I carried over her death go.

"Thank you for your time. You may leave now. You can decide if you want to discuss the case or not when someone asks you," Judge Hayes said to the jury.

Those in the courtroom moved, and most headed out the door. Only a few stayed behind, waiting to take their leave.

"Can we go?" I asked.

"Not yet," Dangers answered.

"Any word from the state?" the Judge asked.

I snapped my head up, and thoughts flooded my brain to flee. Could the state be willing to press more charges? How many murders did Bob and I commit between the lake and the cabin? I'd lost count.

"The jury has spoken," Turnbuckle said. He didn't sound pleased.

"All charges against the defendants are dropped with prejudice. Thank you for your time," Judge Hayes said.

"Now we may go," Dangers said.

"Thank you so much." I gave him a quick hug.

"Thank you for all that you did for my girl," Bob said to him. His hand touched my shoulder and then he offered it to my lawyer. Was he jealous?

"You're welcome. I meant what I said. Thank you for saving Logan Jager." Dangers shook Bob's hand.

I praised York. If she hadn't helped Bob for free, he might not be going home with me. Wherever that was. Did having a home matter? Not really. We had each other.

"The police will bring your personal effects," York said.

"Thank you," I told her. She was considerate. I never imagined she would be, but I was glad I was wrong.

Bob and I waited for our things to be delivered while the lawyers and the judge talked like they hadn't been going head-to-head for the last few weeks. This part amazed me. Would I ever want to be an attorney? Hell, no. I had other plans. I didn't know what, but nothing mattered. My man and I had our whole lives ahead of us.

Someone from the jail brought us our items. I took mine while Bob did the same thing with his. Everything was here except for our weapons. Would we get those back?

"Jolene?" Bob called to me.

Being able to talk to him felt so good. I wanted to ask him a million questions. "Yes?" I answered as I turned to him. I covered my mouth.

Bob kneeled in front of me on one knee. "My life began the moment we met. Will you marry me?" he asked.

"Yes!" I'd been wanting to hear those words for a while now.

After putting the ring on my finger, Bob scooped me into his arms and kissed me. Cheering made us break apart.

My cheeks flushed with heat.

"Shall we go?" Bob offered me his hand.

I nodded at him.

"Congratulations," York and Dangers said at the same time. Even the judge and state lawyers said the same thing.

Bob and I left the court hand in hand.

"This feels strange that we're free. We have killed no one lately," Bob said, once we got into the vehicle Dangers provided for us.

Reporters waited on the curb, being held back by bodyguards that Dangers also hired.

"We did a massacre of sorts. Our biggest one yet," I said to Bob.

"What did we massacre?" Bob's face scrunched up. He was so cute whenever he was confused.

"The justice system."

The end?

Acknowledgements

Thank you for reading my book. Thank you to my editor. Thank you to my writing buddies. Especially, thank you to my niece, Alexis. When I asked her about the concept for this book, she said she would read it.

About K.A. Meng

K. A. Meng lives in North Dakota, in the same town she grew up. Her love for the paranormal started at a young age when she saw her first ghost.

Today, she spends her time writing paranormal romance, fantasy, and everything in between. When life drags her away from it, she hangs out with her son and friends, goes to movies, watches TV, plays board games, walks her dogs, and reads books. She is actively involved in one writing group and wishes to some day visit Disney World.

Social Media Links

Website: http://www.kamengauthor.com

Facebook: https://www.facebook.com/KAMengAuthor

K.A. Meng Books:

https://www.facebook.com/groups/kamengbooks/

(Secret word is HKS.)

Twitter: https://twitter.com/KAMengAuthor

Blog: http://www.kamengauthor.com/blog

Instagram: https://www.instagram.com/kamengauthor/

TikTok: https://www.tiktok.com/@kamengauthor

Email: kamengauthor@gmail.com

Books by K.A. Meng

SWEAR JAR

Imagine if our childhood idioms turned into nightmares...

Cate Barlow and her friends rent a mansion for a week, and a ghost tells the friend who used foul language to place money in a jar. After they refuse, it forcefully hauls them into the wall, leaving a disturbing spectacle behind.

Cate and her friends try to flee, but the security system traps them inside. In order to stay alive, they must work together. If they don't or if they run out of money, they die.

Swear Jar isn't the same we used in our childhood.

https://mybook.to/SJE

ZOZO

Emily Campbell receives a text that her boyfriend, Danny, is cheating on her. When she finally works up the courage to ask him, a drunk driver smashes into their vehicle. She wakes up in the hospital to find out that she is the only survivor of the crash besides the drunk driver.

She is angry and frustrated over how long she's taking to heal and not knowing if Danny was unfaithful or not. Rather than humiliate herself and talk to the other woman for answers; Emily decides to contact Danny through a spirit board. He admits to cheating on her, but something is wrong with his answers to her questions. Emily isn't certain if she has contacted Danny, or something else.

http://getbook.at/zozo

THE WAYWARD STATION

A tornado whisks Kayla Stark into The Wayward Station, a realm between life and death. This special place is in trouble from a ghost with a bad attitude, Jacoby Marone. He has been stealing the precious commodity. If she doesn't stop him, she and The Wayward Station may disappear forever.

http://getbook.at/WS

IMAGINARY FRIEND BOOK 1: AVA

She just wants to play.

Jasmine Cardwell doesn't believe in ghosts...but her niece's imaginary friend Ava may change her mind. Ava destroys the glass shade almost hitting a kid's head. She also talks to Jasmine's niece and writes a deadly message on the computer.

These actions and more begin the Cardwell family's quest to find out if Jasmine or her niece is haunted. Maybe Ava isn't imaginary...maybe she is something much worse.

https://mybook.to/Ava1